A Mormon Motive for Murder

Rural southern Mormons. Mormons with mental illness. Homeless Mormons. Ex-Mormons. Gay and trans Mormons. Mormon murderers. Mormon missionaries. Mormon missionaries who are murderers. There's something for everyone in this collection of short stories from the author of *Mormon Underwear* and *Gayrabian Nights*.

Praise for Johnny Townsend

In *Zombies for Jesus*, "Townsend isn't writing satire, but deeply emotional and revealing portraits of people who are, with a few exceptions, quite lovable."

Kel Munger, *Sacramento News and Review*

In *Sex among the Saints,* "Townsend writes with a deadpan wit and a supple, realistic prose that's full of psychological empathy….he takes his protagonists' moral struggles seriously and invests them with real emotional resonance."

Kirkus Reviews

Inferno in the French Quarter: The UpStairs Lounge Fire is "a gripping account of all the horrors that transpired that night, as well as a respectful remembrance of the victims."

Terry Firma, Patheos

"Johnny Townsend's 'Partying with St. Roch' [in the anthology *Latter-Gay Saints*] tells a beautiful, haunting tale."

Kent Brintnall, Out in Print: Queer Book Reviews

Selling the City of Enoch is "sharply intelligent...pleasingly complex...The stories are full of...doubters, but there's no vindictiveness in these pages; the characters continuously poke holes in Mormonism's more extravagant absurdities, but they take very little pleasure in doing so....Many of Townsend's stories...have a provocative edge to them, but this [book] displays a great deal of insight as well...a playful, biting and surprisingly warm collection."

Kirkus Reviews

Gayrabian Nights is "an allegorical tour de force...a hard-core emotional punch."

Gay. Guy. Reading and Friends

The Washing of Brains has "A lovely writing style, and each story [is] full of unique, engaging characters....immensely entertaining."

Rainbow Awards

In *Dead Mankind Walking*, "Townsend writes in an energetic prose that balances crankiness and humor....A rambunctious volume of short, well-crafted essays..."

Kirkus Reviews

A Mormon Motive for Murder

Johnny Townsend

Print ISBN: 979-8-9883389-0-1
Ebook ISBN: 979-8-9883389-1-8

[Selected stories from *The Circumcision of God*, *Sex among the Saints*, *Dinosaur Perversions*, and *Selling the City of Enoch*.]

Printed on acid-free paper.

2023

First Edition

Cover design by BetiBup33 Studio Design

Contents

Rapture..9
Nanny Princess...22
Ambien Dreams..33
Homework for Hitler...50
A Mormon Motive for Murder.............................66
The Pig Door...82
The Buzzard Tree...120
Mrs. Mariposa..133
Desert Garden..144
Renting Mom and Dad..162
Making Hay..184
The Homeless Bishop..209
Mis ing Parts...225
Becoming an Ammonite.......................................231
Mormon Movie Marathon....................................256
Circumcising the Hivites......................................267
Books by Johnny Townsend..................................284
What Readers Have Said.......................................298

Rapture

Patty Lou sat on the green vinyl sofa, her legs crossed, thumbing through the daily Brookhaven newspaper. She glanced over at Robert, her thirty-year-old grandson, sitting on the brown vinyl sofa, reading the Jackson daily newspaper. It was a ritual they performed every time he came up to visit from New Orleans, three holidays and two extra visits a year.

This was one of the extras, in the middle of the summer, so it was hot, with just a fan blowing in the 90-degree heat. But at least no one else was around to intrude. It was peaceful and quiet, just the sound of insects buzzing outside and cows lowing on the neighbor's dairy farm.

Patty Lou read of a factory outside of town laying off twenty workers, and she worried about her son, Shane, who'd been laid off at the railroad five years now and only had jobs he hated ever since. He didn't complain much, but she could tell he was unhappy. Of course, with that awful wife of his…

But Patty Lou tried not to think of Lisa and her petty lies. She'd been in the family seventeen years now, and at least she'd calmed down a little since they'd adopted a boy through the Church nine years ago. Now, though, they'd taken in Lisa's brother's baby after the brother and his girlfriend had both been put in jail for drugs and stealing.

The boy was a terror, but Patty Lou hoped he'd be okay one day. As it was, the boy's behavior always gave her daughter, Cathy, something to complain about, and to act superior about, too. Cathy, with four children of her own, did have reasonably good children, the oldest fourteen, all on the honor roll, but they had their moments as well. Lisa certainly pointed it out whenever she could.

Patty Lou looked again over at Robert, one of her two grandchildren from her oldest daughter, Marsha. Neither of them had turned out well, the girl divorced, with a son who'd failed the seventh grade three times, and with a nursing degree she refused to use to find work, borrowing money from Patty Lou instead. She lived unmarried with a man in his house, leaving her fifteen-year-old son alone in her own house for days at a time.

And Robert. Patty Lou looked at him again. He was sweet enough, but two years ago he'd told her he was gay, and, well, these things were just too confusing. The Church said he was a sinner, but she liked him. He was the only one in the family who ever asked her about her life, always taking notes when she told him stories. He made negatives of all the family pictures and gave copies to everyone in the family for Christmas, even giving every family an extra copy in case they had another child.

Robert turned to the last page of the newspaper, and when he looked up, Patty Lou said, "Ready to switch?" She laughed, though she didn't know why, and stood up to trade papers. Soon, they'd finished reading the second paper, and now it was time for their next ritual.

"Do Mormons believe in the Rapture?" she asked. For seventy-four years she'd lived as a Methodist, and only in the last four had she been a Mormon. Marhsa had started it, joining the Church with her family over twenty years ago. Then teenage Cathy had become interested, and both Cathy and Patty Lou took the missionary lessons.

But Patty Lou's husband, Webster, who was Baptist, had come home one day with a six-pack of beer and said, "The day you join that church is the day I start drinking." So she hadn't joined, but Cathy had when she turned eighteen, and a few years later Shane and his wife had joined, too.

Then, after Webster died of lung cancer from smoking, Patty Lou waited another couple of years and decided to be baptized. She'd asked Robert to do it, as he'd gone on a mission to Italy. Cathy's husband was the only other one in the family who'd been on a mission, his in Norway, but Patty Lou didn't like him enough to let him baptize her.

Robert had told her she ought to ask her only son, Shane, to do it. Later, when he told her he was gay, Robert explained he couldn't baptize her because he'd just been excommunicated, but he hadn't wanted to tell her right as she was converting.

She didn't know if she believed in the Church or not. She just wanted to make sure they all went to the same place after they died, and with her daughter Marsha dead from leukemia two years before Webster died, she knew which one she wanted to see again most. Not that Webster had been all that bad. He'd been faithful, not like that man on the neighboring farm, and he'd rarely yelled at her.

Still, it was easier to be close to other women. She wondered if that was why she liked Robert. She'd hinted for him to tell her if he was the man or the woman in his relationship, but he said they were both men, so he must not have understood, and Patty Lou couldn't bring herself to ask more directly.

Robert was like a woman in some ways, wanting to talk about important things rather than sports or tractor pulls, so she enjoyed his visits. She liked being with him, even when she did run out of things to say.

She *always* ran out of things to say, of course, but she still liked when her family visited. But if the Church wasn't true, that meant she wouldn't be seeing Robert again, or any of the others. Joining the Church might have been useless.

"No, Grandma," said Robert. "The Church doesn't believe in the Rapture."

Patty Lou sighed. He said that every time she asked. Why couldn't the Church change its mind? She had, as old as she was. "I listen to the preachers on the radio," she said, "and they talk about how bad it's going to get. I'd sure like to go before it gets bad."

"It's already bad."

"But it's going to get worse. How long do you think it'll be before Jesus comes back?"

"I really don't know. Could be just a few years. But it might not be for fifty more."

"I don't know if I want to be here for it or not. It might get real bad first."

They were silent for a moment, Patty Lou thinking about growing up without water or electricity, about seeing planes and rockets and computers all develop during her lifetime. And she knew there was going to be a big nuclear war before she died. She did wish she could die before that happened.

Her sister Fannie Sue, two years older than she was, had died six months ago, of lung cancer, though she'd never smoked a day in her life. That wasn't fair of God. He could give her cancer if he had to, but why lung cancer? That wasn't right.

Fannie Sue would call Patty Lou during her treatment, whispering into the phone that their youngest sister, Virginia, wouldn't take her to her appointments unless Fannie Sue left all her property to Virginia in her will. Fannie Sue had already promised most of it to Patty Lou to give to her grandchildren.

Patty Lou and Webster had owned 200 acres together, and Patty Lou had another sixty acres of her own, so she didn't really need it, but it was the idea. Virginia was the baby of the family and always got everything she wanted. Even when Marsha was lying in the hospital bleeding to death, Virginia had asked for her books to read.

Marsha could hardly talk by then but did manage to stare right at Patty Lou and say, "Don't you give her *anything* of mine." Marsha had died two days later, going into convulsions from a brain hemorrhage during Patty Lou's shift at her bedside.

Virginia had terrorized Fannie Sue for the past forty years, ever since Fannie Sue's marriage ended after only a week, and Virginia had moved back into the family house, to "help." The house had been in Fannie Sue's name, but Virginia acted like it was her own, raising her own family there and making Fannie Sue do most of the chores.

Patty Lou knew she was almost as meek as Fannie Sue, but sometimes, she wanted to shake Fannie Sue and scream, "Slap her!" It was too late now, of course, and Patty Lou wanted to slap Virginia herself, but she could never even manage to say something mean. Patty Lou just smiled and spoke nicely as she always did. It made her mad, but what could she do? After seventy-eight years, how could she say what she wanted to say?

"You know," Robert said then, "the last days don't have to be as bad as we think they'll be."

"What do you mean?" Patty Lou wanted to hear something to believe in, so she quickly tuned back in.

"The scriptures say there'll be wars and plagues, but that doesn't mean *everywhere*. We have AIDS, but the world keeps going on. We have terrorist attacks, but life doesn't change all that much. The scriptures say the sea will die and all the fish, but really, couldn't the prophets have been seeing a few oil spills? Some of those spills go on for miles, and they *are* bad, but life still goes on. It doesn't necessarily have to get much worse than it is now."

"You don't think so?"

"Well, I don't know, but maybe. There are only a handful of prophecies that haven't fully happened yet, and only one of those, the last one, is *really* bad. So that might happen only at the very end."

"But y'all don't believe in the Rapture?"

Robert smiled and shook his head, and Patty Lou sighed.

"The preachers on the radio are always talking about Israel. You don't think they'll get us in a world war?"

Robert shrugged. "It hasn't happened yet. It might not. The preachers don't always interpret things right, do they?"

"No, that's true."

But still, wouldn't it be nice if it was all over? To be taken up in the blink of an eye. Her mother had had a stroke at eighty-seven and lingered on miserably for another year. Patty Lou's older brother, too, at eighty-five. Marsha had suffered just five weeks, but they were a miserable five weeks. Webster had been sick a year, but it was really only the last month he suffered, and only the last two days of that when he had to go to the hospital. And of course, Fannie Sue had suffered quite a bit, too.

Even Shane, healthy now, had had his ribs torn loose when a car broadsided him a couple of years ago. Patty Lou remembered how ribs felt—she'd had two broken when she was eight and a half months pregnant with Cathy, in that terrible accident that had knocked out two of Shane's teeth and cut up the whole family at the very same intersection thirty-five years earlier. Patty Lou didn't want to suffer any more. And she didn't want to have to watch anyone else suffer, either.

"What does Jimmy think about the Church?" she asked, remembering Robert's friend.

"He's Catholic, and he really doesn't believe in any religion. He used to, but you know how it is for us. I'm amazed so many gays still do believe in religion."

"Is he…ready to die if he has to?" She really wanted to ask if he was healthy, but she didn't know how. The two had been together for almost three years. Would they know yet if they were sick? She'd been afraid at first Robert would give AIDS to the other grandchildren, but then she read up on it and learned it wasn't likely. But she still worried for Robert.

Robert shrugged again. "He talks about suicide sometimes."

"Really?"

"His first cousin killed himself right before Christmas. He was depressed because he was out of work, though he still had a pension. They'd grown up together and dated sisters in high school. And you know Jimmy's last partner died of an aneurysm. They'd been together eight years. And his grandmother died last year. Jimmy really loved her. I think the only reason he stays is because of his mother. She has such a jerk of a husband, always threatening to kick her out. Jimmy wants to make sure she's provided for, but if he dies and leaves everything to her, he thinks her husband will somehow manage to get everything and still kick her out."

Patty Lou nodded. "Well, that happens," she said. "But doesn't he worry about leaving you?"

Robert gave kind of a twisted smile. "I guess we've resigned ourselves to losing people."

Patty Lou nodded again. "Eight of my brothers and sisters are dead now. Just two of us left. And Cathy's youngest is so sickly, you never know what to expect. They had a TB outbreak at her school."

They were silent a few moments. Then Robert shifted on the sofa. "We both had blood tests a couple of months ago," he said, and Patty Lou looked up sharply. "We're both still negative, and you know we're monogamous."

"That's good," she said. After a moment, she added, "I hope I die in my sleep."

"I hope you do, too."

Patty Lou sighed. Robert was the only one in the family she could talk to about death. It was comforting. "What do you think about suicide?"

"A friend asked me how to do it painlessly, and I gave him the information."

"Did he do it?"

"No, he hung on as long as he could and then died on his own." He smiled and shook his head. "That was Christmas Eve a year and a half ago. Goodness. Time flies."

Patty Lou looked at her thirty-year-old grandson. Marsha had only been forty-four when she died. And Patty Lou had a great-grandson who was fifteen and already dating girls, so soon there'd be a great-great-grandchild. She loved her family but wondered why the thought of their procreating felt so empty to her. Of course, Shane's children weren't really his, though she loved them, too.

And Cathy's, well, Cathy's children did give her some hope, the only ones who were really being raised in the Church, though Patty Lou knew that Cathy and her husband were having problems. She suspected he was gay, too, like Robert. Robert had certainly hinted about it enough. If that marriage broke up, though, would those kids stay in the Church? And Cathy? Would they be able to believe anymore?

It was so hard to believe. Why did God make it so hard? It wasn't as if Patty Lou were bad and deserved it to be hard. She'd always tried to believe and do what was right. Seventy-eight years of that wasn't enough? What more did God want? What if she gave up at the age of eighty-two and was doomed to hell because of it? That just wasn't *fair*. So she kept trying to believe.

"The preachers say the Lord will be merciful to us in the last days and shorten the time," Patty Lou said. "Do you suppose that means time really is faster? That all the clocks and orbits and everything are faster, so we can't really tell, but that it's all going by quicker?"

"It could be, Grandma," Robert said slowly. "It could be."

But after a moment, Robert asked about the pace of life back in the 1920's and 1930's, and Patty Lou told him a few more stories. She had a list she kept between his visits, so that every time she remembered a story, she could jot it down and then tell him when he came. She knew she remembered the same stories often, but she always threw in a couple of new ones. She could tell by the way Robert took notes.

After a while, they fell silent, and when Robert went to stand on the porch, Patty Lou got together some table scraps from the kitchen and went out to the barn to feed the dogs. She'd tripped over one and sprained her wrist a few years ago, and she never had regained full use of her hand. So she walked carefully to the barn and back, joining Robert on the porch and looking over toward where the neighbor's land started.

He had a gay son, too, who'd tried to kill himself rather than tell his parents. Just how many gays were there? Patty Lou had never even known they existed until she was almost forty. Was this a sign of the last days? There hadn't always been that many gays, had there? The neighbors weren't very pleased with their son, but their oldest boy was schizophrenic, on medication, and their youngest, only twenty-two, was already divorced. Patty Lou guessed parents couldn't be too choosy these days. Kids used to be better, didn't they?

Patty Lou looked at Robert, who was looking off into the garden where the vegetables were planted. Robert was about the only one in the family who liked her cooking. Lisa's son told her that his mother threw out the jars of food Patty Lou put up for her, but Robert always gladly accepted them. The last year or so, he'd also been bringing up desserts from her recipes, but she still liked to cook for him, too, so there were always too many desserts. But he didn't have a garden, and she always loaded him up with fresh vegetables when she could.

It wouldn't be long now. He never stayed overnight anymore since he and Jimmy had moved in together. She missed him staying for a few days at a time. At least Cathy and her children came from McComb for up to a week at a time and her great-grandson had stayed for two weeks earlier this summer.

She worried about him, but he did mow the lawn for her, trimmed the bushes so she could see if anyone was hiding around the house, and he painted the living room. He might turn out okay. But she still wished he'd finish high school. Even Patty Lou had had one semester of college back in 1934, until her father died unexpectedly.

Patty Lou and Robert talked about the dog and the cat on the front steps who were always so friendly and loving to each other, and soon Shane stopped over on his way home from work and fed the three horses he kept here. It gave him a chance to check up on Patty Lou, and she enjoyed seeing him without Lisa.

Shane was the last one in the family Robert had told he was gay, and Shane didn't like it but accepted it, always asking about Jimmy if Jimmy didn't come, and that made Patty Lou feel good.

"Shall I warm up supper?" Patty Lou asked around 6:00.

Robert nodded, and after she asked him to say a blessing on the food, they ate in silence.

And too soon, it was time. They really had very little to say during his visits, but she still worried every time he left she might never see him again, that she'd die before he could come back. And there was *something* she always felt she should tell him first. She simply could never quite figure out what it was.

She loaded some food into brown paper grocery bags for him, and he thanked her and put them in his car. She looked again at the beautiful flowers Jimmy had painted hanging on her walls, remembered how they'd both come up for her last birthday and planted flowers where she could see them from the porch, and she hoped Robert would be okay. Jimmy, too, of course. Was he family now? It was just too confusing.

Robert came back to the porch and gave Patty Lou a hug. She knew he had to force it on her because she'd never been able to initiate a hug, but though she couldn't do it very well, she was glad he insisted.

"I love you, Grandma," he said. "I'll try to come back soon."

She waved from the porch as he drove off, watching the dust from the gravel drift into the air. After a few moments she went back to sit on the sofa, looking through the screen until it was too dark to see any longer. And then she closed the door.

Nanny Princess

"Carlucci, Thibodeaux, and Henderson," Miranda cooed into the phone for the twentieth time that day. She'd been working as the receptionist for the law firm for three years and had learned to make those three names blend so they sounded like parts of a whole entity.

She was proud of her lilting "phone voice," and hardly a week went by that someone didn't compliment her on it, but she couldn't worry about that anymore. People used to tell her she was pretty, too, but she hadn't heard that for a while now, after the thirty pounds she'd gained this past year. The worst part was that Keith was the one who criticized her most for the weight, and he was the one who'd caused it.

Miranda transferred the call to the office of one of the lawyers and hung up her receiver. Then she picked up the book she'd been reading, *Viking Princess*, and found her place. This one was much better than the last one she'd read, *Apache Maiden*. She'd have to look for more by this author.

The phone rang again. "Carlucci, Thibodeaux, and Henderson," she said.

"May I please speak with Miranda Ryan?"

Miranda frowned. Her friends often called her at work, but this was a voice she didn't recognize. Had Keith asked someone to check up on her? Maybe it was Keith's ex-wife. Maybe it was Eric's wife.

"This is Miranda," she answered.

"I'm from Home Search, and I'd like to ask a few questions about your application to be a nanny."

"Oh!" Miranda closed her book and grasped the phone tightly. This was it. This was her chance to move to California and meet a rich, handsome, single Mormon man. This was her chance to finally start living, even if she was already twenty-seven, almost too old now to find a husband. She looked down quickly at her stomach stretching against her dress, and she shoved her thick thighs further under the desk.

She'd had to buy a whole new wardrobe over the past year, using thousands from her inheritance. But she had to look good, didn't she? How else could she attract the right man? Now these clothes were getting a little snug, too. And she was already $100 over her limit at Macy's. She'd have to wait until her next paycheck before she could go shopping again.

"Do you have time to answer some questions?" the woman asked.

"Yes, ma'am, though I may have to put you on hold a few times if I get another call."

"I understand. What I'd—"

"Oops. There's the phone. Hold on." Oh, God, she fretted as she dealt with the other call. What a stupid way to put her on hold. She'd never pass that interview now. That asshole Keith would be glad, though. He didn't want her to leave, anyway, even though he kept saying he didn't want to marry her, either.

"Hello?" asked Miranda, punching back to her own call.

"Yes. First, I'd like to verify some information. You're twenty-seven, adopted at birth, have lived in New Orleans all your life, graduated from a public high school and took two courses at a community college. You worked three months in day care and as a receptionist for three years. Is that correct?"

"Yes." God. It sounded like she'd just loafed around for years after getting out of high school. How could she put on a resume' that she'd been a Sunday School teacher for three years, had been Homemaking teacher at church for a year, that she'd spent over a year taking care of her sick mother? Should she have written that down? Maybe if— "Oops, hold on."

Miranda took a message for one of the lawyers who was out with his secretary for an early lunch and some quick sex. Her fingers pressed the pen harshly onto the paper as she wrote the message. Everyone at the office knew about the affair. The secretary would even return from lunch wearing different clothes, but no one ever told the attorney's wife when she came to the office.

Wasn't that just like men, she thought. Always cheating on their wives. Just like Keith had done when he and Miranda had first started dating. And like Eric had done before Keith, only Eric never did divorce his wife as Keith had.

That bastard Eric! She *had* to get the job. She had to get away from him, too.

"Hello?"

"Yes. Now for those questions, Miss Ryan. Have you ever been pregnant?"

"What? Um, uh, um, no." Oh, God, that woman could *tell*. Miranda was sure of it. Now if she didn't get that job, it would be Eric's fault. If he'd just married her in the first place four years ago when he'd gotten her pregnant, she wouldn't even have to be going through this now.

But he'd dumped her, not even coming to see her in the hospital when she miscarried and almost died from hemorrhaging. And when he'd been in the hospital not four months earlier for an appendicitis attack, she'd brought a card, balloons, ribbons, and streamers to hang up all over his room to cheer him up, even though he'd only been there for a day.

But Eric had married someone else from their congregation shortly after Miranda got out of the hospital, and three years later he'd had the nerve to call her again. She was sure that time she could make him marry her, but after three months of dating, well, sex really, his wife had found out and Eric had disappeared from her life again.

Men, Miranda thought furiously. They were all the same!

"Do you smoke or drink?" asked the woman.

"No, ma'am." Surely a glass of wine every two weeks when Keith came over didn't count. How else could she handle listening to him cry every time after they had sex, moaning about going to hell? She hadn't told her bishop about the wine, so there was no one else who could contradict her story.

"Do you use drugs?"

"Oh, no. Oops, hang on." At least that was one question she could answer honestly. But did the woman have a machine on the other end of the line that could analyze her voice? Could she tell when Miranda was lying? And what if she called all the references Miranda had given? Would they all tell the same story? Miranda took another message, reassuring herself she'd told the same stories to all the people she'd listed as references.

It wasn't that she wanted to lie, of course. Keith was making her do it. He said he didn't want to be excommunicated and told her if she ever told anyone about their relationship, he'd never speak to her again.

Men always lied. Like the time Eric told everyone the reason he didn't marry her was because she'd had an abortion. He never admitted it to Miranda, but she *knew*. Who else would have started such a rumor?

"Hello?"

"Have you ever been physically abused, Miss Ryan?"

Miranda was silent a moment. "Well, no," she said. "Not by my parents." Her father had criticized her every day of her life, but that wasn't physical abuse, was it? Of course, he had thrown chairs at her a few times when she was already an adult and still living at homme, but she'd thrown them right back.

"Have you been physically abused by anyone else?"

Why was she asking that? It must be important, so Miranda figured she'd better lie again. "Oh, no, not by anyone," she replied. Surely, she meant being raped, anyway, didn't she? The woman didn't need to hear about that time three years ago, right before she moved away from home, when a man had smashed through her living room window in the middle of the night completely naked.

Miranda had run to get her father's gun while her father went to see what caused the crash. She'd fired the gun to scare the man away, but the report had instead brought both her father and the man running into the bedroom.

The man had grabbed the gun, pushed Miranda to the floor, and put the gun to her head. He was growling so loudly the neighbors two houses down could hear him. Miranda's father grabbed the gun back and shot the man, who then fell dead on top of her, blood pouring from his chest onto hers.

Twice when Keith had fallen asleep on top of her, she'd experienced the scene all over again and beaten and clawed at his back until he woke up. Both times, he'd yelled at her and left, but she could never bear to tell him why she'd done it. God, why did all these weird things have to happen to her?

"Are you sure there's been no physical abuse?" the woman asked. "We need to know your full background."

"No, ma'am."

There was a pause. Then the woman asked, "Have you ever been mentally abused?"

Oh, God, not as much as this interview is doing, Miranda thought, but she again replied, "No." She knew she wouldn't get the job if she told the truth about her father, and she'd be damned if she'd let him ruin her life any more than he'd already done. What would that woman think if Miranda told her about the time her father had announced to all the relatives that Miranda had killed her mother, who'd died of cancer?

Or about the time after she'd joined the Mormon church as a teenager and he'd thrown all her clothes on the sidewalk and told her to leave? Or the times after she'd moved back when he would turn off the water to the house so she couldn't bathe or put on make-up and would be late for work? Or the time—

"Oops. Hang on." Oh, why were so many calls today? The woman was going to feel like a yo-yo.

"Miranda?"

"Keith?" she asked in return. He almost never called her at work. He said he was afraid she'd be able to tape the conversation and use it against him as evidence in a church court. "What is it? I've got the nanny person on the other line."

"You're not telling her about me, are you?"

"Are you crazy? Of course not. What do you want?"

"I want you to stay here and go to nursing school. You know that. I—"

"I've got to go. I'll call you later."

Oh, God, thought Miranda. All she wanted was a husband to take care of her. Was that asking so much? She thought about the bishop's wife, and the president of the Relief Society in her congregation, and about all the other women at church with children and husbands who took care of them. Didn't the Church say being a wife and mother was the most important thing she could do? Why didn't any of the men at church see that? Why did men always have to shirk their responsibility?

Keith said she didn't make enough money. She knew he wanted her to be able to support *him*. Men! And he said she needed to be a nurse, of all things. He didn't seem to care that Miranda could hardly go out to do her laundry for fear she'd see a lizard, or that she couldn't bear to associate with anyone bald, or fat, or handicapped, or ugly, or like anyone she'd surely see in an emergency room. For goodness' sake, she'd get pale watching a Visine commercial. She wasn't about to go sticking needles in people. "Oh, you'll get desensitized to all that," Keith had told her.

Like hell, she thought. She was going to be a nanny in a rich family in California and take care of children. And some good-looking man rich enough to be friends with the family would see how well she worked with children and see how well dressed she was and want to marry her.

She looked down again at her overweight stomach and bit her lip. She brushed at her eyes quickly and then smoothed down her dress. If that asshole Keith hadn't kept her depressed all the time, she wouldn't be eating so much in the first place. She'd still be pretty. But once she was away from him, she could lose the weight. She was sure of it.

"Hello?"

"Yes, Miss Ryan. Sorry to keep disturbing you at work. Just one more question and we'll be through."

"All right."

"Why do you want this job?"

Well, wasn't that obvious, thought Miranda. She remembered the day care center, when she'd read stories to the children or had them make up stories to tell her. She'd encourage them with their drawings, promising to hang them up in her apartment. She loved seeing her Monet print on one wall and "her" children's drawings on another. She would sometimes bake cookies or brownies to bring to work, and she'd taken pictures of all the children she'd worked with during those three months.

One little girl in particular had always seemed down, and Miranda had eventually decided to give the girl one of her favorite dolls she'd been meaning to save for her own daughter. She'd tried to coax the girl into telling her why she was always so sad, but the girl's parents had taken her out of the day care before Miranda could find out. But if she could get this job in California, she'd have a whole year with the same children. And she could get married and have her own children no one could ever take away.

"I want this job because I love children and I love taking care of them." Miranda sighed in relief but then frowned. What if the woman didn't believe her? Had her answer sounded like one of those phony Miss America answers? What if—

"Thank you for your time, Miss Ryan," the woman said.

"Oh, it was no problem."

"We'll finish checking your references and look for a position suited to your needs and abilities, and then we'll get back to you."

"Thank you."

They both hung up, and Miranda sat staring for a moment, drumming a pen on top of her book. Should she call her bishop and the woman in charge of the day care center to see what they'd told the nanny woman? Would that make things worse? Should she call Keith back? What was she going to do about their date tonight?

She'd let him come over, but only if he brought the condoms this time instead of making her buy them. God, what if someone saw her? And besides, condoms were a man's responsibility. If he didn't want to bring them, he'd just have to take a chance at getting her pregnant and having to marry her. But tonight, she wouldn't argue about the condoms. She'd just tell him she was going to California unless he started going out in public with her. She'd say she was going to leave unless he could offer her a reason to stay. She'd make him realize how much he really loved her.

She picked up the phone and dialed. "Keith?" she asked.

"Can you talk, Miranda?"

"Yeah."

"I just wanted to say I can't make it tonight. I know how you hate it when I don't call to tell you, so I thought I'd let you know. Something came up."

"Oh."

"But I'll give you a call tomorrow or the next day."

"All right."

"Talk to you later."

Miranda hung up and looked at her watch. Still an hour before lunch. She stared at her desk a moment and then picked up *Viking Princess* again. Surely, she'd get the job, she thought. She'd show Keith. She'd show everybody. She smiled and opened the book, but her eyes were still focused on the desktop in front of her, and after a moment, her smile slowly faded away.

Ambien Dreams

The door opened and an attractive young man around thirty-five greeted them. "Hello, Elders," the man said, ushering them inside.

"Mike, this is Jared Martin," said Elder Prusso. "Brother Martin, this is Mike Sobieski."

Jared and Mike shook hands. Jared was impressed. Mike was dark-haired, with a moustache. He had a trim body and a firm handshake. If Jared had still been gay, he'd be attracted to this man. Jared would be fifty-five in a couple of weeks and had been married to Carol for twenty-nine years, but Mike was exactly the kind of guy he'd have been attracted to in the past. Thank God he was beyond that now.

Jared and Elder Prusso sat on the sofa while Mike sat in a chair nearby. Jared was a stake missionary and often worked one evening a week with the full-time missionaries. Elder Prusso was the cuter of the two twenty-year-olds stationed in his ward, so it was always fun when Jared got to work with him. He was able to relive briefly what it had been like to have a permanent, full-time missionary companion so many years ago, which had been the best part of missionary life.

"Mike," Elder Prusso continued, "we thought we'd teach you tonight about the Plan of Salvation. Have you ever asked yourself, 'Where did I come from? Why am I here on the Earth? Where will I go when this life is over?'"

Before they started, Elder Prusso asked Mike to say a prayer, and Jared thought he did a pretty good job for a non-member. He might be in tune enough to accept the gospel. Converts were rare here in Spartanburg. South Carolina was not the largest outpost in Zion.

But it was still Zion. It was where Jared had met Carol thirty years ago. They'd married in the Washington DC temple, the closest temple at the time. And they had two children who'd both turned out fine, both married in the temple themselves. Jared's son, Paul, had even gone on a mission to Uruguay as well.

Ever since Jared's own mission to Germany thirty-three years earlier, he'd dreamed of having a son fill a mission, too. Missionary work was so uplifting. It was the only period in your life you could spend all your time with other men just like yourself. That was why he enjoyed being a stake missionary so much. It was only part-time, but it kept him in touch with dedicated young men like Elder Prusso.

But now that might all be coming to an end. It seemed unfair to have plodded all through life to this point, having overcome so much temptation, having become so much more Christ-like, and still be facing catastrophe. He might not be able to work in the Church at all anymore. How could he tell Carol and their daughter Lisa he couldn't go to the temple next week to witness Lisa's daughter being sealed to her?

"Mike," Elder Prusso said, "before we came to this Earth, we lived as spirits in the Pre-existence with our

Heavenly Father. There, we progressed as much as we could, but there finally came a point where we couldn't progress any further unless we had a body. So God provided a way for us to come to Earth and get one."

A body, thought Jared. Well, he'd certainly done a poor job in the stewardship of his own. Though it was clear spiritual health was more important than physical, he couldn't help but feel a little depressed about his mortal being. He was easily sixty pounds overweight, though he'd lost fifteen since being diagnosed with diabetes last year and starting to watch his diet.

Plus, Jared had a scar on one breast from when he'd had a pre-cancerous tumor removed. How embarrassing to be a man and almost have breast cancer. It was unnatural. In addition to that, Jared also bore ugly scars on his chest and legs from the bypass surgery for his clogged arteries. And he had frequent yeast infections.

But he still never had any trouble finding sex, once he started looking. It just proved that gay men were so decadent they'd do it with anybody. Jared had had sex with at least two dozen men in the past couple of years since he'd finally given in to the temptation. He'd also been to an orgy once and had sex with three guys at one time. One of them had even looked a little like Mike.

God, he hoped he didn't have to tell his family all that.

Of course, technically, Jared knew he was bisexual, not gay. He simply knew that Carol would have felt more betrayed if he'd had sex with a woman, so he'd deliberately passed up several opportunities to have affairs with females at work. Jared was weak, but not so weak he couldn't still consider Carol's feelings when having sex with someone else.

"You're saying we were spirits before we were born?" Mike asked.

"Yes," said Elder Prusso.

"Our intelligences are eternal," Jared interjected, feeling he'd better contribute and not just indulge in his own thoughts all evening. "But God gave us spirit bodies before we came here. He created all things spiritually before giving everything a physical body. Even the Earth has a spirit. All the animals have spirits, too."

"Really? Wow. You guys must believe that environmental conservation is important."

Jared shook his head nonchalantly. "Not really. The Lord gave us dominion over the Earth and everything on it. We have total control of it."

Mike looked confused. "Well," he said, pausing a moment, "isn't that kind of like the father being the head of the family, the one in control? The one with authority to make decisions?"

Jared thought a moment. "I suppose that's a good analogy."

But Mike still looked confused. "So wouldn't destroying the environment be like a man beating his wife and sexually abusing his children? Just because he's the head of the family doesn't mean he doesn't still have a responsibility to be good to them and protect them."

Jared shook his head again and tried to suppress a smile. Non-members always saw things in a distorted way. It was obvious they didn't have the gift of the Holy Ghost like he still did. "The Earth is subject to serving us," he said simply. "We aren't subject to serving the Earth. There's no danger we can hurt the Earth. God gave us an abundance of everything we need. He gave the Earth a spirit so it would be strong enough to serve us faithfully. Nature doesn't need us to be good to it. It's there to be good to us."

Jared noticed Elder Prusso looking at him oddly. Perhaps he didn't agree. But Jared knew that many younger members were influenced by the popular liberal media. And it wasn't as if Jared knew for a fact his opinion was that of Church leaders, since the Church so rarely even broached the subject. But that lack of interest in itself told Jared enough. Nature simply wasn't worth talking about. Spiritual matters were immeasurably more important than natural ones.

Mike still looked uncertain as well, but Jared was always happy to explain the gospel plainly to people. It was why he liked being a stake missionary so much. He hoped he wouldn't lose this opportunity when he talked to his stake president in a few days. Jared looked over at the pleasant young elder next to him, listening as Elder Prusso continued.

"You've heard of near-death experiences, haven't you?"

"Yes, I think I saw a program on that once."

"Almost everyone who has one says they meet up with parents and friends who have died before them. All our spirits are eternal, and just as we existed before this life, we'll still exist afterward."

"Cool."

Mike seemed to be back on track, so Jared returned to his own thoughts, thinking of the new spirit that had just joined his family. His daughter Lisa had married Darren, a great and attractive young man, four years ago, but they hadn't been able to have children.

They were finally able to adopt a baby girl, Hannah, through LDS Social Services from a wayward Mormon girl who'd gotten pregnant as a teenager. The adoption was finalized two weeks ago, and now Lisa and Darren were going to the temple in Atlanta to have Hannah sealed to them for time and all eternity, so they could still be a family even after everyone was old and dead.

Of course, if Jared was excommunicated now, or if Carol divorced him, he'd never be with his family in the next life. He known he'd have to repent sometime, but he'd kept putting it off. Still, he knew that if he were to die in his sins, without real repentance and cleansing by the blood of Christ, he would not have eternal life.

To be consigned to the Telestial kingdom when he knew the rest of his family was happy together in the Celestial—he couldn't face an eternity of that. He wouldn't be able to enjoy that ultimate sociality, that bliss, that perfect life which exalted families enjoyed. He had no choice except to repent.

But Jared knew from his study of the scriptures and the words of the prophets, and even from the whisperings of the Spirit which he still sometimes heard, that true repentance required a change of heart, a genuine change in desires. How could he repent if he still wanted to be with men? Thank God that was no longer the case, now that he'd found the cure for this terrible condition.

"In order to obtain the wisdom that God has," Elder Prusso was saying, "we need many experiences we couldn't have as spirits."

"But I would think a spirit is superior to a physical body," said Mike.

"How can a spirit experience pain and physical suffering?" Elder Prusso asked. "A spirit can't be baptized or married or raise children."

But Jared knew there were also bad things you could do with a body. He remembered about eight years ago, before he'd really done very much sexually, he was serving as first counselor in the bishopric, as his son Paul was doing now in his own ward in Charlotte. A new stake president was being called to serve over nine congregations, and Jared was called in for an interview, almost certainly to be considered as one of the new president's two counselors.

Jared had confessed then to looking at porn on the internet, but he said he'd stopped and wasn't doing it any longer. But even just looking at bodies without touching them was a serious offense. Not only did he not receive a call to the stake presidency, but a week later he was also released from the bishopric, and he was told he'd never be eligible to serve as a bishop or as a sealer in the temple.

Yet he'd repented, he told himself. How could they treat him like a sinner? It wasn't right. Didn't Church leaders believe in the Atonement? Would his repentance now not really count either?

Eventually, since he'd felt condemned anyway, Jared had started looking at porn again. If it didn't help to repent, why bother, he thought. Of course, that was just Satan trying to ensnare him. And he was certainly doing a good job of it. But now he could feel he was finally going to beat Satan, now that he was healed.

If looking at porn, however, were *all* he had to confess to the stake president now. The man had cornered Jared in the hallway at church last week and questioned him intensely. The president knew something was going on because Jared had wriggled out of all interviews for a couple of years, ever since he finally began to hook up with other guys.

"We're here on Earth to be tested?" Mike asked.

"That's right," said Elder Prusso. "That's why we all went through the Veil of Forgetfulness when we were born. It wouldn't be a true test if we could remember our pre-Earth life. We needed to forget so we could develop faith."

Jared turned to the book of Ether in the Book of Mormon and held it out for Mike to read. "Chapter 12, verse 6 explains it pretty well," Jared told him.

"And now, I, Moroni, would speak somewhat concerning these things," Mike read carefully. "I would show unto the world that faith is things which are hoped for and not seen; wherefore, dispute not because ye see not, for ye receive no witness until after the trial of your faith."

"I think I got it," said Mike. He handed the Book of Mormon back to Jared. As he did so, their fingers touched briefly. Their eyes locked for just a second, and suddenly Jared knew that Mike was gay, too.

Jared felt a thrill thinking about it. It was more important than ever that he help Mike be baptized. If Jared could help save another gay man, it would be at least *some* kind of atonement for his own sins. He offered a quick prayer for the Holy Ghost to testify to Mike tonight.

Should he tell Carol about Mike when he got home, to sort of buffer the way to his big revelation later this week? Of course, he'd told Carol ten years ago he was gay. He'd said gay and not bisexual because he didn't want her to worry he was lusting after other women.

She had to have suspected his inclinations anyway, since he had so many long conversations alone with Tad, Carol's gay younger brother, who'd been excommunicated a few years after his mission to Japan. But all Jared had had to confess to ten years ago was a couple of episodes of mutual masturbation with other guys. He'd thought the news would be shocking, but while Carol had cried at first, she soon dried her tears and said, "Well, that explains a lot. And at least we don't need to have sex anymore."

Goodness knows they hardly ever had sex as it was. Carol had hated it right from the start twenty-nine years ago, and its frequency had decreased steadily over the years, finally petering out to just once a month, always at Jared's insistence against Carol's reluctance. But they hadn't had sex even once in ten years now. How in the world could she have expected him to be faithful under those conditions? It was unnatural.

Of course, it was a sin no matter how stressful the situation. Jared was still going to hell if he didn't repent.

Jared wondered if maybe he'd had sex just once early in his life with a really good-looking man, someone like Mike, if he could have gotten it out of his system, instead of spending three decades fantasizing about it.

Two years ago, internet-arranged meetings had just become too much of a temptation, and he'd met a guy at his place, "just to talk." It was the first time Jared had ever tasted semen. He didn't particularly like it, but he was more willing to give a blow job than have someone enter him anally, so he soon got used to it.

"Because we came to Earth to get a body and be tested," Elder Prusso went on, "it was inevitable we'd sin. God sent his son Jesus Christ to atone for our sins so we could be cleansed and be able to enter again into his presence."

"Yes, well, Catholics believe that, too." Mike looked at Jared, and Jared could tell Mike understood that he was gay as well. If Jared could only help get Mike into the Church, maybe Mike would be able to testify on Jared's behalf on Judgment Day. That plus the atonement should get him into heaven.

But even the atonement itself might not be enough to keep him in the Church once he confessed. Yet confession was part of repentance. He had to do it, even if it meant excommunication. Just the idea of what lay ahead made him tired.

But Jared smiled anyway. At least being tired these days wasn't the end of the world anymore. Over the years, he noticed that whenever he was tired, his mind automatically turned to gay fantasies and he longed to see gay images. When he was rested, he felt few or no urges. As his sleep apnea and weight problems and heart disease worsened, Jared was more and more drawn to gay images. Finally, however, images weren't enough, and he had to have actual contact.

But while the encounters were satisfying, the satisfaction never lasted for long. Jared always needed more. That was the nature of carnal sin, he realized. And after two cases of crabs, followed by a genital wart on his penis, he knew he was being physically punished for his sins, as was appropriate.

Then a couple of months ago, after his faith had been tested to the limit, a miracle happened. Jared did another sleep study, and his doctor, an attractive, gray-haired man his own age, had prescribed Ambien for three weeks to help with the central episodes. The doctor didn't know what was causing those spikes on the EEG but thought Ambien might help Jared sleep better.

When he began taking the drug, Jared felt like a blind man seeing for the first time. Not only did he sleep much better and feel more energetic and happy, but *all* homosexual desires and thoughts left him completely and actually became unpleasant to him. After the three-week course of Ambien, a few of the desires and thoughts returned, but not to the same degree as before.

So now Jared knew that homosexuality was caused by a lack of proper sleep.

It meant he could finally be cured. He just had to get his doctor to prescribe Ambien permanently, and he could lead a happy life for the first time in fifty years.

You couldn't expect someone with Down syndrome to earn a PhD in Physics. You couldn't expect someone with schizophrenia to stop hearing voices without medication.

Maybe if Jared could tell his family all this, the good news would somehow moderate the bad.

What would Jared do, though, if he was kicked out of his family and kicked out of the Church at the same time? He was getting old and sick and would have no one to turn to. He'd brought it on himself, of course, but the idea of being abandoned by everyone and everything he ever held dear was almost too much to bear.

Yet he couldn't lie about it and go to the temple unworthily. His family had a right to know. And Jared would have to confess everything to the bishop and stake president. So far, all he'd said to his leaders was that he was unworthy, but he hadn't gone into detail. Now he'd have to. It was time.

Being honest was better than sneaking around. And now, with Ambien, he wouldn't even have to sneak around anymore. Life could be good, after all. Heavenly Father was merciful. He'd tried Jared sorely, and Jared hadn't passed the test very well, but everything was going to be okay.

"There are three degrees in heaven," Elder Prusso was telling Mike. "And getting married in the temple will allow us to be with our spouse not just till death do us part but for time and all eternity, if we live worthily and make it to the highest degree of heaven, which is the Celestial Kingdom."

"What if you're worthy but your spouse isn't?" Mike asked.

"That's why marriage is a true partnership. You both want to make it there together."

"But if you do make it and your spouse doesn't?" Mike insisted. It was as if he could read Jared's mind, so Jared thought he'd better answer this one.

"You can go to the Celestial Kingdom without your spouse. And God will probably let you be with someone else whose spouse didn't make it either. But eternal marriage is reserved for those who make it to the highest degree in the Celestial Kingdom. No one else in the lower kingdoms will enjoy the benefits of eternal marriage."

"Benefits?"

"Well, we don't want to get into really heavy doctrine just yet," Elder Prusso said.

No, Mike needed to hear the whole story, Jared thought. It was the only way to be strong. "Sex, for one thing," he said. "And the creation of spirits to people our own planets that we'll be gods over."

"Wow."

"The whole purpose of life is to learn, grow, be tested, and eventually become like God himself. He wants us to become like him. It's the whole purpose of life, the reason God created our spirits in the Pre-existence, the reason we came to Earth to get bodies and be tested, the reason for Christ's atonement, the reason for everything."

Sex with two dozen men couldn't compare to a family's love, couldn't compare to the joy and privilege of becoming a god. Jared knew now what was important in this life. And the only way he could have that love for eternity was to be honest with his family and bishop.

Fortunately, with the Ambien, he could face repentance with a willing heart. It would be better if he could do it by himself, without drugs, but homosexuality was clearly a medical condition, just like diabetes, and simply needed treatment with the right drugs.

Of course, Jared couldn't help remembering something he'd heard St. Augustine once say: "To abstain from sin when a man cannot sin is to be forsaken by sin, not to forsake it."

That wouldn't apply in his case, though. God would be happy he'd quit fooling around, no matter what the reason. Nature had gone astray in him for a while, but God had created Nature, and Nature was now taking care of him as it was programmed to do. He was going to be all right.

"Well, I certainly want to hear more," Mike said. "Do you think you could come by again next week?"

"Sure." Elder Prusso smiled. "And you can come to church Sunday if you like. It starts at 10:00."

"I can give you a ride if you want," Jared offered. It would be nice if they could end up being friends. A true friendship was better than sex anyway.

"Okay. I think I'd like that. Is it okay if I bring my girlfriend, too?"

Jared felt a chill run down his spine. Elder Prusso smiled again, but Jared had to fight to keep the disappointment from showing on his face. If Mike wasn't gay, they could never be true friends. Jared was sure that a true, platonic friendship with another gay man would be all he really needed now that most of his sexual desires were gone.

Maybe if he took a larger dose of Ambien, or a combination of two drugs, he wouldn't even need the friendship. Perhaps Mike was bisexual, though, like he was. They could still have a special friendship. God could still be responsible for their meeting like this.

But Jared knew he'd also need to get to the Celestial Kingdom as Carol's friend, and once there, they'd be happy together for eternity. They'd enjoy sex finally and the creation of spirit children. That would entail billions upon billions of acts of sexual intercourse over the eons. It was God's plan. It would all work out.

Elder Prusso asked Mike to offer another prayer, and again it was a good one, Jared noticed. Mike seemed to be a spiritual man, even if he were fornicating regularly with his girlfriend. Jared himself still felt the Holy Ghost despite his own fornication, so he wasn't surprised Mike was still a good guy. Sex was bad, but when you were truly good deep down, even illicit sex couldn't dampen the Spirit completely.

Jared shook Mike's hand firmly as he left. Then he drove Elder Prusso back to his apartment and headed on home himself. After a spiritual evening like tonight, he'd never be better in tune to talk to Carol. It would have to be this evening. And then tomorrow he'd need to talk to Lisa.

Thank God his parents had both died in a car accident two years ago and wouldn't have to know. He wondered if they got reports on him in the spirit world, but he hoped that could all wait till Judgment Day.

Jared pulled into the driveway and turned off the motor, keeping his hand on the steering wheel another minute. Yes, he was going to tell Carol tonight.

He breathed deeply and reached for the keys, but he noticed his hand was shaking, the way it had shaken the first time he'd had sex with a man.

How would he ever have the strength to make it to the Celestial Kingdom by himself if Carol turned him away?

He got out of the car and shut the door. As he started toward the house, he felt his heart beating quickly.

Because he'd been in college in the early 70's, Jared hadn't had to go to Viet Nam. But now he understood how courageous soldiers were. He felt he was walking into the deadliest battle scene anyone could face. But he was doing it with a brave heart. He was a hero really.

He was going to be honest and face whatever fallout came from it.

As Jared reached the front door, his heart beat so hard it hurt. He hoped the bypass was working.

He thought of Mike, and he wished he had a sleeping pill to take tonight.

Jared unlocked the door and went to the kitchen. "That you, Jared?" Carol called out from the living room where he could hear the TV in the background.

He walked into the living room and stood there, preparing himself. This might be the end of the world, but even without an Ambien, Jared was sure to get a good night's sleep if he unburdened himself.

"You have a good evening with the elders?" Carol asked, looking up briefly from the TV but not waiting for a response.

Jared suddenly felt at peace. Yes, he was going to get a decent night's sleep. But he definitely needed to renew that Ambien prescription. He couldn't face the next twenty years without it. "Carol," he said, and from his tone, she turned to look at him sharply, "we need to talk."

He took another deep breath and began.

Homework for Hitler

"Come on, Lester, you can help out just this once," Cathy's uncle Willie Ray urged Cathy's father. They were outside on the porch discussing something personal. Cathy sneaked over to the front door and listened as hard as she could through the thick wood. She knew something was up. Willie Ray never came over at all unless he needed something.

"You know I can't," her father said firmly.

"It's that damn religion of yours again, isn't it? You've been a real deadbeat ever since you joined. You're lucky we don't bomb *your* church."

"I've got to go, Willie Ray. You need to get out of the Klan. It'll destroy your soul."

"You standing up for Jews now? *You're* the one who's going to hell."

Cathy heard footsteps and realized her father was heading for the door. She turned and ran to the bathroom so he wouldn't catch her listening. The front door opened just as she reached the commode. She waited in the room for several minutes and then flushed.

When she went back to the kitchen, her father was sitting at the table with her mother. Tommy, her eight-year-old brother, was probably in his room reading a book.

"Cathy," her father said. "Sit down."

"Yes, Daddy."

"You'll be thirteen next week. You're old enough to hear this."

Cathy sat down across from her father, her heart beating faster. She'd so looked forward to her first cup of coffee to show she was all grown up, but when they joined the Mormon Church the year before, she was told she could never drink coffee at all. Ever. She hadn't been happy about that then and still found it irritating.

But her father had stopped smoking those awful Picayunes almost overnight, so that was something.

"What is it, Daddy?"

He smiled. "You know darn well what it is. I heard you at the front door."

Cathy could feel her face starting to burn, and she looked at the floor.

"Cathy, you know I used to belong to the Klan?"

She shook her head. "No, Daddy."

"Well, you know now that we're Mormon, we can't belong to any secret combinations. It's a sin." He sighed. "Of course, colored folks still bear the mark of Cain. That's why they can't hold the priesthood. But we can't treat them like they're not human."

"Yes, Daddy." Cathy still heard her mother use a common slur pretty often, but her father never did anymore.

Tommy still said it, too. Cathy was scared of colored folks, but while most of her friends hated them, she didn't exactly hate them herself. She just wished they'd go away.

"The Klan is planning another bombing," her father explained.

"Lester, do we really have to tell the child all this? I don't want Cathy getting in trouble."

"Annie Mae, she needs—"

"What does this have to do with Uncle Willie Ray?" Cathy interrupted. "He was talking about Jews."

Her father sighed again. "The Klan is going to bomb the synagogue here in Brookhaven, like they bombed the one in Meridian last week."

Cathy didn't much like Jews. The ones at school always acted so stuck up.

"Daddy, why are you telling me this?"

He sighed again and closed his eyes. When he opened them again, he looked right at Cathy. "I need you to be a grown up."

"Lester, what are you—"

"Yes, Daddy."

"That Liverman girl's in your class, isn't she?"

"Yes," Cathy said carefully.

"Lester—"

"I need you to tell her what the Klan is planning to do."

"Oh my god. Lester, she can't!"

Cathy felt a chill run down her spine. It was like being a spy. A secret agent. But wasn't that kind of like being in a secret combination, too?

"Daddy, I don't like Linda Liverman."

"You don't have to like her. Just pull her aside tomorrow and tell her to warn her father."

"Lester, Willie Ray'll know it was you who told. You'll still get in trouble. And now you want Cathy—"

"I'll tell Willie Ray I didn't say a word to any Jews. I'll swear on the Bible. He'll know I'm telling the truth."

"But Lester—"

Cathy's parents kept talking about it, and Cathy didn't know what to think. There were kids in her class whose fathers and older brothers were in the Klan, and if anyone got wind of what she was doing, life could get plenty ugly for her. Of course, they only had a little more than a week left before summer vacation started. Maybe everyone would forget before school started back up in three months.

Still, that colored man Martin Luther King had been killed just a couple of months ago. And those two Jews and that other colored man had been killed here in Mississippi a few years before. If Cathy said something to mess up the Klan's plans, maybe *she* would be killed. Maybe *their* house would be burned.

"Daddy, can't you just tell the police? Can't they take care of it?"

Her father looked at Cathy sadly and smiled again.

"No, honey, I can't go to the police."

"Lester, I forbid it! Cathy, I forbid you to say a word to that girl!"

"It's up to Cathy, Annie Mae. Cathy's a young woman now. She can make up her own mind."

Cathy didn't know what to think about that, either. It made her feel mature and proud that her father was putting this on her shoulders. But he never let Cathy's mother make up her own mind about anything. Why was Cathy old enough to think for herself but her mother wasn't? Cathy wasn't quite sure she trusted her father.

"Lester, what if they find out?"

"Annie Mae, what if they kill four little Jewish girls like they killed those four little colored girls in that church in Alabama?"

"That's not our problem. If the Jews hadn't crucified Christ, everyone wouldn't hate them so."

"Annie Mae, we're practically Jews ourselves now. We—"

"No, no, no, no, no!"

"Daddy, I'll think about it, but I'm not promising anything." Cathy got up and walked slowly to her room and closed the door. She turned her radio on softly and sat on her bed. She was in the middle of a Nancy Drew book, and she'd always wanted an adventure of her own. Nancy was always finding clues and catching bad guys. She was always getting in trouble, too, but things always worked out for her.

But those were just books. The Klan was mean. They meant business. What if Willie Ray figured out what happened? He wouldn't turn on his own family, would he?

But those men were pretty serious about race traitors. And Linda was such a creep sometimes. Always snooty. Just because she had nice clothes and made good grades. She didn't know the first thing about being nice to people. What did Cathy care if the Klan blew out a couple of windows of that synagogue?

But then what about Jeanette and Libby? They'd been Cathy's best friends until her father made the family join the Mormon Church. Now those girls wouldn't even talk to her anymore. So Cathy knew being mean to folks just because of their religion was bad, but at the same time, other people *did* act that way, and she didn't need any more trouble than she already had.

Cathy read a few more pages of Nancy Drew. Her mind kept wandering, though, and she had to reread one paragraph three times before she put the book down.

An adventure of her own. But it wasn't exciting. It was scary. She'd wanted to do something incredible on her own just once in her life. But maybe it was better to read about adventure than to live it.

Still, it didn't feel good to be a scaredy-cat like her mother, either.

Cathy stared at blond-haired Nancy for the next twenty minutes, thinking. When Louis Armstrong started singing "What a wonderful world," she snapped off the radio.

The next day at school, Cathy noticed that Linda Liverman looked upset, as if she'd been crying. Had someone already told her? Cathy smiled. She wouldn't have to say anything, after all.

She was curious, though, and at lunch she sat next to Linda for the first time ever. Linda did have a couple of friends here at school, other snobs. But Linda had sat by herself today, so Cathy felt she could risk it.

"Linda? Are you all right?"

Linda looked at Cathy with an expression Cathy couldn't quite figure out. It was half despair but also half anger. Did she know it was Cathy's uncle who was involved?

"Why aren't *you* upset?" Linda demanded.

It was a good question, Cathy realized. Shouldn't she be more disturbed that her uncle was a criminal? That he seemed happy to hurt other people, even if they were snobs?

"Well, we never even talk to my uncle anymore," Cathy explained, feeling that somehow this still didn't fully absolve her.

"Huh?" Linda looked puzzled. "I'm talking about Robert Kennedy."

"What about him?"

"He was assassinated last night."

"Oh." Cathy suddenly felt cold. People *were* terrible, she realized. She had better keep her mouth shut.

"Is that it? 'Oh'?"

"I don't get involved in politics."

"That figures."

Now, wasn't that a snobby thing to say? Cathy picked up her lunch and moved to another table.

That night as supper ended, Tommy asked if he could be excused and went to his room. Cathy was about to do the same thing when her father said, "Did you talk to the Liverman girl today?"

"Yes."

"You told her about the bomb?" her mother asked sharply, looking quickly at Cathy's father.

"No. We talked about Robert Kennedy."

"You didn't warn her?" asked her father wearily.

"No."

"Good for you! I knew I'd raised a smart daughter."

"Cathy—"

"No, I won't hear any more about it. The girl's made up her mind. You said she was old enough to think for herself. Now she has. So you leave her be."

"May I be excused?"

"Of course, dear."

Cathy read a couple more chapters of Nancy Drew, but she couldn't get really interested. She turned the radio on to listen to some music. "Classical Gas" always put her in a good mood. She wished her parents would get her a record player for her birthday in a few days, but that was probably hoping for too much. She wondered if she could bargain with her father. "I'll talk to Linda if you get me a phonograph." But somehow that didn't feel quite right.

The next day, Linda was back to normal, talking and laughing with her girlfriends, pointing and giggling at the other girls in the class. Cathy wanted to slap her. So what if her synagogue did get blown up? Linda would just get what she deserved. What a pill.

Cathy didn't sit with her friends at lunch, feeling a little blue, but to her surprise, Linda came over and sat next to her. "It'll be nice when school lets out next week," she said. "You doing anything fun?"

"I'm having my birthday party right after our last day." She said it almost defiantly, wanting Linda to feel jealous that she was getting such a good start to the summer.

"Oh. You'll be thirteen?"

"Yes."

"How nice. You'll be a real woman then."

Cathy frowned.

"Thirteen is the age of adulthood for Jews. Boys get to become a bar mitzvah." She shrugged. "Girls don't get anything, but we're adults, too. It'll be July for me."

"What happened to your brother last year when he turned thirteen?"

"He got a record player."

"Ooh." Cathy didn't know whether she should feel impressed or just mad.

"Yeah, I probably won't get much of anything. I never do."

"You always get nice clothes," Cathy pointed out.

Linda shrugged. "But that's not special. You should get something special for your birthday."

Stuck up.

"I've been asking for a nice book, though. Maybe I'll get that."

"You like books?"

"Yeah. You?"

"Me, too. I love those Mary Jane mysteries."

"My favorite book is *To Kill a Mockingbird*."

Jews, thought Cathy.

"You want to come to my party?" Cathy asked. She had no idea why she'd said such a thing. But Linda's family had money. Maybe Linda would get her a nice gift.

"Really?"

"Sure. Unless you don't want to."

"Oh, no. I think it'd be fun. Gee, I always thought you were too stuck up to say hi."

Cathy finished her lunch and walked away, confused.

During the rest of the period, Cathy went to the school library and looked for a book about Jews. There was only one she could find, called *The Jewish Problem*. She skimmed through it, reading a few paragraphs here and there, about how Jews had poisoned wells in the Middle Ages and had had secret ceremonies during something called Passover during which they sacrificed Gentile children, and how they had a book that taught Jews how to take over banks and governments.

"What're you studying, Cathy?" asked Miss Kyzar, the librarian. "You're not usually in here during lunch."

"Just doing some homework."

Cathy looked at a few more sections of the book and wondered if this was why Linda was so snooty sometimes, because her father expected to help take over the world. He was a doctor, after all. He had power and money. She suspected he donated to all the wrong candidates, too. Still, it seemed hard to believe Linda would've ever been a part of a hidden ceremony to kill children.

But you never really knew what people did in secret, did you? No one would suspect that Willie Ray was in the Klan, would they?

Cathy frowned.

Then again, anyone who knew Willie Ray at all could probably figure that out pretty quickly.

Supper was tense and awkward that night. Even Tommy noticed, looking around at everyone. But he asked to be excused before dessert and went to his room.

"Cathy," began her father.

"Don't start," her mother warned.

"I talked to Linda today," Cathy said, sipping her milk.

There was silence a moment.

"I invited her to my birthday party next week."

"Do Jews celebrate birthdays?" asked her mother.

"Oh, Mama, of course they do."

"Cathy, tomorrow is Friday. If you don't talk to that poor girl before Saturday…"

"Lester, if it means so much to you, you do it."

"I can't, Annie Mae."

"Well, Cathy can't, either."

Cathy stood up, her napkin falling into her plate. "I'm so sick of all this! Who cares what happens to a bunch of Jews? If they were good, wouldn't they be Mormon? Y'all keep saying we're the only ones with the truth."

"That gives us a greater obligation to others," Cathy's father said.

"Oh, Daddy."

"My baby girl isn't going to risk her life because you're a coward!"

"Annie Mae…"

Cathy's mother got up and walked out of the kitchen. Cathy heard the bathroom door close and lock.

"Cathy…"

"No! Mama's right! You're being mean to make me do this. I don't like it. It feels like you're giving me a terrible homework assignment. Or like you're asking me to do all *your* homework for you. Just like the bullies at school." She left the table, too, and stalked off to her room. She turned her radio up, loud, and listened to the Rascals. "It's a beautiful morning." Cathy almost threw the radio across the room.

She sat on her bed and fumed.

Cathy only got a few hours of sleep, but by morning, she knew what she was going to do. While her parents were in the kitchen, she called Willie Ray at home and woke him up. She hoped no one was listening in on the party line. Cathy told him what she had decided and hung up, with Willie Ray still yelling into the phone.

The kids were all excited at school. After this weekend, they only had two more days of class. They were already celebrating and giving the teacher a headache. Cathy paid more attention than usual, though, and she noticed that Linda was still as attentive as ever, too.

Cathy saw that Linda was sitting with her snobby friends again at lunch, and she almost decided to ignore her, but then she took a deep breath and joined the three girls. "Hey, Cathy," said Linda.

"Hey, Linda."

"I can't wait till Wednesday."

Cathy knew her birthday party was the first day of summer vacation, and she wasn't quite sure which event Linda was referring to. She didn't want to say anything about the party in front of these other girls, who she hadn't invited and didn't want to invite now.

"Do you think you could pick me up tomorrow morning?" asked Cathy.

Linda's brow furrowed. "What for?"

"I'd like to go to synagogue with you." Cathy felt like an idiot. "Would that be okay?"

Linda stared at her a moment. The other girls stared, too. "I guess so. Why do you want to come?"

Cathy shrugged. "Oh, I don't know. Just because." She smiled impishly. "If I'm going to be a woman this week, I want to go somewhere I'll be considered an adult."

Linda's two friends snickered, and Cathy felt her face burning, but Linda smiled. "Sure. We can come pick you up. Then you can eat with us afterward if you like."

Things were still a little tense at supper that night, though Cathy was feeling fine now. Tommy noticed the strain on his parents' faces, though, and again asked to be excused before dessert.

This time, Cathy's parents didn't take advantage of the opportunity to say anything. Cathy slowly ate her lemon meringue pie, rather enjoying her parents' discomfort.

Finally, she put her milk down. "I talked to Linda today. Everything is taken care of."

To her surprise, both her parents looked relieved. "I'm so glad," her mother said.

Cathy felt confused.

"Your father and I decided the best way to get you to help was for me to pretend I was against it," her mother went on, laughing. "You never do what I want you to do."

Another secret combination, Cathy thought. But she didn't feel particularly upset, because she knew she hadn't been completely honest, either.

"So the Jews will be on the lookout tonight?" Cathy's father asked.

Cathy smiled. "There's not going to be any bombing," she said confidently.

"I'm glad," said her mother.

"You did a brave thing, Cathy. Thank you."

Cathy smiled again.

After supper, while her parents were watching channel 3, the only station they got from Jackson, Cathy went to the spare bedroom and set up the ironing board and started ironing her best dress. Her mother usually did the ironing, but it was probably time for Cathy to start doing some things herself.

She went to her room and hung the dress on her closet door. Then she sat in bed and picked up Nancy Drew again.

Bobby Goldsboro sang "Honey" in the background, and Cathy turned the page of her book eagerly to see what would happen next.

A Mormon Motive for Murder

"Salve, Sorella Tolman," Sister Covino said as Cindy Tolman opened the mission home door.

"Oh, I told you to stop that," Sister Tolman chided, playfully slapping at the air in Sister Covino's direction. Then she grimaced and massaged her wrist. "Use the *tu* with me," she said, forcing a smile.

It was a mission rule that elders and sisters address those of the opposite sex using the *lei*. That and anyone else they needed to show special deference to, like the mission president and his wife.

"Ciao, Sorella Tolman," said Sister Showalter, Sister Covino's companion, smiling sweetly.

"That's what I want to hear." Sister Tolman nodded at Sister Showalter.

Sister Tolman struggled to pull her shopping cart out the door, and Sister Covino jumped forward to take over. "Let me get that, Sister."

Sister Carla Covino was a missionary for The Church of Jesus Christ of Latter-day Saints, called to serve for eighteen months in the Italy Rome Mission. She'd been here for fourteen months and was senior companion to Sister Kelly Showalter, of Miami. Twenty years old, Sister Covino was from Sioux City. She was half Native American and half Italian. The Italians she worked with here were always dismayed by her name since she looked 100% Native American. She was tall and lean, with high cheekbones and black, smooth hair that fell to her shoulders.

Italian men frequently ogled her, despite an ugly scar on her arm where her brother had shot her with an arrow once when they were kids. Sister Covino usually wore long sleeves, except at the height of summer, when she just couldn't bear it. It was summer now.

Sister Covino grabbed the large red basket on wheels and lifted it down the steps in front of 95 Via Cimone. Though not technically part of the MOPS, the Mission Office Proselytizing Staff, Sisters Covino and Showalter spent the first couple of work hours every morning helping Sister Tolman with her shopping. Sister Tolman did all the cooking by herself, of course, but after meals the young elders in the office did the dishwashing.

"Where to this morning?" Sister Covino asked as Sister Showalter helped Sister Tolman down the steps.

"I want some fresh fruit, some fresh bread, some cheese, and maybe some clams. I feel like spaghetti alle vongole sta sera." She giggled. "I mean, this evening. President Tolman never lets me get away with speaking English. He's so enamored of everything Italian. It's such a relief to spend some time with you sisters."

They strolled slowly down the sidewalk, Sister Covino deliberately making her long legs take short strides, so as not to aggravate Sister Tolman's arthritis. There was no point in the president allowing Sister Tolman to use the mission van, since there was never any place to park near the market. Piazza Sempione would allow them to gather most of Sister Tolman's meal for tonight.

Meandering about the open market was always fun. The truth was that Sister Covino was not too excited about early morning missionary work, which consisted almost totally in performing "24-hour work," which meant walking up and down busy Roman streets, stopping people cold and asking them if they wanted to hear more about the Mormon Church. She described it in her emails home as "24-hour torture."

"Umph." It was Sister Tolman, stopping for a moment to rub her hip.

"When's your next doctor appointment?" asked Sister Covino.

Sister Tolman smiled. "I see Dr. Vardeu this afternoon. It's the best part of each week."

"Do you have trouble understanding him?"

"Oh, he speaks English wonderfully," Sister Tolman replied, "with a lovely accent. He's from Sardegna."

Before long, they'd reached the main road, and it was just a few more minutes before they stood at the bus stop. Like any main road in Rome, traffic was non-stop, and pedestrians were everywhere. At the bus stop itself, there were already fifteen people waiting to board.

It wasn't as bad as Napoli, where Sister Covino had started her mission, but Rome buses could fill up pretty quickly, too. Sister Covino had learned to navigate crowds by this point and started squeezing Sister Tolman in closer to the front of the line. Sister Showalter followed a few feet behind.

"It's good to get out of the house," Sister Tolman said, "even if it hurts. You young sisters are lucky to be out on the streets all day every day. It sounds heavenly."

Sister Covino stole a quick glance at Sister Showalter and smiled. While Sister Covino hated 24-hour work, Sister Showalter hated tracting, which they did in the afternoons and evenings. "What if some guy grabs us and drags us into his apartment?" Sister Showalter always complained.

Sister Covino knew karate, though, and wasn't worried. And they never entered a home without a woman present, which helped decrease their risk. But they were always aware of their vulnerability. Sister Covino simply relied on Heavenly Father to protect her.

If only…

If only she wasn't starting to doubt the very existence of God these days. A couple of weeks ago, one of their investigators had showed her that Lehi's dream from the Book of Mormon was taken almost word for word from a dream that Joseph Smith's father had had. Joseph had simply incorporated the dream when he translated the Book of Mormon.

When he *wrote* it, Sister Covino corrected herself.

She didn't even know any more if she was really a Lamanite.

"Autobus," Sister Showalter announced.

Sister Covino got ready to push onboard with Sister Tolman and the cart the moment the doors opened. But just a second before the bus arrived, Sister Tolman screamed and fell right in front of the bus. Before Sister Covino could react, the bus rolled right on top of her.

Everyone in the crowd waiting to board started shouting. Sister Covino struggled to find her companion in the crowd and vaguely noticed a young man running away. Someone else in the crowd was pointing at him.

"L'ha spinta!" shouted a woman in her mid-fifties, about the same age as Sister Tolman. "He pushed her! I saw him!"

Sister Covino fell to her knees and tried to reach under the bus. Even a quick glance told her there was no hope. Sister Tolman's chest was crushed. She stood and put her hand over her mouth. Sister Showalter hugged her and started crying.

But Sister Covino was confused. Why would anyone want to kill a mission president's wife? If someone hated the Mormons, it would be easier and make a bigger splash to kill one of the missionaries. If it was an anti-American statement, it would be better, and again, probably easier, to kill a tourist. She looked off into the distance but there was no sign of the running man. Damn.

"Sister Showalter, you go back to the mission home and tell them what happened. I'll stay with Sister Tolman."

"By myself?" Sister Showalter said nervously. "We're supposed to always stay together." She looked at Sister Tolman's feet jutting out from beneath the bus. "For...for safety."

"Oh, for God's sake," Sister Covino said brusquely. "President Tolman needs to know, and I certainly can't leave Sister Tolman here by herself."

"All—all right."

Sister Covino waited patiently for the police and ambulance to arrive. She answered questions and then went along with the body to the hospital. She felt a stab of guilt when she realized she was enjoying the freedom of being without her constant companion.

Sister Showalter was nice enough, but even a pleasant companion could be a pain when they were with you every second of the day. Sister Covino almost welcomed her periods because they gave her a few extra moments alone in the bathroom.

Poor Sister Tolman. She hadn't wanted to come on a mission to begin with. It had been her husband's idea, and of course, the priesthood must be respected. Sister Tolman had wanted to remain in Phoenix, where the warm weather helped alleviate her arthritis, which had grown steadily worse over the long months she'd spent in Rome. Since mission presidents served for three years, she still had another year left before she could return to the desert.

And now she never would.

Sister Covino wasn't even sure anymore that dying while serving a mission would gain her any extra points up in heaven. If the Book of Mormon wasn't true, if Joseph Smith wasn't a real prophet, if the Church itself wasn't true…was *any* of it true? Maybe there wasn't even a God.

Sister Covino only had four months left. She loved speaking Italian and living in Rome. She loved meeting the Italian people in their apartments and talking with them. She loved going to see the Coliseum and the Vatican on P-Day. She would stay for her full time, regardless of her doubts. It had just been more fun when she believed.

But it would be nice to see her mother again.

President Tolman hadn't arrived at the hospital yet. Maybe it was best if Sister Covino left before he arrived. If she waited, Sister Showalter might come along, and she'd be trapped again. Better to leave now and not let everyone know how long it took her to get back to the mission home. She walked out the front door, looking ahead to make sure she didn't see any of the MOPS heading her way. Then she hurried for the bus stop and hopped on the first bus that came her way.

The murder itself was too confusing. She still couldn't figure out why anyone would kill the wife of a mission president. It just didn't make any sense. Had Sister Tolman unknowingly witnessed a crime? She had certainly never said anything about it. So what could be the reason for killing her?

Sister Covino saw a sign out the window and immediately pulled on the red cord to ring the bell. A block later, the bus pulled to a stop and Sister Covino hopped off. She walked slowly back toward the sign, wondering if she was making a mistake. She stood on the sidewalk staring at the sign for almost five minutes before making a decision.

"Francesco Vardeu. Medico."

It was Sister Tolman's doctor's office. It was a long shot he'd know anything. But then, maybe something nefarious was going on in his office, and the woman had witnessed something without even realizing it. At the very least, the man needed to know why his patient wouldn't be arriving later this afternoon.

Sister Covino pushed the button on the citofono.

"Chi é?"

"Sono qui per la Signora Tolman."

The door buzzed and Sister Covino pulled it open. "You're not Signora Tolman," said the receptionist at the front desk.

"No, but I need to see Dr. Vardeu about her. It's very important."

The woman looked at her computer screen. "The appointment's not until 1:00."

Sister Covino looked at her watch. Being AWOL that long was bound to cause suspicion. She might even be sent home if the president thought she was out sinning. But then, he had other things on his mind right now, didn't he?

"I'll wait."

Sister Covino decided to tell the other sisters she'd been so traumatized she'd needed a long walk. She'd still be back at the apartment in time for lunch, which lasted from 1:30 to 3:30 every day. She picked up a *Gente* magazine and flipped absentmindedly through the pages, thinking of her brother, at eighteen just now deciding if he wanted to serve a mission as well. Should she tell him what she knew? Maybe he'd go someplace like Tokyo and get a real education. It would be good for him, regardless of whether the Church was a great big lie.

Sister Covino noticed that the last three patients to come out of Dr. Vardeu's examining rooms were attractive women in their fifties. She looked about the waiting room. Two more women were seated near her, both attractive, both in their fifties.

What kind of doctor specialized in attractive fifty-year-old women?

Finally, it was 1:00, and Dr. Vardeu called for Signora Tolman. Sister Covino stood and walked toward him. He frowned but waved her into his office. "Where is Signora Tolman?" he asked immediately.

"She was murdered this morning," Sister Covino replied, studying his reaction. He looked genuinely surprised. "She was pushed under a bus and run over."

"Madonna!"

"Were you having an affair with Signora Tolman?" Sister Covino asked.

"What?!" His eyes bugged out. "Of course not!"

"She spoke very highly of you." Sister Covino kept looking at Dr. Vardeu. "Very highly."

Dr. Vardeu shook his head. "We—we got along well. She didn't come here just to talk about her arthritis." He looked nervously toward the window.

"Yes?"

"She also came to talk about how much she wanted to go home. She had trouble learning Italian, and she didn't like our cold winters."

"So you talked about the weather?"

Dr. Vardeu looked irritated. "To tell you the truth, she talked most of the time about how unhappy she was with her husband."

Now it was Sister Covino's turn to look surprised.

"She said he'd grown very distant lately and spent a lot of time with the local Mormons. He was either with the young men in the house or out of the house with congregants."

That sounded odd. It wasn't really the mission president's job to interact daily with local members. Was Dr. Vardeu making something up to hide the truth?

"Did she tell you why she thought he was becoming so distant?"

Dr. Vardeu shrugged. "She did tell me something in confidence."

Sister Covino leaned forward and put her hand on his desk. "Well, I'm not the police. You certainly don't have to tell me anything. But if you know anything at all that might be helpful…"

He shook his head. "This won't be helpful, but I don't suppose I need to keep any secrets any longer." He sighed.

"Signora Tolman told me her arthritis gave her such pain she was no longer able to…able to…you know…make love."

Sister Covino blinked. She knew technically that people as old as the Tolmans still had sex, but the couple always seemed so asexual when she saw them together that she was surprised to discover Sister Tolman had found this to be a concern.

"Signora Tolman was a lonely woman," the doctor went on. "I sometimes put on a little extra charm when she was here, to make her feel special. It seemed the least I could do."

Sister Covino thought of all the other attractive middle-aged women she'd seen in the office today. Was charming them his way of getting a steady income? Or was it his way of getting something else steadily?

What if Sister Tolman simply thought he was flirting and became clingy, as lonely people sometimes did? What if Dr. Vardeu had hired some young thug to push Sister Tolman in front of a bus to get rid of her?

Sister Covino decided she'd better not act too suspicious or she might end up under a bus herself. "Thank you for your time, Dr. Vardeu." She stood and offered her hand. He held it just a little too long.

Back on the street, Sister Covino tried to decide if she should head back to her own apartment or go directly to the mission home. Sister Showalter could be at either location. The mission home was sure to be in an uproar, but that might work to her advantage. She caught the bus back to Piazza Sempione and walked the rest of the way to Via Cimone.

She knocked on the door timidly, and it was opened a moment later by Elder Sorenson. Sister Covino had always been fond of Eric. They'd grown up in the same districts, first in Napoli Two and then in Cagliari. He was now an AP, Assistant to the President. You couldn't rise any higher than that in the mission. Some of the other missionaries complained that the power had gone to his head, but Sister Covino still liked him.

"Salve, Sorella Covino."

"Salve, Anziano Sorenson."

"What a day, huh?"

"Unbelievable."

He put a finger to his lips and motioned her inside. People were walking back and forth throughout the house. It looked like the other three sister missionaries from Covino's district were either cooking or cleaning, and the MOPS seemed like bees buzzing about from place to place.

Elder Sorenson pulled Sister Covino into an empty office. She was surprised he didn't keep the door wide open for propriety, leaving it open only a crack. "They've been talking about you being gone so long. You had everyone worried."

"I went to see Sorella Tolman's doctor."

"Why?"

"He said she and the President haven't been having sex, and it bothered her."

Elder Sorenson frowned. He put his hand to his mouth, looked at Sister Covino, then turned away and sat down.

"What are you thinking?" Sister Covino asked. "You're thinking something."

Elder Sorenson shook his head. "It's just that…"

"Yes?"

He shook his head again. "I'm wondering how much you know."

"Is there something to know?"

Elder Sorenson gave her an appraising look. Sister Covino wasn't sure if it was a look to gauge how must he could trust her, or something else. "President Tolman has been humming and singing a lot lately," he said carefully.

"Singing?"

"Italian songs."

"Hymns?"

Elder Sorenson shook his head. "Love songs. Like from the radio."

Sister Covino frowned. Elder Sorenson studied something on the floor. "There's more?"

Elder Sorenson glanced at the nearly closed door and leaned forward toward Sister Covino. "I know it's nothing," he whispered, "but…"

"Spit it out."

"It's just a coincidence. But the other night, President Tolman and us MOPS were sitting in his office after a meeting. And the president started talking about life in the Celestial Kingdom." He paused. "In particular, whether there would be polygamy."

"Everyone knows there will be polygamy there," Sister Covino said. It was a relief in some ways to be able to doubt the Church. Maybe that meant heaven wouldn't be hell for eternity. "So what?"

Elder Sorenson stood up and moved deeper into the study. Sister Covino followed. "The president said it would be a blessing if Sister Tolman died, to relieve her suffering. And that if he married again in the temple, he'd have at least two wives in the Celestial Kingdom." He shook his head. "He has to be beating himself up now for saying such things."

Sister Covino blinked again. She heard a lilting female voice out in the hall, speaking clear Italian, not one of the sister missionaries. "Who's that?" she asked.

"It's Sister Di Prima. She came over to help with the cooking."

Sister Covino stared at the almost occluded doorway, a meager inch allowing sound to filter softly into the study. She heard clattering in the kitchen. And footsteps. And a radio on. She looked at Elder Sorenson, who was looking at her intently.

The president couldn't be *that* stupid, could he? Was he having an affair with one of the local members? Sister Di Prima was Relief Society president for the Trionfale ward. A widow. Sister Covino looked into Elder Sorenson's eyes. There was a shadow there.

"Why are you trembling?" she asked. "You know perfectly well what happened, don't you?"

Elder Sorenson shook his head. "I don't know anything." He paused. "Just that the president is a great man. No one can say anything different."

"Uh-huh." She headed for the door. "I've got to leave. I'll be back shortly."

"Where are you going?" Elder Sorenson looked anxious.

"I need to take a walk."

"You're not going to say anything to anyone, are you?"

Sister Covino smiled bitterly. "What would I say?"

"We follow the priesthood," Elder Sorenson said. "And there are lots of anti-Mormons out there who will say and do anything to hurt the Church."

Sister Covino thought back to the investigator who'd ambushed her with that damn article. She nodded slowly and walked out. She'd go back to her apartment while the other sisters were at the mission home and call the police. She knew there might be nothing to her suspicions. She might just be a silly fool. Or she might simply be mad at the Church for deceiving her and be trying to get back at them any way she could. But the police could sort through all that.

She stood at the bus stop, looking impatiently down the street. Ah, there was the bus. She'd be home soon. And maybe she'd call her parents and *really* go home, leave *all* her doubts behind, even about what might have happened to Sister Tolman.

She smiled grimly as the bus approached. But just as the vehicle was about to pull over, she felt a shove from behind and was thrown out flatly into the street. The last thing she saw before the darkness were wheels heading right toward her head.

The Pig Door

"Is your name Jeff Landers?" asked a young man on the other end of the phone.

"Yes," Jeff replied hesitantly. Was this another telemarketer? He was on the Do Not Call registry, but some calls still seemed to get through.

"Did you used to live in Houston twenty years ago?"

"Yes," Jeff said again, even more cautiously. Was this a bill collector? His finances had always been in good order. But he'd moved to Dallas eighteen years ago, when he was twenty-five. Who could be looking for him there? Had someone stolen his identity and was causing trouble now?

"Did you ever donate sperm at the Greendale clinic?"

What the hell was this? Jeff stared at the phone in his hand. Had the Church found out what he'd done? Was he about to get in trouble? He'd been disfellowshipped once eighteen years ago for having sex with his girlfriend, which was one of the main reasons he'd left Houston. And he'd been disfellowshipped here in Dallas a year later for having sex with his fianceé in this city before they married.

He'd tried to be good after their divorce and was working hard to resist his new girlfriend until he could convince her to marry him, but it wasn't easy. He certainly didn't want to get in trouble now for donating sperm twenty years ago.

"Why would you need to know a thing like that?" asked Jeff.

"Well, if you did, then you're my father."

Jeff was speechless. He looked at the phone again. Could this be real? Was he really talking to his son?

Jeff never had any children of his own. His girlfriend back in Houston had been a single mom with two kids and didn't want more children. When things started getting serious, he felt such a longing for children of his own he decided to donate sperm, just so he could always feel that maybe somewhere out in the world was a kid with his genes.

"Are you there?" asked the young man.

"Y-yes, I'm here," Jeff said. "It might be me, but we'd have to do a DNA test before I'll say any more."

"Really? You'll do a DNA test? That's great!"

Had Jeff made a mistake in offering that so soon? Was this guy just after his money? Even if this man was biologically his son, Jeff clearly had no financial obligations, did he? Besides, the boy must be almost an adult by now.

"Are you down in Houston?" Jeff asked.

"Yes, but you tell me when you want me to come up for a blood test, and I'll be there."

They talked a couple more minutes. The young man said his name was Sweeney. It seemed an odd name, but Jeff didn't comment. After he hung up, he sat at his kitchen table, staring at the floor. When he'd moved to Dallas and eventually married Sherry, Jeff still never fathered any kids. They'd been married fifteen years, breaking up two years ago. Now he'd been dating Kristen for several months. She had two kids as well, so it looked like he was never going to have any children. Only now it seemed he'd had one eighteen years ago. It was kind of scary, but he hoped it might be true.

He wondered briefly if he'd get in trouble with the Church for having a child outside of marriage. But it was years ago, and it wasn't as if he'd physically had sex with the boy's mother.

Jeff heard a grunting noise and felt a nudge at his feet. Penelope was hungry. He reached down and scratched behind Penelope's ears. He'd had the pot-bellied pig for two years, since breaking up with Sherry. He'd thought for a while she might be his only real "child." Sherry's kids had never liked him and hadn't spoken to him once since the temple divorce. They attended a different Mormon congregation now and he never saw them anymore.

It was another two hours before Jeff could see Kristen for dinner. She always brought the kids, Tim, aged eight, baptized a month ago by Kristen's ex-husband, and Lizbeth, aged ten, already wearing sexy outfits at her age. When Jeff said something to Kristen about it, she told him, "They're my kids. Don't worry about it."

But they certainly seemed like Jeff's kids when the check came at the restaurant, or when it was movie night. The children had even started bringing their friends along on movie night, and Jeff found himself paying for them, too.

They sat at Denny's for the buffet. Jeff only saw his girlfriend twice a week, and they ate out each time. Kristen was a flight attendant for American Airlines, where Jeff worked as a baggage handler. She said she was too tired to both go on a date *and* cook, so he'd have to take everyone to dinner if he wanted to see her.

But he did want to see her, so they went to Denny's a lot.

Tonight, Jeff made an effort to ask the kids about their day, but they answered in monosyllables, and Jeff didn't have the energy to draw them out. Kristen, on the other hand, went on in detail about her day.

"First, the other crew and I decided we didn't want to serve alcohol today and deal with the money, so we told people there was a new policy that this was a non-drinking flight. One man insisted he'd flown on this flight just last week, and there was alcohol then. So I said the new rule just went into effect today. But he said he was going to call and complain, so we had to get out the alcohol just for him, and then other people saw us, and we had to let everyone buy drinks who wanted one. What a bother."

"Maybe it's better not to lie in the first place," Jeff suggested, smiling.

"Drinking alcohol is a sin. It's my duty to discourage it whenever I can."

"So that's the reason the other crew members didn't want to serve alcohol today?"

"Whose side are you on?"

"Oh, yours, always, sweetie." Jeff smiled again, but Kristen gave him an annoyed glance.

They were almost finished dinner when Kristen looked at her watch and said in a bored tone, "And how was your day, Jeff?"

"Well," Jeff said, taking a deep breath. "I got a call from a man who claims he's my son."

Kristen froze with her glass halfway to her lips. She looked at him quickly.

"I thought you had a vasectomy."

"Well, I wasn't born with one." Jeff laughed.

"Oh, gross, Tim!" said Lizbeth, hitting her brother. "Don't eat like a pig!"

Kristen ignored the fight and put her glass down. She looked at Jeff, her eyes narrowing. "If you have a kid, that puts things in a different light."

"How do you mean?"

"It means you're not all mine. I don't want to share you."

Jeff glanced briefly at the two kids, still fighting, but he didn't say anything.

"You believe him?" Kristen asked.

Jeff shrugged. "I don't know. I guess we'll have to do a blood test."

"Don't open that door." Kristen shook her head firmly. "Just refuse to see him. He'll go away."

"And if he *is* my son?"

"He's not your responsibility. His mother never told you about him. You have other responsibilities now."

Jeff didn't know what to say. He'd never actually proposed, but every time he started hinting that he wanted to, Kristen would change the subject. Was she saying now she felt they were committed to each other?

Kristen was a beautiful woman. She could have any man she wanted. She'd married once outside the temple, and she and her husband never did get sealed there because he could never stop drinking coffee. Kristen herself drank tea. She was drinking it tonight.

But Jeff wanted a temple marriage. He wanted to know he was going to be with his wife forever. Kristen could be a little harsh, but she'd had a hard life, abandoned by her father, who she referred to as "the pig fucker," when she was ten. So Jeff was willing to cut her a little slack.

She could also be quite pleasant. They'd all play Sorry with the kids sometimes, or Clue, or Life. She seemed to be at her best when she was in a playful mood. Jeff sometimes pushed her on the swing at the park or took her and the kids to jump on trampolines or took them to the waterpark. One weekend, he'd taken everyone down to Astroworld. He loved seeing Kristen smile. She seemed so sweet and innocent then.

"Come on. We're done. Take me home. I'm getting a headache."

Jeff drove to Kristen's apartment, where she unlocked her door and let the kids go in. Then she turned to Jeff.

"Can I come in for a few minutes?"

"I have an early flight."

"Well, I have to be at work at 5:30."

"So you'd better get home and get to sleep."

Jeff leaned forward, but Kristen pulled back. "For God's sake, Jeff. Do I have to kiss you all the time just because you paid for dinner? You make me feel like a prostitute."

"You don't want to kiss me just because you like me?"

"I don't want to kiss you if I can't know you're all mine." She turned around and went inside, closing the door behind her.

Jeff drove back home slowly, thinking about how to get Kristen to warm up. He needed to convince her he was really committed, that he wouldn't leave her like her last husband did. If he could get her to understand he truly loved her, she'd relax and let the sweeter part of her nature take over. She was just mean sometimes now because she was afraid. If Jeff could only get her to understand there was nothing to be afraid of, she'd be fine.

Jeff took a cold shower, but as he lay in bed later, he still found himself fondling his penis. He'd had a vasectomy while he was with Sherry because she kept avoiding sex, afraid the condom would break. Still, he'd always hoped he could have it reversed.

But this penis, this very penis, may have already sired a child.

Jeff smiled, thinking about it. Then he kept stroking his member, as if to reward it. But soon he was tugging forcefully at it, and before long, he was sighing in relief.

He instantly felt guilty. He no longer believed masturbation was a terrible sin. But he didn't want anything to keep him out of the temple if he and Kristen did finally decide to marry.

The next day at work, Jeff couldn't help but look at some of his younger coworkers. Did his son look like any of them? That is, if it really was his son, he kept reminding himself.

On his lunch break, Jeff called a clinic that could do the DNA test. Thank God, the appointment was only a week away. When he got home, he called Sweeney to see if the time was acceptable.

"I'll be there." Jeff could hear the smile in the boy's voice. "Thanks!"

But Kristen was livid when she learned Jeff had made an appointment for the blood test. "You're living your life in the past. You have to think of your future. You have other obligations now."

"Obligations?"

"I don't want to talk about it. I need to feel special. You're not making me feel special."

"Well, can I come over? You're my pet, sweetie. I can make you feel special in person."

"No," she said. "You're always causing trouble. Don't talk to me again till you're ready to put me first."

She hung up and Jeff felt a tremendous weight on his chest. Was he lousing things up just for some egotistical thrill in knowing he had sperm that worked? Was it really that important to have biological offspring? There were plenty of kids already here that needed tending. And this kid was probably close to eighteen. Why ruin what could be a lifelong relationship, an eternal relationship, just to see a kid who would probably at best only call twice a year even if he did turn out to be related?

Jeff heard some grunting and looked down. Penelope was after some attention again. Jeff leaned over and scratched her back. Penelope was always good to him, no matter what. Why couldn't people be like that?

Jeff watched as Penelope ran off and pushed her way through the pet door to get outside. He'd installed the door after his divorce. He was lucky to have been able to keep the house, of course. He'd had to pay Sherry off, but this was his house, and he liked being here. It was true the place was a little lonely at times with just Penelope, but it had been lonely far too often even when Sherry and her kids were here.

No one was perfect, but Jeff understood Kristen wanting to feel special. So he decided on a plan. He set up his video camera and spent $300 on flowers. He placed them all around the gas fireplace and then, wearing a rented tux, he turned on the camera and started talking.

"Kristen, you're the best thing that ever happened to me. When you come home, all these flowers are yours." He motioned around the room. Then he patted his chest once. "And *I'm* all yours, too," he said. He got down on one knee and looked right at the camera, offering it a bouquet of roses. "Kristen, will you marry me?"

The next morning at the airport, Jeff pulled aside one of the other flight attendants scheduled for the same flight as Kristen. He explained that he wanted her to substitute his DVD for the regular movie they were going to show on their return trip. She giggled when he told her it was a proposal, but she agreed.

By the time Kristen's flight returned later, Jeff had finished his shift at work, gone home to clean up, and had put on the tux again. He was waiting at the airport with the roses when Kristen walked past security and into the main terminal.

Two other flight attendants were with her, and they were laughing when they saw Jeff. But one of them gave him a thumbs up as they moved off to the side to let Jeff approach Kristen in person. Jeff gathered his courage when he saw Kristen was smiling.

She came up to him, and he got down on one knee again and offered the flowers to her. "Will you marry me?"

Kristen smelled the roses and looked around to see everyone's reaction, enjoying the attention. "You'll always put me first?" she said.

"Always." He handed her a small box, which she took with a gleam in her eye. He couldn't quite gauge her reaction when she saw the engagement ring, but she carefully put it on her finger and nodded.

"Okay," she said. "I accept. Tomorrow I'll go pick out a wedding ring."

Jeff stood up and moved to kiss her. She put a hand up, though, and said, "How much are you willing to pay for the wedding ring?"

Jeff had already thought about it and knew he couldn't hesitate, even though he was going to offer spending more than he could really afford. "$5000," he said confidently. He'd only spent $600 on the engagement ring, but he knew she'd want to spend more on the permanent ring.

Kristen considered for a moment. "Okay," she said, smiling. Then she let Jeff kiss her. "And you might want to see about getting that vasectomy reversed," she whispered in his ear.

"Really?"

"I want *all* of you."

That kept Jeff on a high until Tuesday, when he was supposed to meet Sweeney at the doctor's office. He'd given Sweeney the clinic's address, not sure he wanted this guy to know his home address just yet. When Jeff arrived at the office shortly before 11:30, he saw a young man already seated in the waiting area.

Jeff had brown hair now, but it had been sandy blond when he was younger, and the young man sitting there also had sandy blond hair. He was slim, like Jeff, but otherwise didn't look particularly like him. Still, he was a good-looking kid, and for some strange reason, Jeff felt proud of that.

The young man looked up and smiled immediately. A sweet smile, thought Jeff.

"Sweeney?"

"Hi, Jeff! It's good to meet you." He stood up and offered his hand. "I won't call you Dad till the results are back." He laughed pleasantly.

"Did you have trouble finding the place?"

"I used Mapquest."

"Sorry about the gas money. I know that's a long trip."

"Oh, I hitchhiked. Just one old fat man who drove me the whole way, and all he wanted in return was a blow job." Sweeney laughed again.

"What?"

"Oh, I didn't give him one, of course. How gross. I have my standards."

Jeff looked at the young man, not knowing what to say to all that. He suddenly felt very protective of this boy and wanted to punch the old man for trying to take advantage of him. "Some people just wallow in filth, don't they?"

"Oh, live and let live, I suppose. But I certainly wouldn't have sex with a strange man in a car." He smiled again. "I'm still a virgin, but I have to admit, when I found out a couple of months ago how I was conceived, I did go to the sperm bank and donate a couple of times."

"Like father, like son?" Jeff smiled.

Soon they both had their blood drawn and were told it would be several days before the results were in. Jeff had to get back to work but asked Sweeney if he wanted to have dinner with him that evening.

"Sure! I'll just do some sightseeing by bus and meet you at the restaurant. What time?"

"6:00." Jeff paused. "But how about dinner at my place?"

"Your wife won't mind?"

"Oh, I'm not married, though I did just get engaged."

"Congratulations. That's wonderful. I'm engaged, too."

"And you're still a virgin?" Jeff laughed. "Isn't that a little retro?"

"You disapprove?"

"Oh, no. Kristen and I are waiting till we get married."

"We are, too."

What were the odds that in today's world, Jeff would have a son with any kind of moral standards at all? Maybe he could get the kid into the Church. Maybe they could be sealed together. He smiled again.

A couple of times that afternoon, Jeff's coworkers had to ask him to stop whistling while he tossed bags around, but he was just in too good a mood. He hoped the DNA results matched.

Sweeney showed up right at 6:00, and Jeff gave him a tour of the house. Sweeney laughed when he saw Penelope burst through the pet door, but he petted her affectionately, and she seemed to like him, too. Not that she didn't like most people. Though she never did seem to take to Kristen, he thought. Probably just jealous.

Jeff had the dinner almost ready before Sweeney arrived, so it didn't take long to get it on the table. But when he saw Sweeney's face, he grew concerned. "What is it?"

"You're serving pork chops," Sweeney said. "I should have told you earlier. I don't eat pork. I'm sorry."

"Are you Jewish?"

Sweeney nodded. "I'm not very observant, but I won't eat pork. This salad looks good, though. I'll be fine."

"You sure? I have vegetable soup in a can."

"No, no, I'm good. As a rule, I'm not very demanding."

They started eating, and Sweeney asked for Jeff's life story. He talked of his boyhood with three brothers, of his days as a missionary in Thailand, and of his unsuccessful first marriage. He decided to omit the fact he had a bit of a strained relationship with his own father.

The man had often tried to humiliate him in front of others. "Can't you mow the lawn like a real man?" he'd say while Jeff's brothers watched. "Don't throw the ball to Jeff. He can't shoot."

And there was the time in the sauna at the YMCA when Jeff's towel had fallen off. His father had laughed and said, in front of two other men, "If it gets any smaller, Jeff, it'll just disappear." Jeff could never quite forgive his father for that one, and they didn't talk much these days.

But Jeff did tell the story of the time his father had sent his mother to a fat farm, not because he was upset with her weight, but because it bothered her so much. She'd gained two pounds while she was there, but when she returned, his father made a fuss about how good she looked. He even had her go out and buy a new dress so they could have a professional portrait taken together.

Jeff told a few other pleasant anecdotes, and then he asked for Sweeney's story.

"An idyllic childhood, too," he said, and Jeff wondered if he was editing as well. "Though I was always getting in trouble at school."

"For what?"

"For punching kids who made fun of me."

"You were teased a lot?"

Sweeney shrugged. "Comes with the territory, I suppose. It wasn't as bad as getting kicked out of the house by my father two months ago."

Jeff paused with a half-eaten bite of pork chop in his mouth. He quickly swallowed. "Why on earth did he kick you out?"

"I told him Jeremy and I were engaged."

Jeff stared.

"When I told him I was gay, he said I wasn't welcome there anymore. That's when he told me how I was conceived, and I decided to look for you."

"Where are you living? Are you doing okay?" Jeff wasn't going to get sucked into supporting this stranger, but he still couldn't help but feel concerned. This might really be his son.

"I'm staying with a friend. Not Jeremy," he added quickly. "That would be too hard since we can't get to California to be married for a few more months yet."

Jeff looked at the boy, a sweet, attractive young man. He hated to see his life ruined by this filth. "You haven't had sex at all with another man yet?"

"No."

"Then don't open that door. You can still find a good woman and have a good life."

Sweeney's eyes narrowed. "Are you going to kick me out of your life, too?"

Jeff looked down at his plate for a moment. "No," he said slowly. "But I would like you to get some help. I can pay for a psychiatrist."

Sweeney laughed. "I'm just fine, Jeff. Really. But thanks for the offer."

Sweeney switched the subject then, talking about his work rehabilitating mentally disabled adults and his hope to get a degree in Special Education, to teach the kids nobody else wanted. Jeremy taught sign language, and taking a class in sign was how Sweeney had first met him.

Jeff offered Sweeney the spare bedroom but told him he'd have to leave early in the morning when Jeff left for work. Sweeney nodded, smiling.

It took Jeff a while to fall asleep. It was his worst fear. Having a kid who was making some very wrong decisions. But how could you be loving and supportive yet firm enough to guide someone down the right path? Door number one led to one prize, but door number two led to a completely different one.

Jeff felt a pain he'd never felt before over any of his stepchildren. He'd truly tried to be a real father to the others, but somehow, this was different. He wanted to make everything right for Sweeney.

In the morning, Sweeney shook Jeff's hand and gave Penelope a scratch behind the ears. Jeff drove the boy to the interstate and then headed on to work. He moved about in a daze most the day, but he wasn't whistling. He called Kristen on his lunch break and left a message on her machine.

When he saw the light flashing on his own when he got home, he smiled in anticipation. Kristen hardly ever called. She must finally be loosening up.

"Hey, Jeff," said the machine. It was Sweeney. "I'm afraid I got in trouble. I was picked up for hitchhiking. Could you come get me at the police station?"

Jeff closed his eyes and groaned. What in the world was he being caught up in?

Jeff drove down to the police station and soon they were on their way out of the building. Sweeney literally ran when he reached the door. Jeff caught up with him outside.

"I normally like a man in uniform," Sweeney said. "But that police officer was a real jerk."

"Let me take you to the bus station," Jeff said wearily. "I'll get you a ticket."

"I'm sorry, Jeff. I didn't mean to cause any trouble. You must be regretting you ever met me."

"Don't worry about it."

Jeff saw Sweeney off and then drove back home slowly. There was still no message from Kristen, and Jeff didn't feel like calling again. But he thought more about that vasectomy reversal. Maybe it wouldn't be a bad idea to have more than one kid. Maybe at least one of them would turn out okay. Mormons weren't supposed to gamble, but there seemed to be some value in hedging his bets.

The next day on his break at work, Jeff called a doctor and made an appointment for an evaluation. He was excited that the appointment was only two days away. God obviously knew he needed some good news right now and was giving it to him. Heavenly Father was a good father.

That evening, Jeff picked Kristen up so she could show him the ring she'd picked out. They went to the mall and stopped in what looked to Jeff like a dangerously expensive jewelry store. Even a plain band here probably cost $2000. Kristen might have gone over her limit a little. But if she had found something she liked here, it had to be reasonably modest in design to fall within the range he'd given her. Jeff was a little surprised she was going to show some restraint. Tasteful but simple. He felt bad for doubting her.

Kristen gave her name to the saleswoman, who went immediately to the ring Kristen had selected earlier. When the woman put it on the counter, Jeff felt he'd been kicked in the groin.

"Do you like it?" asked Kristen.

"How much is that?"

"Jeff, you said you'd always put me first. How can you be so crass?"

"How much is that?"

"This ring is $20,000," the saleswoman said. "That's with a 20% discount. A steal."

Jeff's knees almost buckled. "Kristen, I absolutely can't afford something like that."

"But it's the ring I want. This is the marriage that's going to take, and I want something to show its permanence."

"Emma Smith didn't have a ring like that."

"This is the ring I want," she repeated. "If you're serious about committing yourself to me, you need to put your money where your mouth is."

Jeff sighed and tried to bargain with the store manager. "Trying to Jew us down?" the manager asked, smiling politely.

"I'm trying to Mormon you down." Should he have said more to stand up for his son? Too much was happening in his head to concentrate.

Jeff was able to get the price reduced to $10,000, but he was still miffed to be spending twice what was already an overly generous amount. He did want Kristen to feel loved, and he understood this was symbolic for her rather than just an aesthetic decision. But he still felt miffed.

As they left the store, Kristen held onto Jeff's arm and whispered in his ear, "Now you have too much invested in me to ever leave." She giggled to show she was joking, but somehow, it didn't seem funny.

When he got home, Jeff took his mother's wedding ring out of its box and looked at it. It was a modest ring, and he'd known Kristen would never wear it. Jeff had loved his mother, who'd been nothing but good to him. He'd been devastated when she died five years earlier of breast cancer. He always kind of hoped he'd have a son or daughter he could pass the ring on to.

Now he took out his digital camera and took several pictures of the ring and posted it on eBay. He wouldn't get enough to make even a dent in the extra $5000 he'd just spent, but he had to start somewhere. He'd need to start working more overtime, too.

Jeff sat glumly looking at his computer screen, wondering what was happening to him. He was getting married and maybe about to have a good life for a change, and yet somehow, he didn't feel happy. Was Sweeney the problem?

There was a possibility Sweeney was the only child he'd ever have, that his DNA stopped right there. Even if Sweeney did donate sperm and it was used, Jeff would never know his grandchild. The chances that that child would look for Sweeney twenty years from now were pretty slim, and even if he did, Jeff would be in his sixties by then. What sense of family could you have under those circumstances? He certainly didn't want to go through that door. He'd simply have to try harder with Kristen's kids.

The doctor took a biopsy from one of Jeff's testicles to see if there were viable sperm, and then he did an MRI of Jeff's groin. After looking at it carefully, he smiled. "It looks promising, Jeff. I think we can do it."

"I told them fifteen years ago I might want to reverse it one day, so I think they were extra careful."

"Well, there are no guarantees, and fifteen years is pushing it, but I have a cancellation four days from now. That's normally too soon, because we need to make sure you haven't taken any aspirin or ibuprofen for at least two weeks. Have you?"

"No, I hardly ever take pain killers. Nothing in a couple of months."

"Do you think you're up for some minor surgery that soon?"

Jeff nodded and they set up the schedule. There was no time to think, but you needed to take advantage of an opening when you had the chance.

When he got home from work, Jeff saw there was a message on his machine. It was his dad. He wished he could talk to him about everything that was happening, ask for some advice. His father had seemed to make a tiny effort at being nicer to him these last few years.

But he deleted the message and went to fix something to eat.

Two days later, the DNA results were back. Jeff didn't know if he should be happy or sad. He called Sweeney in Houston.

"Hi, Sweeney. How are you, son?"

"Son? You mean it?"

"That's right. I just got the results."

"That's fabulous news. You'll have to send me your picture so I can put it in my wallet. I'll send you one of me, too. That is, if you want one."

"I want one."

"I'll send you one of me and Jeremy together, too. After all, in four months and three days, he'll be your son-in-law."

Jeff felt as if he'd been kicked in the stomach. Even after the revelation that he had a gay son, it had never occurred to him there might be even more included in the package.

"Sweeney, I know after only four minutes as your father, I've hardly earned the right to give you advice."

"But…"

"But I think you'll have a better life if you don't behave like an animal." Jeff was afraid that sounded too harsh, but how could he stand by and let his son open the door to hell and rush right in?

Sweeney laughed. "I *do* behave like an animal," he said, still laughing. "I just read a book from the library called *Biological Exuberance.* It talks about how there is documented homosexuality in over two hundred other species."

"Really?" Jeff was intrigued despite himself.

"Even pigs," said Sweeney. "Your Penelope might be a lesbian." He laughed again, that sweet laugh, Jeff noticed. "But maybe I shouldn't go there."

They talked about other things and stayed on the phone another forty-five minutes. Sweeney was really a pleasant young man. Jeff wasn't sure he could accept the homosexuality, but he didn't understand how the boy's other father could just kick him out, either, or how his mother could have permitted it.

But after everything that happened this week, it was a relief to be back in church on Sunday. Kristen didn't have to work that day, so he picked her and the kids up, and they were all able to sit together. Kristen went around showing everyone her engagement ring and describing in detail the wedding ring she'd soon have. All the women congratulated her, and all the men congratulated him. And they were all teasing the kids about having a "new father."

The bishop, a heavyset man, pulled Jeff aside. "We'll need to set up an interview to make sure your temple recommend is still valid. Wouldn't want you to find the temple doors closed in your face." He chuckled. "Let's set up a time to talk in the next couple of weeks. You know *my* door is always open to you."

Jeff started worrying again about getting in trouble for fathering a son, and having a gay son to boot. Would he get in trouble for not disowning him?

The surgery later that week took just over two hours, performed on Jeff as an outpatient, and he had one of his home teachers from church give him a ride home afterward. He'd had the doctor take a sample of his sperm during the procedure and freeze it, just in case the surgery wasn't successful.

His scrotum was extremely tender. He'd need to wear a jockstrap at all times for at least a month, and for a month more while at work. He decided to wear it on the outside of his garments, not wanting anything to come between him and his Mormon underwear.

The surgery cost Jeff another $8500, making him feel guilty. His credit card was maxed to the limit, all because he was wasting so much money on vanity. He didn't *need* more biological children. Even if he and Kristen wanted a child together, they could always adopt. His cousin had adopted a baby through the Church. They could, too.

Jeff didn't see Kristen for a couple of days. He was afraid he'd get aroused if he saw her, and it was too soon to let that happen. He wasn't supposed to even ejaculate for a month, so he certainly didn't want to start having erections yet.

Kristen called him on Friday night. "Have you forgotten about me, Jeff? You aren't getting cold feet, are you? You can always warm them up on that damn pig of yours, can't you?" She laughed.

"No cold feet," said Jeff. "You and the kids want to go eat tonight?"

Jeff didn't mention the surgery over dinner. He didn't know why. He'd tell her soon, of course, but not yet. And he didn't tell her about the DNA results, either. She needed this time right after their engagement to think about herself. Jeff felt funny, though, keeping such important information from her. Weren't you supposed to share everything with your partner? Well, he would, soon enough. Just not yet.

Jeff tried extra hard to connect to the kids tonight, but Tim looked sullen, and Lizbeth yawned right in his face when he asked her a question. What was he doing wrong?

It was ten days after the surgery before Jeff could go back to work. So much for getting overtime. He was afraid of pulling or tearing something and wanted to be careful, yet he was never a loafer at work and couldn't help but toss more than his fair share of bags once he got back.

That night, Jeff finally decided to tell Kristen about the surgery, over supper at Denny's. "Well, that's wonderful, Jeff. Does it take right away? Does it hurt?"

"Yes, it's still tender. And the doctor said it could be three months before any sperm appear in the semen." He felt a little funny saying all this in front of the kids, but they seemed oblivious. "It should be okay by the time we get married."

"And just when do you think that will be? You haven't given me a date yet."

Jeff hesitated. "Well, it depends on how long the bishop will want you to wait after you start obeying the Word of Wisdom." He looked at the glass of tea next to Kristen's plate.

"You're going to use *this* as an excuse not to get married? That's pretty low. The bishop doesn't need to know everything."

"I'll know. The marriage won't be valid in God's eyes if we're not worthy to go to the temple."

Kristen made a disgusted snort. "Okay, okay, Mr. Holier Than Thou. I'll stop drinking tea." She picked up her water glass and took a sip. "Jeez."

Jeff smiled. "I'll talk to the bishop this week and see what kind of timeline we're looking at."

Kristen's eyes narrowed slightly, and then she looked off at a waiter walking by. "Whatever."

Jeff hated to see Kristen upset, but since she was already mad, he decided he might as well tell her all the bad news at one time, and he knew she'd see the next part as bad, too. "You never asked," he said, "but I got the DNA results back the other day."

Kristen quickly looked at him again. "Yeah?"

"Sweeney really is my biological son."

Kristen slammed her fork on the table, and the kids jumped. "You are not to see that boy again! I forbid it!" She took a deep breath and put her palms flat on the table. "He'll come up with some sad story and try to suck all your money away. I know the type. He'll have you wallowing in pity for him. I won't have it. He'll distract you from your real family, which is us. We've known you longer than he has. You belong to us, not to him."

"I promised I'd always put you first, but that doesn't mean he can't be somewhere on the list."

"We need to go now. I'm getting a headache."

Jeff drove them home, and after the kids went inside, Kristen stayed with him at the door for a moment. "You know I love you, don't you?" he asked.

"I'm not sure I believe you."

"Doesn't the ring prove it?"

"That's just money."

"What do you need me to do?"

"I need you to close the door on your past and focus on your future."

Jeff didn't say anything. Then Kristen moved forward and kissed him slowly. She pressed her body against him, and for the first time, he felt her hand groping his manhood. He tried to pull back, but she had her other arm across his back. Within seconds, Jeff had an erection, and he felt terribly embarrassed.

Then she squeezed his sac, and he grunted in pain.

"Oh, I'm sorry. I forgot it's still sore."

"It's okay."

"I'll see you in a couple of days. You go home and think about what I said. I need to know you love me. You do things for people you love that you know will make them happy."

Jeff sat on his sofa when he got home, staring at the floor. He thought Kristen was being unreasonable, but he remembered Abraham. He'd been asked to sacrifice Isaac to please God. He hadn't had to go through with it, but he didn't know that at the time. He had to be willing to do it, he had to accept the demand.

Jeff picked up the phone and called Sweeney.

"Hi, Dad."

"How're you doing? They ever give you any hassle at work for missing a couple of days when you were up here?"

"No, my boss is cool. I told her about your pet pig. Now she's thinking of getting one, too."

"It's nice to be a trend setter."

Sweeney laughed. It was such a sweet laugh, Jeff thought.

"I know I'm being kind of pushy, Jeff, but I was wondering if next month I could come up for a couple of days. I'd like you to meet Jeremy. He's Jewish, too, so no pork. He's asked his rabbi to perform a commitment ceremony after we get back from California. I certainly don't expect you to come to California, but I did hope you could make it to the commitment ceremony here in Houston. But first I'd like to give you and Jeremy a chance to meet each other. Is it okay if we come up?"

How was Jeff going to tell Sweeney he couldn't see him anymore? He didn't want all this perversion in his life. And he had to be good to Kristen.

It was like pulling off a band-aid. You just had to do it.

"Sure, you guys can come up any time."

Sweeney told him more about his week, and they talked about this and that for another thirty minutes. He seemed so easy to talk to, and he always asked about Jeff, too, what his hobbies were, what shows he liked, what kind of music he listened to, how things were going with Kristen. He supposed the young man could be manipulating him, but it didn't *feel* like it.

Jeff realized he couldn't remember if Kristen had ever asked him about his hobbies. Jeff liked to collect old, vintage photographs. There was something pleasant about seeing all those quaintly dressed people in their sepia tones, wondering if they were related to him, if there was another whole world he might be connected with.

Jeff had dutifully done his genealogy as he was commanded to do, and he'd gone to the temple to do work for many of his ancestors. He loved being baptized for them, but it was even more fun doing the marriages and the sealings, connecting people together throughout the centuries, making everyone into one huge family.

He could never be sealed to Sweeney, though, if Sweeney was both gay and Jewish. How could he feel connected to this boy if there was always going to be that huge gap?

Jeff hung up after their conversation, feeling more confused than ever. He called and left a message for the bishop about setting up an interview for next week, and then he let Penelope get in his lap while he scratched her back.

The interview went well. The bishop wasn't upset Jeff had donated sperm so many years ago, and he thought Jeff could be a positive influence in the young man's life, as he'd been with Kristen by getting her to give up tea.

A month after the surgery, Jeff was too curious to wait any longer and masturbated one night after dropping Kristen off, shooting onto his chest. Everything seemed to work okay. He breathed a sigh of relief and sent up a prayer of gratitude.

Sweeney and Jeremy came to stay a couple of days the following week, and Jeff found himself liking Jeremy despite his better judgment. He tried to talk them into staying platonic friends, but Jeremy took Sweeney's hand and said, "Do you only want to be platonic friends with Kristen forever?"

Jeff didn't know what to say to that.

"Jeremy wants to get in my back door."

"I need your man pussy."

"I can hardly wait."

"Uh, guys, you aren't alone in the room."

"Sorry, Jeff."

"No one thinks Maria von Trapp was a slut for having sex with her husband. And I'm not a slut for wanting to have sex with mine."

"Okay, okay. Let's talk about something else. How long have you been signing, Jeremy? How did you get interested in that?"

Jeff tried to get Kristen to have dinner with him and Sweeney, but she hung up the phone when he suggested it. He called her a couple of days later to see if he could make it up to her. "Want to go see a movie tonight? The new Harry Potter is playing. We could bring the kids, too."

They went to the Cineplex, and everyone seemed to have a good time. Kristen even let Jeff hold her hand throughout most of the movie. Then he drove them home, and the kids ran inside while Kristen stayed with Jeff at the door. "I was thinking of making an appointment at the Dallas temple for the 25th of the month after next," Jeff said. "Does that sound like a good day for a wedding?"

"Oh, do we have to get married in Dallas? Our temple is so plain. Can't we go to a pretty one? It's not like we can't get good flights."

"Where would you like to get married?"

"I think the Hawaii temple is pretty."

"Okay, I'll see what I can arrange."

"You're not still planning to go to Sweeney's Jewish wedding, are you?"

"I'm thinking about it."

"You're condoning their deplorable lifestyle. If you encourage them to sin, you're guilty, too."

"I know. I've thought about all that. But what can you do? You can't live other people's lives for them. You can't stop loving someone because they do something you don't like."

"I could."

"Kristen, he's my son. I love him. Don't you love your kids even when they're not perfect?"

"My kids are angels! Your kid is a dirty animal! You're being nice to him just to upset me. You don't really care about him, or *you'd* have tried to find *him*. You just have some juvenile macho need to think your sperm is better than other men's."

"Kristen, he's a part of my family."

"No, he's not. He's a complete stranger. Are you're mean for putting me through this."

"You'll feel better when we have a child of our own. Then you'll be glad I'm not the kind of father you had, someone who abandons his own kid."

"You're a beast."

She went inside and slammed the door.

Jeff drove home slowly and sat on his sofa, staring at the floor and scratching his ears absentmindedly. Maybe marrying Kristen wasn't such a good idea, after all. Maybe he was wrong to think she'd eventually calm down. Maybe she'd never come around.

Maybe she was just a bitch.

Jeff immediately felt ashamed. No one was perfect, he realized, and he was trying her beyond her abilities right now. He had to be patient.

He called Kristen, and she answered on the second ring. "I think we ought to call off the engagement for a while," he said. "Just till things get settled."

Kristen hung up the phone.

Jeff walked slowly to the kitchen and opened the refrigerator. It was time for the hard stuff. He took out a 16-ounce bottle of Coke and opened it. He kept the bottle in there for emergencies, for when he needed the forbidden caffeine. He turned the radio to a smooth jazz station and sat on the sofa, thinking. Penelope snuffled around his feet, and he patted her on the back.

Finally, around 10:30, Jeff trudged off to bed. 5:30 would come around soon enough. He had a hard time falling asleep, but sometime later, perhaps around midnight, he thought he heard something in the living room. It didn't sound like Penelope, and Jeff tensed up. Had someone broken in? He had a gun, but he didn't know if it was loaded. What was he going to do?

He heard another noise and then saw a shadow in the doorway. His heart jumped in his throat.

The shadow moved toward him, and Jeff felt an almost uncontrollable urge to scream like a girl.

"I'm going to show you what you're missing."

It was Kristen, and she slipped into the bed next to Jeff, pulling his hand onto her naked breast.

"How did you get in here?"

"I crawled through the pig door."

"You're naked."

"My clothes are in the bedroom doorway. You want me to put them back on?" She put his hand on her crotch, and Jeff could feel the soft moistness.

"Oh my god."

Kristen crawled up on top of Jeff and pulled his T-shirt up over his head. Then she unstraddled him and pulled his shorts off, too. His penis was pointing directly skyward.

"I see you want me to stay."

Jeff never even thought about a condom until after they finished, when Kristen said, "I should be ovulating now. If I get pregnant, you'll want to marry me before I start showing."

"Oh, my god, we're going to hell."

"No, we're getting married in the temple. And you're going to put me first, and our baby, just like you said."

"I'll lose my temple recommend. I'll be disfellowshipped."

"Not if you keep your mouth shut."

Jeff suddenly remembered the doctor had said it might be three months after the surgery before he had much sperm in his semen. He hoped it was true.

"You need to leave now."

"If you make a fuss, I'll tell everyone you seduced me."

Jeff looked at her in the dim light. He seemed to see her very clearly for the first time.

"You need to leave now."

"Just like a man. You come, and then all you want to do is roll over and go to sleep. I don't know what I ever saw in you."

Jeff stood up and pulled his garments back on, even though he knew he wasn't worthy to wear them any longer. How could Heavenly Father love a person like him?

Kristen stood up, too, and started putting her clothes back on. "You're not even any good," she said savagely, zipping up her pants. "And you have a little dick, too!"

Better than having a small soul, Jeff thought, but he didn't say anything. He turned on the light, and Kristen hurriedly pulled on her blouse. Jeff walked out to the living room and waited for her. He was just about to unlock the front door when Kristen stalked over and came right up to him.

"No wonder you have a faggot son. You're not much of a man yourself. God only knows why your wife didn't leave sooner."

Jeff looked at her calmly.

"So now you're not speaking to me? You have a bigger pussy than I do. I'm going to tell the bishop I came over to discuss our wedding, and you put something in my drink and hog-tied me and raped me. I'll get you in trouble."

Jeff pointed wearily toward the back door.

"If I go out that door, I'm not coming back."

He kept pointing, and she clenched her jaws and stomped to the door. "The deadbolt's locked. Unlock this door so I can leave." She glared at him.

This time Jeff did speak. "You can go out the way you came in."

Kristen's face turned pink, and Jeff thought she was going to hit him. But instead she got down on her hands and knees and forced her way back out through the pet door.

Jeff left the lights on and went back to his bedroom. He got down on his knees and apologized to God, but when he stood back up, he thought maybe Kristen was right about one thing. He didn't particularly feel the need to talk with the bishop. Now that Kristen was out of his life, he somehow felt clean again. He could *tell* that God was okay with him. He climbed back into bed and was asleep within minutes.

The next day after work, Jeff got online and found a site for PFLAG, Parents and Friends of Lesbians and Gays. They met once a month, it turned out, at a church not too far away. They'd be meeting next week. Jeff marked it on his calendar.

He sat on the sofa and opened the box with the new wedding ring and looked at it for a few minutes.

Well, he was prepared now if he ever did get married again.

Or maybe, he considered, turning the ring so that it sparkled in the light, maybe Sweeney and Jeremy would adopt a child, and he could give his grandchild the ring one day.

Jeff picked up the phone and called Houston.

"Hi, Dad! How're you doing?"

"Oh, I'm fine. And you guys?"

"We're good, too. Trying to decide what neighborhood to live in once we get married and can share an apartment."

Jeff thought for a moment.

"You will come visit us, won't you?"

"Yes," said Jeff. "But I was wondering. If you guys wanted to find jobs up here, you could stay in the house with me for a year or so, rent-free, so you could save up for a down payment on a home of your own. There's plenty of room here."

There was silence on the other end of the phone.

"Sweeney? You there?"

"Yes, Jeff." There was another pause. "You know, Jeremy's been telling me we really have to understand the difference between biological family and chosen family." He paused again. "But sometimes, they turn out to be the same thing."

"Well, you guys think about it for a while and let me know."

"We will, Jeff."

They talked for another half hour, about nothing of any real importance, Jeff rubbing Penelope's back as they chatted. After they hung up, Jeff turned the radio to some smooth jazz.

It wasn't good for man to be alone, he thought. But even if you weren't married, you were never really alone if you had someone in your life you loved.

Jeff picked up the phone and dialed his father.

The Buzzard Tree

Patty Lou looked out the door. She was waiting for her grandson Robert to come. She hadn't seen him since her 90th birthday three months earlier, when the whole family had come out to Brookhaven to celebrate with her. Robert only came up from New Orleans to see her three or four times a year, and she was looking forward to seeing him.

She looked out at the sky. There were four buzzards circling slowly and gently over the farm. She remembered the rhyme she'd learned some eighty years earlier. "One for sorrow. Two for joy. Three for a letter. Four for a boy." Well, she'd be getting a boy today. Robert. She'd actually be getting two boys. Robert would be coming with his friend, Joseph.

Patty Lou had long since stopped worrying about Robert being gay. At first, being Mormon, she'd worried he'd go to hell, but he still seemed like a decent man. Then she'd worried about him catching AIDS. But he'd told her six years ago he had the AIDS virus, and he still seemed okay. Now she just worried she wouldn't see him enough.

Patty Lou sat back down on her sofa. She had a window unit air conditioner, which the family had forced her into buying five years ago, threatening not to visit her again during the long summer months unless she got one, but even though it was 90 degrees outside, she decided to wait until closer to the time Robert and Joseph were coming before turning it on.

She still believed natural air was healthier. She'd lived eighty-five years before getting an air conditioner, hadn't she? And now, facing leukemia, she needed all the natural air she could get.

It wasn't the same kind of leukemia her daughter, Marsha, had died of twenty-one years earlier. Patty Lou still remembered seeing her daughter in her temple clothes in her casket. She herself hadn't converted till after Marsha's death, doing so largely so she could be with her daughter again. Marsha had had acute leukemia, while Patty Lou had chronic. There was more to the name than that, but she couldn't remember it.

When Patty Lou had been diagnosed ten years earlier, the doctor had said, "With this disease, I'm afraid you've probably only got ten years to live."

Patty Lou had replied, "Well, I'm eighty. I'll take it." But now that the ten years had passed and the Leukeran pills no longer worked, ten years didn't seem like enough.

She knew heaven would be nice, and it would be great to be with Marsha again. Patty Lou had had Marsha sealed to her in the temple by proxy after joining the Church, and she felt that the afterlife would be pleasant enough. She just wasn't ready to go yet. Was it selfish to still want to live when you were ninety years old? Maybe, but she couldn't help it. She liked being alive.

As it neared noon, Patty Lou turned on the air conditioner in the living room, and she heated some field peas and green beans on the stove. She also heated some mashed potatoes and a pot roast she'd cooked earlier. The family had always loved her cooking, though it was simple enough. It was one thing she could still do, so she did it. She ate well, even though she was cooking for one most days. She wanted to stay healthy, and she was in pretty good shape, except perhaps for a bruise or two.

Around 12:30, Patty Lou heard the dogs barking outside. She went to the door and saw Robert and Joseph walking up. Robert had dark hair and a graying beard, and Joseph was short and Italian-looking. Robert was forty-three, the same age his mother had been when she died, and Joseph was fifty-five. How could her grandson be so old?

"Hi!" Robert said cheerily as she opened the screen door. "How're you doing?"

"Okay." They hugged, and both boys gave her a kiss.

"Here. We brought you some treats." Robert handed her a bag, and she saw inside it a pack of chocolate-covered peanuts, some peanut butter cups, and a pack of maple-covered peanuts. She loved peanuts.

"Thank you," she said. "Come on in the kitchen. Dinner's ready."

The boys went in the bathroom to freshen up after their two-and-a-half hour trip while Patty Lou poured some Coke. She knew the Church frowned on caffeine, but she also knew Robert liked Coke, so she always served it when he came to visit. The boys soon joined her at the kitchen table, which was already set.

Robert's father, Henry, had made the table some forty-five years earlier. He'd left New Orleans to come back to the country after Marsha died and married a local woman, Joann, a Baptist, a few years later. He no longer came to the Mormon meetings, but he still came by Patty Lou's house every few months to bush-hog her weeds.

"Would you like to say the blessing?" Patty Lou asked Robert.

He nodded and bowed his head. "Dear Heavenly Father. We thank thee for this food, and we ask thee to bless it that it will be good for us. And we ask thee to please bless Grandma that her medicine will work and she'll be okay. And we ask this in Jesus' name. Amen."

Patty Lou liked to hear him use Jesus' name. Robert had started going to the Jewish church in New Orleans when he'd been with his last friend, a Jew. She wasn't sure God would take him to heaven as a gay person, but there was no sense making it worse by being a Jew. Of course, her doctor was Jewish, and he seemed nice enough. Maybe being a Jew didn't matter, either.

"Your sister Joyce was up here last night for your dad's tractor pull. She came by for fifteen minutes with Veronica before going to your dad's place." Joyce was a year older than Robert and lived in New Orleans. She came up to see her even less than Robert, usually just for Christmas and maybe one other time a year.

While Veronica was seventeen and still lived at home, Joyce's oldest child, Mark, was now twenty-seven. He also lived in New Orleans and came up to visit his grandfather

Henry several times a year. Patty Lou knew and couldn't help but feel hurt that he rarely stopped by to see her as well.

"They're doing okay?" asked Robert.

"Yeah, I think so."

"Did Mark come up, too?"

"I don't know."

Mark usually rode in each of Henry's tractor pulls, but Patty Lou hadn't asked Joyce if he was coming up yesterday. If he didn't show up to visit, it was better not to know he was in town. They were all still active in the Church, at least, and that was some comfort. If they couldn't be together now, they might still be together later. Maybe she'd be more fun to be with in heaven.

"Veronica still in the ROTC?"

"I think so. They were only here fifteen minutes." She took a sip of her Coke. She had to admit, she liked it once in a while, too. "Y'all didn't want to come up for the tractor pull?"

"It's not really our thing."

After the meal, Patty Lou went out on the back porch and brought in a yellow cake with chocolate icing. She brushed a few ants off the plate and set it down on the table. "I've got some Robbie-cake for you." As a child, this was the only one of several kinds of cake Patty Lou made that Robert would eat, so it became known in the family as Robbie-cake. She still made it every time he came to visit.

"Thanks, Grandma."

When they'd finished eating, Robert washed the dishes in the sink. The other grandkids never helped clean up. Patty Lou felt awkward about it, not liking to impose when they were visiting, but appreciating the thought. If they helped, it made her feel they thought she was weak, but not helping made her feel unappreciated. It was bad either way. When Robert was through, they all went back in the living room to sit down on the two sofas.

"How's work?" Patty Lou asked, hoping she'd be able to hear over the sound of the air conditioner.

"It's okay," Robert replied. "A new girl just started at the library. She's obsessive-compulsive, so she drives me crazy."

Patty Lou didn't know what that meant and didn't really care to ask. She was sorry Robert didn't do something more important with his life, but no one in the family really had. Being a good person was more important than being successful, but why couldn't you be both? "And how's work for you, Joseph?"

"I just finished teaching summer school. I had some good students. The fall semester starts in three weeks."

"Y'all going anywhere?"

"We're heading to San Francisco for several days next week," said Robert.

Patty Lou nodded. The boys had spent two weeks in Europe in the spring and now were going to California for a week, but they were only coming to see her for the afternoon.

They weren't even staying the night. Of course, she knew she was boring. She never had anything interesting to talk about. She never did anything different. Robert used to ask her to tell stories about when she was growing up, and he'd written her early history up in a forty-page booklet and given copies to everyone in the family, but there were no new stories to tell.

At first, seeing the printed booklet had made her feel important. But after a while, she felt dismayed that her whole life, her whole being, had been reduced to a mere forty pages. It seemed somehow disappointing.

"How's your blood count?" asked Robert.

"It's at 100,000. It was at 160,000, but it's supposed to be 4,000, so they want me to start chemotherapy tomorrow."

"You have to go to the hospital?"

"No, I just go to the doctor's office for a half hour. They'll give me an IV for thirty minutes a day every day this week. Then I'll be off it for three weeks, and then we repeat it again the next month the same way, for four months."

"What's the name of the drug?"

Patty Lou got up and went to her dresser, returning a moment later with a piece of paper. "It's called Fludara." She handed him the paper and let him read about the drug.

"Possible kidney problems," said Robert. "I guess you better drink lots of water. Unless your feet swell up. I expect the doctor will tell you what to do."

"I just hope it doesn't make me sick. Remember your mother? I think the chemotherapy killed her before the leukemia would have."

"Well, diarrhea isn't supposed to be a problem," Robert said, still reading the paper, "but nausea might. You could be okay, though. The paper doesn't say what percentage of people experience these side effects."

"I'm just glad I don't have to go to the hospital. People die in hospitals. You never knew my sister Margaret Missouri. She went in the hospital to have a tumor removed, and she got lockjaw and died. She was only thirty-eight."

"Tetanus," said Robert. "How awful. Your whole body is just one big charley horse for two days and then you die."

"And my sister Nelda Sue. She was forty-four when she went in to have her tonsils out. And she bled to death on the operating table."

Patty Lou thought about the rest of her family. She was the ninth of ten children, and now she was the only one left. James had died of diphtheria when he was three, and Aubrey had died in his twenties when the glass in the back of the truck he was driving caved in and the dirt he was carrying suffocated him.

Virginia, the youngest, was the last to go five years ago, of cancer. Patty Lou's parents were gone, her brothers and sisters were gone, her husband was gone, her daughter was gone. She should be ready to go, too, shouldn't she?

It wasn't that the grandkids were so good to her, but she still liked being around to see that they were okay. Her son,

Shane, lived a couple of miles away and either he or his wife Lisa stopped by to see her every day for at least five minutes, but their two teenage sons didn't come by any more often than Robert or Joyce.

No one called her, but she knew that was her fault. She could never think of anything to say over the phone, and the conversation never lasted more than two minutes. But Robert did write her every few months. Her eyesight was still good, so she enjoyed that. He often wrote about his gay friends, but that was okay. They seemed to be nice to him, and that made her feel good. She didn't know if he was going to hell, but she still wanted him to have a good life. A good life was important.

"They'll probably stick you in a different vein every day this week," said Robert, "but I'm sure they have someone who will do it right and won't hurt you."

"You think they'll use a big needle?"

"I expect it'll be about medium."

"I hope I don't start going downhill," Patty Lou said. "I don't want a lingering death. I want to go in my sleep."

"I hope you go in your sleep, too."

Patty Lou smiled. The others wouldn't even talk about death, but Robert did, and they pretty much said the same thing every time. She liked that. She wasn't deeply afraid of death. She felt she was going to heaven, maybe not the highest degree in the Celestial Kingdom, but heaven nevertheless. She'd always tried to be a good Christian back when she was Methodist, and she tried to be a good Mormon now.

So she believed the afterlife would be good. She simply wasn't ready to go just yet. When she was a girl, they didn't have running water. They had a horse and buggy to get to town. They had kerosene lanterns for light in the evening. The world had changed so drastically since then. It certainly wasn't all good, but it was *interesting*. She didn't want to miss it.

They managed to talk till 3:00. So often when the grandkids visited, they would all just sit on the sofa in silence, struggling for something to say. But today it had gone pretty well. Then at 3:00, Robert said he and Joseph had to go over and see Henry for an hour but would be back.

Patty Lou quietly sat on the sofa waiting for them. She didn't really like to read, and there was never anything good on TV on Sunday afternoon. She could listen to music or watch one of the videos the kids had given her, but she preferred just sitting and thinking. She always had lots of thoughts.

She simply never had anything to *say*. She thought again of the possibility of death. She had her will made out already. She'd had it done twenty years ago. Everyone got an equal portion. Of course, they'd have to sell the 200 acres as a unit and then divide the money. She couldn't divide the land seven or eight different ways.

Robert and Joseph came back around 4:30. The dogs barked again but let them pass. "We went by the old buzzard tree down near the creek," said Robert. "There must have been seventy-five buzzards in it. It was incredible."

"They're always out circling, waiting for something to die."

Patty Lou opened the pack of chocolate-covered peanuts, and everyone ate a couple. She used a twist tie to close the package, and though the conversation had flowed pretty well before, now it seemed to flounder. "So you like San Francisco?" she asked.

"It's great," Robert said. "The weather's always nice, in the sixties in the day and fifties at night. The hills are pretty. And the city is clean and lively, not at all like New Orleans."

Patty Lou had never been out of Mississippi, but of course she'd seen a lot on television. "Y'all planning any other trips?"

"We'll probably go see my mom in New York for Thanksgiving," Joseph said. "She's eighty-five and having trouble walking."

"Oh, that's too bad."

They found a couple more things to talk about, and at 5:30, Patty Lou heated up the supper. They ate mostly in silence.

"I want you to be one of my pallbearers," Patty Lou said. It sounded too abrupt.

Robert stopped eating and nodded. "Okay. If I'm not too old by then."

"You won't be."

He nodded and put his hand on her wrist.

They had cake, drinking milk with the evening meal instead of Coke. Then they went back to the living room.

"Joann said she could take you to your doctor's appointment a couple of times this week if it was too hard for Lisa to take you every day," said Robert. "She's a retired nurse, so she could probably answer some of your questions, too."

"I'll think about it." It was nice of Joann to offer, but Patty Lou thought she'd feel too awkward with her, the woman who had replaced her daughter.

They sat in silence a while, looking at the wooden floor. Robert had varnished it a few years ago on one of his trips up, but it was starting to get worn in places. Maybe if she was still alive next spring, he could do the floor again.

Around 6:30, Robert stood. "I guess we better go before it gets too dark. We'll be praying for you tomorrow."

Patty Lou hugged Robert and Joseph and opened the door for them. "Will I see you before Christmas?"

"We'll have to see what our schedule is like."

"All right."

Patty Lou gave Robert a jar of homemade pickles. She stood on the porch with the dogs as he and Joseph got in their car. They all waved, and soon the car had gone off down the curving gravel drive. Patty Lou stood on the porch a moment longer after they left. There were still three buzzards circling in the sky overhead. Three for a letter. Maybe someone would write to her soon.

Patty Lou went back inside and turned off the air conditioner. Then she sat back down on the sofa and stared at the floor. An hour later when the sun went down, she was still sitting there, thinking.

Chemotherapy started tomorrow at 9:00, and she wanted to live. She went to the kitchen, took out the pack of chocolate-covered peanuts, and brushed the ants off. She didn't usually have two desserts, but if she was going to be nauseated this week, putting on a few extra ounces now wouldn't hurt. She poured some milk and sat down to eat.

Mrs. Mariposa

I waited in the hall outside of the bishop's office, my palms sweating. I was twenty-six and hadn't had more than a handful of talks with my bishop since I was twelve. Naturally, there'd been the worthiness interviews, and as embarrassing as they were, I'd always told the truth: I never smoked, I never drank, I never used drugs, I didn't drink coffee or tea, I never had sex with girls, I never petted, and I didn't watch R-rated movies. I did, however, masturbate on occasion.

By "on occasion," I meant five times a week.

It was my one moral failing, and it bothered me tremendously. I was afraid my sexuality would be my Achilles' heel and destroy me. I tried singing hymns, I tried listening to classical music, I tried exercise, I tried reading the scriptures, I even tried tying one hand to my bedpost. But you can see the problem—there was always one hand still free.

Nevertheless, while the five bishops I'd had over the past fourteen years had told me what I was doing was a sin, they hadn't driven me to the brink of suicide over my depravity. My current bishop even told me, only eight months ago, "Hector, this is a problem that plagues many young men." Then he'd sighed heavily, as if this was the third time he'd heard a similar confession that day. "Why don't you marry that pretty girl, Angelica, who just moved into the ward? That'll solve all your problems."

I was an Eagle Scout. I was third in my graduating class in high school. When I learned to drive, I looked in my rear view mirror every fifteen seconds as I was instructed. I never went over the speed limit. At Arizona State, I had a 3.6 average. I gave my non-Mormon professors a Book of Mormon at the end of each semester. I never cheated on my taxes or my tithes.

I'd always thought of myself as living an A- life, or maybe a B+ one. Some days, I felt I'd be barred from the Celestial Kingdom and be sent down to the Terrestrial. Other days, I believed I might just slip through before the doors shut. I might not be worthy of earning godhood, but I could certainly become a ministering angel. I would happily accept bottom of the barrel Celestial status.

But now…

I rubbed the side of my face. I was sweating. Married four months ago in the Mesa temple, I had to confess tonight perhaps the worst sin a Mormon could commit. What I had done to my wife was unspeakable. I was going to be excommunicated, that was clear. What wasn't clear was just how far the repercussions would go.

Would I now even be eligible for the Telestial Kingdom? Or was even that no longer within my reach? Perhaps Outer Darkness was all that eternity offered.

The door opened, and the bishop's secretary waved me in. "Brother Mariposa, Bishop Wright will see you now."

I walked through the door into a tiny office. Inside was a door leading to the bishop's private office. That door was open now, too, Bishop Wright holding out his hand with a concerned expression on his face. "Hector, you all right? You sounded very upset over the phone."

I looked at Brother Lopez, the secretary, and then back at the bishop. "Can we talk in your office, Bishop?" I asked.

Bishop Wright and Brother Lopez exchanged glances, and the bishop ushered me in and closed the door. "Have a seat, Hector."

I sat down in a tiny wooden chair with a thin cushion. The bishop sat down behind his desk in a larger chair. His head was now a few inches above mine. I felt like shrinking into the floor.

"What seems to be the problem?" Bishop Wright asked gently.

I rubbed my hands together, trying to wipe off the sweat. I looked back at the bishop. I wished I were dead. Maybe I should just leave. I took a deep breath. "It's about Angelica," I said.

"Yes? How is she? I heard from my wife that she announced her pregnancy last week in Sunday School. Everything going okay?"

I felt my face burning in shame.

"Hector?"

"You know I was a virgin when I married," I began.

"Yes. I interviewed you before the stake president did to give you your temple recommend."

"You know I've never seen even one porn magazine. I've never looked at porn on the internet even once."

"Hector, what are you trying to tell me? Have you become addicted?" Bishop Wright sighed. "I'm afraid we see far too much of this in our young men." He looked down at a paperweight on his desk. "Even among our older men."

"No, no." I shook my head. "I'm telling you I'm ignorant. I didn't know any better."

"Any better than what?" Bishop Wright tilted his head in confusion.

"Angelica and I never even petted while we were dating," I said. "She was the purest girl I'd ever met. It's what drew me to her." I paused. "We did a lot of French kissing, but that was it." I looked at the floor in embarrassment. "I know some General Authorities say the first time you kiss your wife should be over the altar, but really, as much as I *wanted* to do, I felt I was holding back."

Bishop Wright chuckled. "That's like saying fornicating only once a week is better than four times a week. But yes, I see your point. Kissing, even French kissing, is a fairly minor issue. It leads to temptation, which is bad, but if you were still a virgin when you married in the temple, that's the important thing." He looked at me sharply. "You *were* still a virgin?"

"Yes, yes, I already told you."

The bishop sat back, looking flustered. "I don't understand what the problem is, Hector."

"I'm a good boy," I said. "I never park in handicapped parking spaces. I drive five miles under the speed limit. I always check my rearview mirror."

"Hector…"

"It was Angelica," I went on. "She insisted on chastity even after we were married. I found it…frustrating."

"What do mean?"

"She still wouldn't let me fondle her breasts. Or touch her…down there."

The bishop chuckled again. "Well, you must have managed it *sometime*. When is the baby due?"

"There's not going to be a baby," I said morosely. "Not now. Not really."

"Oh, my heck," Bishop Wright murmured. "What in the world happened?"

"Angelica always insisted the lights be turned off when we had sex," I said unhappily, wishing I could have a stroke or heart attack before I had to explain further. "Even the curtains had to be drawn. It had to be pitch black in the bedroom."

"She's a sweet girl. I liked her ever since she moved into the ward nine months ago."

"And she never let me…" I couldn't say it.

"What?"

"She never let me…"

"Oh, for goodness' sake, Hector, I'll keep anything you say in complete confidentiality."

No, he wouldn't. He'd be calling the stake president before I left his office tonight. "She never let me be on top," I blurted out. "I couldn't even touch her. Not at all. Nothing. I had to just lie there while she…while she lowered herself onto my…my penis." I put my face in my hands. It was all too mortifying to explain.

There was silence for a moment. Then the bishop said, "Hmmph," and looked perplexed. "Well," he said slowly, "that certainly is unusual for a timid girl like Angelica. But I've certainly heard stranger tales from some of the married members of the congregation. I wouldn't worry about it too much. She'll loosen up eventually and let you touch her."

I looked up into the bishop's eyes, my own filling with tears. "I *did* touch her, Bishop. Last night."

Suddenly, the bishop's face grew pale. "You didn't lose control and rape her, did you? Oh, Hector."

I buried my face in my hands again. Why couldn't Heavenly Father strike me down right this very minute before I had to go on?

"We were married in the temple," I said. "We have a temple marriage."

"Yes, but…"

"Bishop, you don't understand. I'm going to hell for what I've done."

"And just what have you done? Tell me, for Pete's sake!"

I sighed. There was no way to drag out the story any further. "When I reached up to feel Angelica while we were having sex last night…"

"Yes?"

"I grabbed her penis."

The bishop's mouth fell open, and I started to cry. "We had a same-sex marriage in the temple!" I said, sobbing, "but I didn't know! I swear! All this time, I thought Angelica was a woman! She never let me touch her! I thought she was just extraordinarily righteous. I thought we'd make it to the Celestial Kingdom together. I thought we'd be gods and populate our own planet. I never thought… I never thought…"

"Oh, my heck," breathed the bishop.

"What am I going to do?" I wailed.

The bishop put his palms flat on his desk and breathed heavily for a moment. "Are you gay?" he finally asked.

I sobbed again. "Aren't you listening, Bishop? I thought she was a woman."

The bishop rubbed his chin, frowning as he stared at me, and then he looked at a photo of the prophet on the wall beside him. He opened a drawer and glanced inside it, then shut it and picked up a piece of paper on his desk and put it down again. "Hector, this will require serious action. Your wife will be excommunicated. You'll almost certainly have to attend a Church court yourself." Then he looked startled as a new idea apparently struck him. "What happened last night? After you found out?"

I swallowed and tried to regain my composure, though I knew I could never regain my dignity. "I was already inside her." I paused. "Inside *him*. She was—he was moving up and down. It felt so good. Even after I realized Angelica was a man, I—I let him keep going. I came inside a man, knowing it was a man." I felt I was driving a car that was completely out of control. I kept trying to look in the rearview mirror to save myself, but there was nothing there.

Bishop Wright puffed out his cheeks and blew out a long breath of air. "You didn't hit him?" asked the bishop carefully. "Perhaps if there was some evidence you were truly angry…"

"Bishop," I said slowly, "when I was a boy, I had a pet ferret I named Sarah. I loved Sarah, and I got another ferret for her to play with, Samuel. They were both fixed, of course, but I thought they made a great couple. They played together so happily. I always thought after the Resurrection, they'd be in heaven together and have babies then."

"I don't understand where you're going with this, Hector."

"One day, I brought Sarah to the vet, and the vet told me that Sarah was a boy. It came as a complete shock to me, even though Sarah had always been larger than Samuel. I just thought she was a big girl."

"Hector…"

"Bishop, ferrets don't live a long time, only about five years. But for the next few years, I could never think of Sarah as a boy. In my mind, she was always a girl. Angelica told me last night her parents can never think of her as a girl, only as a boy, because that's how they knew her. But Bishop, I can only think of Angelica as a girl. I know she has a penis, but to me, she's still a woman."

"Hector, we'll definitely have to hold a court for you, too."

"Bishop, I'm not gay. I'm not. It's just that…I love Angelica." I shook my head. That was the worst of it all. The unforgiveable sin. "She's my first love, my only love. I married her in the temple. She's my *eternal* love."

"I'll have to report all this at your court."

"We had a long talk last night. We're going to try to adopt privately. Time it with her 'pregnancy.'"

The bishop put his hands over his ears.

I stood up and leaned on his desk. "Bishop, I've simply got to know. I'm not going to lose the Church, am I? I'm not going to hell, am I? Just for loving somebody with all my heart?"

"You need to leave my office. This interview is over."

"I've always been a good boy," I said.

The bishop stood up and walked over to the door, swinging it open brusquely.

"Bishop…"

"The stake president will call you to let you know the date of your court."

I walked through the door and felt it shut firmly behind me. I could hear the bishop pick up the phone in his office. I looked at Brother Lopez, who frowned. He didn't know what was going on, but if the bishop was mad, he knew he needed to be, too.

I stumbled out into the hall and made my way toward the foyer, pushing open the glass doors. I walked out into the parking lot, feeling light-headed. Angelica was leaning against the door of our car, in a tight yellow dress. She nodded when she saw me. "I told you," she said.

I hesitated a moment and then hugged her. "It's okay," I breathed into her ear. "It's okay."

"What's okay, honey?" she breathed back into mine. I felt my crotch tightening.

"I'll go to hell for you," I said, my voice thick. "I will."

She pulled me tight against her body. "Oh, why did you have to tell?" she moaned. "Now they'll annul our wedding. Our lovely temple wedding."

Another car pulled into the parking lot, probably the bishop's next scheduled interview. A fortyish woman from the Relief Society stepped out. "Hi, Sister Mariposa," she called out cheerily.

"It's Mrs. Mariposa," Angelica said calmly.

"Huh?"

"Let's go home, sweetheart," I told my wife, kissing her on the lips. I opened the car door for her, noticing her beautiful legs as she slid into the seat. "We need to spend some time together with the lights on."

Angelica smiled.

"And this time, I want to be on top."

We pulled out of the parking lot, the Relief Society sister still looking at us quizzically, and drove off down the street away from the church. As we headed home, I kept glancing over at my wife and smiling. I never looked even once in the rearview mirror.

Desert Garden

"There's a snake in here, Leland," Arlette said.

"What?" Leland replied sleepily, turning in the oversized chair in the living room. He'd gone to sleep a half hour earlier, but Arlette had stayed up with a kerosene lamp a while longer to read. When she stood from the couch to walk over to the lamp and turn it out, she'd seen a shadow move across the floor and under Leland's chair.

"Leland," she said a little louder and more firmly. "Don't move. There's a snake under your chair."

This time, the words sank in more deeply, and Leland opened his eyes. He didn't move but looked across the room at Arlette. "What kind?" he asked.

"I don't know," she replied in an exasperated but still subdued tone. "We don't have as many snakes in St. Louis as they do here in Snowflake."

They were several miles outside of Snowflake, Arizona, in the desert, down a narrow dirt road which had taken forty-five minutes to travel. Arlette hadn't understood the reason for Leland's mumbled prayer as they'd started down the road until they were halfway to the Petersons' house. The road was little more than a cleared space with no bushes on it. There were several places where water had washed over the path, taking some of the ground with it and leaving sharp drop-offs, though each was usually only a few inches deep. Sometimes, one side of the road would drop half a foot while the other stayed at its normal level. For one stretch, the holes alternated sides almost continually for a hundred yards. Arlette had jokingly complained of seasickness, carsickness, and even morning sickness, though it was mid-afternoon and she wasn't pregnant. Then a more fully realized sickness came over her when they came to a six-foot deep pit.

"We have to go across that?" she'd asked incredulously. "In this car?"

"At least it hasn't been raining. We'd never make it." He closed his eyes for a moment. "Hang on." Then he started down the steep slope in the road. The sharp angle continued for about fifteen feet, gave four feet of level ground, and climbed at another thirty degree angle back up again on the other side. The Toyota Corona jostled and complained, but the tires didn't slide and they'd soon made it back up to the "good" part of the road.

"How did you ever find these people to baptize them?" Arlette had asked.

Leland smiled, apparently pleased that Arlette was beginning to appreciate his experiences here better. Arlette had known Leland now for eight months, and they'd been married three. He'd told her all about his two years as a missionary in Arizona, and when the opportunity had come to go back and visit the area, they'd both been pleased with the idea of sharing some new experiences in his old mission field. Besides, they wouldn't be able to do things like this once they started having kids.

They'd already been through East Phoenix, Paradise Valley, Scottsdale, and South Phoenix, an area Leland had particularly loved because of the open and friendly people. When they'd left there for Snowflake, though, Arlette had found an even greater friendliness. Everybody in the whole town seemed to know Leland, who hadn't been there in almost a year. People would come up to him and say, "Hi, Elder Miller!" When Arlette would ask later, "Why didn't you introduce me?" he would just laugh and say, "I have no idea who that was!"

One family with six children took them in for two days, feeding them and washing their clothes. Then they'd stayed a night with a family of twelve children who'd taken them horseback riding and to a luau. Arlette wondered if Leland had purposely saved this part of the trip for last to help convince her not to wait any longer to become pregnant. She had said she wanted to wait until they'd been married a couple of years, but she had to admit that seeing all those huge and surprisingly happy families was tempting.

When the following day they attended a Flake family reunion, it seemed at least half the town was there. If one wasn't a Snow or a Flake by name, he was related by his mother.

"Talk about multiplying and replenishing!" Arlette had joked. "They're like rabbits!"

"That's why they put a temple here," said Leland admiringly.

Arlette had been raised a Protestant, but her family had never attended church very often. She'd felt the need to be involved in a cause, though, and had investigated and adopted Greenpeace, Zero Population, and Doctors Without Borders to feel she was a contributing member of society. She'd been reluctant to listen to the two LDS missionaries who'd shown up at her parents' home one day when she was seventeen, and while Arlette liked some of the doctrine in the discussions, she felt apathetic toward much of it. She had never quite come to a full decision regarding abortion, for instance, but she didn't approve of large families and supported the idea of birth control and voluntary sterilization.

"It is our duty to provide bodies for the spirits who are waiting for their turn on Earth," she was told. Once Arlette could believe in the idea of a purpose to life, of course, she could see why those spirits needed to come. But so many? What was the harm in making those spirits wait another generation? Why did so many members of the Church insist on having five or six children?

She wondered if the idea was really to keep members so busy they didn't have time to question anything. Arlette wasn't pregnant yet, though, and still had time. The question of raising children petrified her.

Only two months after she began dating Leland, he'd proposed to her. He'd have been happy to get married within another month, but Arlette had wanted to wait a year, to give them both a little more time to get further along in school. He was persistent, however, repeating the prophet's words that it was wrong to wait until their situation was completely "right." She finally relented, and they'd soon gone up to the temple and were sealed for "time and all eternity."

Not a month later, Leland was asking if he could stop using condoms. "Only if I can go on the pill," Arlette had replied. Arlette had wanted to do that anyway. It was more expensive but also more reliable, she felt.

Now, however, it didn't look like any of that was going to make much difference if they were both about to be bitten by a poisonous snake an hour away from the nearest help. She was hoping to go into nursing or radiology or some other health-related field, but she had yet to take so much as a first aid course. She knew enough to realize that snake venom caused hemolysis, but not enough to know what to do about it. What was that scripture those fanatics used who purposely let snakes bite them? Unfortunately, she realized nervously as she peered across the room, knowing the answer to that wouldn't help them now, either.

"Leland, do you see it?" Arlette asked.

"No, but I think I heard something." He looked around his chair and then at the walls and table near him. "There's nothing to hit it with. We better call for help." Then he shouted loudly, "Brother Peterson! There's a snake in here!"

There was a fumbling sound from the bedroom, followed by a muffled, "Just a minute." The door opened and Brother Peterson stepped out wearing boots and his Mormon undergarments. He was carrying a rifle.

Arlette pointed to the chair and Brother Peterson prodded underneath it with the barrel of the gun. All three of them then could hear the rattling. A few seconds later, the snake lunged forward, and Arlette could see the head of the snake. It missed Brother Peterson and coiled up again, rattling away.

"Shit!"

"Arlette!" Leland said, frowning at her.

Brother Peterson poked underneath the chair again, and the snake lunged a second time. This time, it stayed far enough out that he could take aim, and he shot. One blast, and the snake was dead.

Arlette sank back into the couch and breathed deeply.

"Don't worry," said Brother Peterson. "I'll put something over the hole in the floor so another one doesn't come in."

How comforting, Arlette thought, but she managed a polite, "Thank you."

Later, after Brother Peterson was back in bed and Arlette had turned out the kerosene lamp, she heard Leland tiptoeing across the floor. He crawled onto the couch beside her and kissed her.

"You know we can't both sleep here," she said. "There's no room."

"I wasn't thinking of sleeping," he replied. "Seeing that snake gave me some ideas." He slid his hand underneath her nightgown.

"And are you wearing a snakeskin?" she asked.

"Oh, Arlette, just once won't matter."

"You'd better get that snake away from me, or I'll call Brother Peterson again."

"One baby won't destroy your Zero Population Growth."

"Someone's got to make up for all these people with twelve kids."

"That's what nuns and old maids are for."

"Goodnight, Leland."

Leland sighed and walked back to his chair, and Arlette slowly drifted off into a fretful, restless sleep.

The next morning, Sister Peterson cooked breakfast, and afterwards, Brother Peterson and Leland traded stories back and forth while Arlette listened. Then Brother Peterson took Arlette and Leland outside to his shed to show them a piece of wood he'd carved into a scorpion.

"My God," said Arlette, ignoring Leland's frown. "It's beautiful. That must have taken forever." It seemed a morbid thing to carve, but the details were incredible. She wanted to touch it but held back.

"Thanks. Not much else to do out here in your spare time." He pointed to a shelf in the shed with other wood carvings, of a pear, an apple, a banana, and a bird.

"Do you sell these?" asked Arlette. "People would appreciate your craftsmanship."

Brother Peterson shrugged. "Too much trouble to drive into town. Besides, I like looking at them. They pretty up the place." He motioned expansively around the small, tin shed. "This is as close as I'm going to get to Paradise."

He began to rummage around, and Leland brought Arlette back outside. They stood near a fence, and Leland pointed off into the distance. "His land goes on for ten miles in that direction. Isn't that incredible?"

"It's only a desert, Leland." She looked at the vast expanse of slightly rolling, tan landscape. She saw a few bushes and lots of rocks, wondering where Brother Peterson found any wood to carve. Still, there was something liberating about seeing so much space. It must be why the people in Snowflake didn't feel criminal about having so many kids. But this land wouldn't support much of a family.

Leland took her hand, and they walked slowly along the fence. "See that house?" He pointed to a small building in the distance. "Witches live there."

"Witches?"

"Druids, I think."

Arlette laughed. "Druids? In the desert?"

"Well, they're some kind of Satan worshipper."

"You've just mentioned three very different kinds of people." She hoped Leland wouldn't take offense at her "uppitiness," but she resolved again to finish school before she became pregnant. How could she teach her kids properly if she didn't know anything herself? And what if Leland had been killed last night? How would she support a family if she had no education and no career?

"Except for them," Leland went on, "this place is great. But one bad apple doesn't spoil the whole bunch. I know I could live out here."

"I'd write to you as often as I could."

Leland smiled and shrugged, and they walked along a little further. Arlette looked down to watch where she stepped, and she noticed a beautiful, tan rock with red and purple lines. She stooped down to pick it up. "How interesting," she said, looking at the pattern the lines made. "It almost looks like…"

She looked up and began searching for other rocks like this one. They were everywhere, and they almost all had similar markings. Why, there must be a thousand, ten thousand of them. "My God," she said. "We're in a petrified forest."

"I know." Leland picked up a large piece of fossilized wood. "Aren't they pretty?"

"Fascinating."

"Found it," they heard Brother Peterson saying from the shed entrance. "Come on and see."

Arlette picked up a few pieces of the petrified wood as they walked back, slipping them into her pocket.

"Here," said Brother Peterson, pointing to another wood carving. "I did these several years ago."

Before them was a nativity scene, a woman lying down, a man kneeling beside her, two other men standing, part of a barn wall and floor, and a baby on a clump of straw. Arlette leaned close to see the eyes and mouths, the fingers, the straws. There was so much detail.

"Brother Peterson," she breathed. "This is museum-quality art. These would be worth a fortune, hundreds at least, maybe more."

Brother Peterson laughed. "What do I need with money?" he asked. "I've got everything I need. I'd rather just enjoy the beauty. Besides, these are my babies. I can't part with them."

Arlette glanced at Leland and then back at Brother Peterson. "Do you have any children?" she asked.

"A son," Peterson said with a shrug. "He joined the Navy when he was seventeen and has only come back to visit twice in the last fifteen years."

"I'm sorry," said Arlette.

"Oh, he likes us well enough," said Peterson. "He just hates the desert. When I look out there, I see the lush garden this once was. But he can't see through my eyes."

Arlette looked out at the brown hills.

"He writes," Brother Peterson went on, "but I don't go into town to pick up my mail often enough to keep any kind of conversation going." He shrugged again. "Lizabeth and I have made our contribution to the world, though. John is a good boy."

Brother Peterson returned to his wood, turning over a couple of rough pieces as if trying to guess which figures might be hiding inside them. Arlette wondered why he felt his contribution to the world had to do with DNA rather than his talent. Almost anyone could have sex and make a baby. Not many, however, could make any other kind of significant offering. Arlette bit her lip and determined she would apply to medical school as well as nursing school and see just how far she could go. She had to do something useful to the world.

Leland stayed to watch Brother Peterson, but Arlette stepped away and walked behind the shed. In one corral, there were two horses, and in a smaller corral next to it a few goats. Arlette looked again at the bleak, beige landscape. How could these animals stay alive? There wasn't enough vegetation to support a mouse. Well, probably it could support mice. And then snakes would eat the mice.

So did people eat the snakes? Arlette never did see what Brother Peterson had done with that snake, but come to think of it, Lizabeth had announced they were having "chicken" soup for lunch today. Arlette swallowed, trying not to feel sick.

Behind the shed, she stooped and found a large, beautiful piece of fossilized wood. She counted the rings. That tree had been a good fifty-five years old. The same age as Brother Peterson. She stood again and looked out over the desert. This had all been a forest once. The Book of Mormon had a story about the people killing all the trees in their community by not caring properly for their resources, but this petrified forest, of course, was natural. Still, as stupid as humans were, and as unpredictable as nature was, could it be right to bring ten kids into the world? The Church said that having a large family proved responsibility. But didn't they have a responsibility to all of mankind, and to the planet itself?

Why didn't the Church encourage each couple to have perhaps one or two children and then adopt abandoned children? Surely, teaching abused or disabled children was every bit as important to society as simply reproducing. Cats could reproduce exponentially. Didn't humans have an obligation to be more than mere copying machines? Did Arlette have to use her own eggs to be considered righteous?

Arlette stood and walked down a gently sloping hill, staying away from bushes where a snake might be hiding. A couple of the bushes had rather lovely flowers, and the colored wood was pretty, too. She could see how the Petersons liked it out here. Still, St. Louis was Eden compared to this bleakness. She'd have to stop complaining about how fast the weeds grew back home.

Arlette found another large, spectacular chunk of petrified tree, and after checking around it for scorpions, she sat down, looking at a small, woody bush a few feet away. The plant wasn't beautiful, but it lived. It found a way amidst all this nothingness to survive. When this whole area had died for whatever reason umpteen millennia ago, this plant's ancestors had struggled on. There was something beautiful in that. She wondered briefly about her own genealogical tree. Was her branch going to grow any further?

"Arlette? You okay?" It was Leland, walking over from the shed.

She nodded and lifted her arm to hold his hand when he came close.

"What are you thinking about?" he asked, squatting beside her.

"You don't want to know."

Leland laughed but then frowned when she didn't elaborate. "Of course I do," he said. "We're husband and wife. We can talk about anything."

She looked at him, wondering if they would ever be "one." "There are over six billion people on this planet," she said, gesturing toward the desert. "How many more can it support?"

Leland patted her hand. "There is enough and to spare," he said. "The planet is big. It isn't all like this. Our having a few babies isn't going to destroy the world."

"Don't hunters say they're doing the deer a favor because the deer reproduce too much and would starve when there isn't enough food for them all?"

"We're not animals. God has provided this world for *us*. He *wants* us to use it."

"By the time our first-born could go on a mission, there will be ten billion people on this planet. Can the Earth sustain that?"

"You need to have faith, Arlette. We can't understand the ways of God. He'll see to it. He commanded us to multiply and replenish the Earth."

"And haven't we? If someone asks you to refill his glass of 7-Up, do you fill it to the very top? Do you keep pouring even after the soda is spilling out over the sides?"

"We haven't reached the top."

Arlette groaned. "When my dad would pour me a glass of milk, he'd tell me, 'Say when.' Of course, I'd say, 'Stop!' 'That's enough!' 'Okay!' and the milk would pour all over the counter because I didn't say 'When.'"

"Well, we have prophets. God can say 'when' anytime He wants."

"Maybe He's already shouting 'Stop!' by giving us droughts and famines and expects us not to be so stupid we don't understand this isn't some silly game."

"Will one child turn the rain forests into deserts? Can't we at least have one child? We can worry about more after that. You might find you like being a mother. Let's just have the first one and concentrate on that."

Arlette smiled and then looked out again over the desolate land. "Yes," she said, "let's concentrate on the immediate future and forget about the rest of our lives."

"Look, the Millennium will come before things get out of control."

"If it's coming so soon, why not let the kids be born then, when they won't have to deal with so much crime and drugs and war? Isn't it selfish to want children now, when they'll be better off if we wait?"

There was silence for a few moments, and Arlette knew she'd been mean to say it like that, but she couldn't quite bring herself to apologize, either. Maybe that just showed she was too selfish herself to be a good mother in the first place. There did seem to be an awful lot of women in her ward who were reproducing without following up on the "raising them well" part.

The kids ran around like wild animals. The young couples she visited had kids that screamed and hit each other and threw tantrums. The innocence of childhood could be corrupted pretty quickly. A baptismal certificate or even a temple marriage certificate still didn't erase the need for some kind of parenting license.

"Are you saying you never want to have children?" asked Leland slowly. "We'd better resolve this once and for all."

"I want God to tend His own damn garden," Arlette said. "Can't He thin out some weeds, do a little pruning? Do we have to live in the Jungle of Eden?"

"He does weed. That's what AIDS and Ebola are for."

Arlette pulled her hand away. "Well, good grief. Who put a jerk like that in charge?"

"What?" Leland stood up, and so did Arlette.

"I don't want to be one of those sheep like I see at church every week."

"Following God doesn't make you a robot."

"If God only wanted creatures to reproduce, He could have stopped Creation after He made bacteria. If He allowed a brain to evolve, He must value that as well."

"What good is the best brain in the world if you keep it all greedily to yourself? Don't you see some of these great celebrities who've never had children? Don't you think what a waste it is all that greatness stops with them?"

Arlette shrugged. "I don't seem to be reading much in the news about Shakespeare's great-great-great-granddaughter. Wasn't his contribution to culture worthwhile regardless of what he did with his dick?"

Leland turned and walked several feet away, stopping at a little dry gully. Arlette didn't know if she wanted to go to him or not. Their eternal marriage might not even last six months, she realized.

She still had another year and a half of undergraduate school before she could think of professional school. She wanted a biology degree first rather than a nursing degree, so she could teach high school if it turned out she didn't like nursing. And it seemed like a better background if she did decide on medicine or something else more daunting. How could she make a lifelong commitment to a baby when she didn't even know for sure what she wanted to be doing three years from now?

Arlette finally moved over to Leland's side. She let her fingers brush against his hand, but he didn't respond.

"I'm quitting school," he said. "I'm tired of waiting for my life to begin. I'm going to get a job and start living now."

That didn't sound very inclusive, Arlette thought. She wasn't sure if she was glad about that fact or not.

"I'm moving to Snowflake. This is Zion out here."

Arlette looked about at the dead forest all around her, still somehow beautiful despite its lifelessness. "Maybe I could be a gynecologist," she said slowly. "This town could probably use one more."

"Let's make love just once without a condom," said Leland, turning to her. "If you get pregnant, it was meant to be. If you don't…"

"You'll wait five years without pestering me?"

Leland was silent a moment. "I guess not."

Arlette held his hand and squeezed it gently. Then she let it go. "I can catch a bus from Snowflake to Phoenix and get a plane from there."

"You're no Shakespeare, you know," he said. "Or Einstein."

"No," she agreed softly. "And I suppose you're no Abraham, either."

"If you start walking now, you can get to Snowflake before dark."

Arlette turned and stared at Leland in disbelief for a moment, and then she suddenly laughed. "You're casting me out of the Garden?"

"We have nothing more to talk about."

What kind of father would this man have made, thought Arlette? She looked across the desert. It couldn't be more than seven or eight miles to town, despite how long it had taken to get here. She'd been a Girl Scout in her youth and knew she could follow the trail back easily enough. Thank God it wasn't the middle of summer.

"Mind if I get some water first?"

Leland didn't say anything. Arlette laughed again and walked back toward the house.

"Don't get weeded out," Leland called after her.

Arlette asked Lizabeth for a few bottles of water. She left her overnight bag in the living room, just taking her wallet with her ID and credit card. She kept the petrified wood in her pockets.

Medical school, thought Arlette, nodding. Maybe genetics. Or psychiatry. Perhaps she'd work on curing cancer. She was determined to do something beyond herself. And it didn't mean she wouldn't also be a good mother one day as well.

Arlette stepped aside to avoid the hole in the floor, still covered by a small piece of wood. Maybe she'd work on finding better treatments for venomous attacks, she thought.

Arlette walked out of the house and into the desert. She started down the road, following the ruts in the hard earth. She passed another lovely piece of petrified wood and put that one in her pocket, too. She hadn't had a chance to say goodbye to Brother Peterson, but she had his address. He might not get to town to pick up his mail for a while, but she'd send a thank you note for his hospitality, and maybe she'd ask him for a custom order, perhaps of a coiled snake. He did such beautiful work.

Arlette smiled and, looking up into the bright morning sky, headed slowly off for the small town in the distance.

Renting Mom and Dad

I can't whistle.

I can't tie a balloon.

I can't even blow my nose.

My parents never taught me any of these things. There were quite a few things my parents didn't do for me. First of all, my dad didn't stick around. He left when I was five. I have just the vaguest memories of the man, mostly him coming home drunk and yelling. My mom says he used to hit me, but I don't remember that. I remember him hitting *her*.

I do have this odd dream occasionally of a grizzly bear breaking into my apartment and attacking me.

I live in downtown Seattle and have never been out in the countryside, and I've never seen a bear except in a zoo. My mom didn't take me, of course. I went on a field trip with my class.

My parents were both part of the Swinomish tribe, though I was born and raised in Seattle. I didn't grow up speaking our native language, however, and during our long Seattle winters, I would dream of one day learning the language and even adding words to it. If the Inuit could have twenty-five different words for "snow," I could have twenty-five different words for "gray."

Mom didn't drink. But she did smoke non-stop. I can remember her telling me when I was just six, "Lucy, go buy me a pack." She didn't even have to specify a pack of what. I already knew. I would walk the two blocks from our First Hill apartment over to Broadway to the dumpy convenience store on the corner of Jefferson. The clerk never batted an eye.

Mom often had boyfriends over, usually white guys, though as often as not, I'd only see them one, two, or maybe three times before they disappeared.

I suppose I was fortunate not to end up with five or six siblings. It was always just me and Mom.

And the TV she watched incessantly when she was home from the job she hated, swatting me if I interrupted her favorite show.

Every show seemed to be her favorite show.

Mom died of ovarian cancer when I was eighteen.

I couldn't afford to attend UW, and frankly, my grades weren't good enough anyway, but I did enroll in community college. Working as a waitress, I kept the apartment, and Central was only a five-minute bus ride north on Broadway. My second quarter on campus, I saw two Mormon sister missionaries. They told me they had a book of scripture written by the native peoples of America. I took the lessons and was baptized a month later.

But that was when my troubles really began. I hadn't had many friends growing up, and the few I did have came from homes not terribly different from my own. Mormons, though, showed me a different world, where families were full and loving and committed to staying together not only for this life but throughout the eternities. It was something I'd never even considered before.

I read about the Lamanite men who loved their wives more than the Nephite men loved theirs. I read about Alma the Elder who loved his son Alma. I read about Mosiah who loved his four sons. I was a little miffed there wasn't more talk of daughters.

There was no reason Mom and Dad had to be such rotten parents. Of course, I understood it wasn't because they were Swinomish. Lots of white parents and black parents and Hispanic parents in my neighborhood were just as rotten. Probably other parents, too, though I didn't know many Asian kids personally. Or Indians. Real Indians, I mean.

What with work and all, it took me three years to finish community college, but my grades were strong enough now to get me into the University of Washington, and with student loans, I decided to jump in and do it, though I still needed to wait tables part-time to make ends meet. What I really wanted was be a counselor and help other young people struggling to improve their lives.

But there was one problem.

I was an emotional mess. How could *I* ever help someone else?

For the past few years since I'd joined the Church, I struggled during the holidays. It was clearly such an important time for families, and I didn't have any fond memories to get me through. As well-meaning as the other

Church members were, they were unable to avoid making single members of the Church feel like crap during these times. They were so happy to have great families of their own they didn't have any time or energy left over to help the rest of us. Even the singles didn't stick together. They became "children" again and ran off to their parents. Those of us with nothing were left with…nothing.

So this year, I had an idea. It was December 17, only a few days left until the big event. But there might still be time to do something about it. I went on Craigslist and posted an ad:

Wanted—Mom and Dad. Willing to rent for $8 an hour during the holidays.

I thought about adding more details, but I figured I'd just see who responded and explain further if necessary. There might simply be three or four crackpots and no one else. I posted the ad and picked up my Book of Mormon to comfort me. It was family history, after all.

The very next day, I got my first response. "Our daughter is spending Christmas with her boyfriend's family this year," said a woman. "My husband and I would love to have you over for Christmas Eve. You don't need to bring anything. We'll do all the cooking."

"Could I come over early and help you?" I asked. Since my mother and I had never done anything special for Christmas, helping with the holiday meal wasn't part of my tradition. I simply felt it *should* be.

The woman laughed. "We may have to trade you for our own daughter." She laughed again.

I calculated my funds. "I could come over and stay for a total of five hours," I said hesitantly. It sounded like an enormous chunk of time, but if I was going to do this, I wanted a full family experience. "That's all I can afford."

"Don't be ridiculous. We certainly aren't going to charge you for a thing like this. You're perfectly welcome to come."

They weren't going to charge me! How wonderful. Maybe I should use my funds to buy them Christmas presents. What did one buy for people one didn't know?

But then I got a second response. Greedy as I was, I made a second appointment, this one for Christmas Day. And when I got yet a third response, I decided to make a date for the day after Christmas, when I heard everyone always felt the after-Christmas blues. Best yet, neither of the other two sets of "parents" were going to charge me, either. Of course, I wasn't sure I had enough money to buy gifts for six people.

I sat on my futon sofa and hugged myself. I was finally going to experience the Christmas of my dreams. I wanted to call someone and tell them, but there was no one to call.

To my surprise, the responses didn't stop at three. Or thirty. Or three hundred. By the end of the week, over a thousand people had responded to my ad, everyone sounding truly generous and thoughtful. There really were good people out there. I smiled as I prayed to Heavenly Father in gratitude.

Not one of the respondents was Mormon, however, but that was another matter. When I'd hesitantly told my Visiting Teachers earlier in the month I was worried about another lonely Christmas, one of them said, "'There must needs be opposition in all things.' It'll be good for you in the long run."

Then her companion chimed in. "Well, we need to go now. I've still got lots of Christmas shopping to do. It was so good seeing you, dear."

Before they left, they hugged me as if we were good friends.

On December 24, I caught the bus to Ballard and knocked on the door of the Millers. "You must be Lucy," said a white woman around forty. "Come in, come in."

I handed her two poorly wrapped gifts. "You didn't have to do that," Mr. Miller chided, standing beside his wife. I was glad no one could tell when I blushed. "I'm Jerry," he said, offering his hand.

"And I'm Charlene," said Mrs. Miller.

"Can I call you Mom and Dad?" I asked, feeling like an idiot. What if they were about to murder me?

"Of course, of course."

I followed them into the house. They had real furniture, without patches. They had real artwork on the walls. They had a whole room just for the kitchen table.

How did they make so much money, I wondered. I hoped they weren't going to sell me into sexual slavery. There were a lot of missing indigenous women.

Don't be ridiculous, I told myself, studying their hands for any sign of menace.

"The turkey's almost done," said Charlene, "but you can help with the apple pie."

I felt a thrill run through my body. This was really happening.

"You're not vegetarian, are you? Oh, dear, I should have asked."

"No, no, turkey is fine."

Jerry stood by while I cut apples and Charlene made pie dough. "So, what do you do, Lucy?" Charlene asked.

"Well, Mom, I transferred to UW this quarter, where I'll finish my degree in Psychology. Then I'll go on to get a Masters, either in Social Work or Counseling."

"How wonderful."

"I want to talk to young people who feel there's no hope in their futures. I had friends steal cars or do drugs or do all sorts of things, just because they felt like nothing they did mattered."

Charlene shook her head. "I slept with one of my professors once. Just to get a grade."

"Oh, for God's sake, don't tell the girl that!" said Jerry.

"We told Cathy, didn't we?" she countered. "When she went off to college."

Jerry looked like he was about to say something but bit his lip instead. I suddenly felt uneasy again. Then Jerry smiled and said, "Welcome to the family." Everyone laughed, and I sighed in relief.

Charlene and I chatted about nothing of substance. She shared some of her favorite recipes and I told her about the one dish my mother made well, salmon, which really was hard to ruin even for bad cooks. I talked about how I loved to read Sherman Alexie stories, and Jerry threw in that he loved James Patterson. When we finally sat down to eat, there wasn't even one moment of awkward silence. We just kept talking, Jerry about his work at NOAA, and Charlene about volunteering with the Sierra Club.

Finally, after the pie was served, I smiled and said, "You two should open the presents I brought. They're not much, but…"

"We found something for you, too, Lucy."

Somehow, I hadn't expected that. First, Charlene opened her gift with a smile. "Nutella. I love it."

Then Jerry opened his, his eyes widening in surprise. "A jar of pickled okra." He was clearly trying to keep his voice neutral.

"You'll love them," I said. "I promise. And if you don't, you can serve them as hors d'oeuvres at your next party."

Then Charlene handed me a gift wrapped in bright red paper, with snowflakes and stars sprinkled on top. Don't read too much into this, I told myself. It's just one gift. It doesn't have to make up for twenty years of no gifts. I smiled and carefully pulled back the paper.

"Rip it off," Jerry encouraged.

I smiled again and ripped off the paper. It was a book. *The Secret Garden.* I'd never heard of it. But I would certainly read it. It must be good if that's what they were giving me.

"It's about a girl whose parents are dead," Charlene said softly. "Who feels unloved. But then she finds people who care about her."

I smiled. "I'll read it this weekend," I said.

And then it was time to go home. "Can I help with the dishes?" I asked, wanting to prolong the visit.

Charlene smiled and shook her head firmly. "You have our number," she said. "Call us any time. And for sure call us for Easter."

We all hugged, and I walked back to the bus stop, feeling warm in the cold air. I had to wait an extra half hour because of the holiday schedule, but I finally made it home and wrote in my journal. I felt like a blind child who'd just had a miraculous operation and could now see for the first time.

The world was wonderful.

Mormons said that "Families are Forever." But even if they only lasted five hours, it wasn't bad.

I woke up the next morning knowing I had yet another exciting day with a family ahead of me. It seemed unfair to have two such great presents for one Christmas. I arrived at the Smiths' house in the Central District around noon. They'd be having Christmas dinner in an hour. "Hello!" said a Latina around forty-five. "I'm Erlinda. You're Lucy?"

I nodded happily.

A black man appeared beside Mrs. Smith. "I'm Carl," he said, offering his hand.

"Hug the girl!" Mrs. Smith commanded. I remembered reading an article about a woman who procured young women for her husband to torture.

After the slightly awkward hugs, I followed the Smiths inside, putting a bright smile on my face. Another childless couple, it seemed. I decided I might as well address the issue. "Do you guys have kids?"

Erlinda and Carl looked at each other for a long moment. Finally, Erlinda spoke. "Carl has a son, and I have two daughters. But none of our kids will speak to us. We won't go into that now."

It had always been clear to me that parents could neglect their children, but it only just now occurred to me children could neglect their parents, too. I wanted to ask why, but I was afraid the question would upset the Smiths.

Erlinda refused my help in the kitchen, so I sat with Carl in the living room and listened to him talk about his work at Boeing. I didn't understand a word of it and struggled to look attentive. He didn't ask anything about me.

Just after 1:00, Erlinda announced dinner, and we sat at the table. I jumped when Carl slapped the table so hard the cutlery jumped in the air. "Ham?" he asked. "You know I don't like ham. You said you were going to fry me some bacon."

"Bacon…ham…it's all pork," Erlinda said, motioning with her hand as if shooing away a fly. "Besides, we have company. Of course we need the ham."

"You guys can have all the ham you want. I'm going to fry me some bacon." Carl stood up and stalked off to the kitchen.

"He's such a baby sometimes," Erlinda whispered. "He's lucky we aren't having tamales."

I forced a smile.

"At least you're getting a real family for Christmas," she said, smiling. "No fake stuff here."

"Yes," I said, not sure if that was a good thing or not. I suppose in a way I was asking these people to prostitute themselves. You might have real sexual problems with your spouse, but when you hired a hooker, you wanted everything to go smoothly. Surely, though, the real thing was better, even if imperfect.

"Goddamn it!" muttered Carl from the kitchen. He'd probably been splattered with bacon grease. Was he going to come out with a knife and kill us both? I realized I didn't know the first thing about these people.

Carl was gone a long time, perhaps eating his bacon in the kitchen alone. Erlinda spoke about her job at Bartell. Only her seniority had allowed her to take the day off from the drugstore. She'd been there twenty years and had met Carl when he was a customer. She'd had an affair with him while still married to Augusto.

I sensed why the daughters might still be upset.

Erlinda never asked a single question about me.

Carl finally came out and rejoined us, and the conversation drifted along for another hour. After the meal was over, I half-heartedly offered to help clean up, accepting Erlinda's initial refusal immediately and saying I had to go. The Smiths still hadn't opened the token gifts I'd brought, and they offered nothing to me. They didn't need to, of course. All they were obligated to do was have dinner with me and talk, and they'd done that.

Nevertheless, I almost ran once I was out the door. Jogging toward the bus stop, it occurred to me this was how a great many children felt when spending time with their parents. It was certainly "the real deal."

I wanted a real eternal family. Right now.

Ridiculous.

I had to work a short shift this evening at the restaurant, and I watched as couples and families ate happily. One man sat by himself at our smallest table and ordered a steak. Feeling sorry for him, I was extra attentive, always making sure his water glass was filled, and even sneaking him a slice of chocolate cake which I paid for myself, hoping he'd feel he wasn't all alone in the world. He was about forty-five, the age my father would be right now. I wondered where my father was, and how he was doing.

The man smiled, and I smiled back.

After he left, I picked up his credit slip and gasped. He'd left me a $2000 tip. I sat down at his table and cried. Another server had to help me to the kitchen.

Maybe one didn't need a family, I thought. Perhaps all one really needed was to band together with other cast-offs.

After the unpleasant afternoon I'd spent with the Smiths, I was dreading my last holiday event the following day. I stayed up late, my Book of Mormon in my lap unopened, thinking about what my own future family might be like. As damaged as I was, how much ground could I reasonably make up? Would my own kids hate me? Would they abandon me? Would my husband leave me? What if I left him?

If I couldn't ensure I had the ability to create the kind of family my husband and kids would flourish in, would I be better off not starting a family in the first place?

Maybe it would be better to be permanently lonely than eternally tortured.

Perhaps those were the same thing.

The next morning around 10:00, I started off for my final family adventure. I thought about canceling, but it didn't seem right to let one bad experience put me off my dream. I arrived on Beacon Hill just after 11:00 and knocked on the Carters' door. Mr. Carter answered.

"Hi, Lucy, how are you?" He was a white man about fifty, with smile lines around his eyes.

A Eurasian woman appeared next to him. "I'm so glad you could come," she said. "I'm Amy, and this is Dexter."

I thought about serial killers.

"Come in, come in." I smiled and entered the house, noticing Dexter lock the door after I was inside.

"We're having leftovers, I'm afraid," Amy said, "so there isn't much cooking to do. Let's all go in the living room."

We sat down, and I noticed that the house was furnished more nicely than mine, but not as nicely as the Millers'. It was good to be able to see how lots of different people lived. Perhaps I should go on a mission like my bishop suggested. He said learning to live with my companions would prepare me for getting along with my husband. Perhaps eighteen months of practice wasn't a bad idea.

"Did you get your nap in, honey?" Amy asked her husband, touching his shoulder.

"I had a partial nap," he replied.

Amy laughed. "How can you have a partial nap?"

"My foot fell asleep."

Ignoring her husband and leaning forward slightly, Amy asked, "And Lucy, did you have a good Christmas?"

"Yes, it was lovely, thank you." I decided it best not to mention the tip money. They might ask to be paid, after all, and that would somehow cheapen the experience. Maybe I'd use the money to start a mission fund. "And how was yours?"

"Oh, we had both kids over," said Dexter, "with their spouses and their children. Nine of us altogether. Quite an experience."

Maybe I should have picked the Carters for Christmas Day, I thought. Next year…

Who even knew what I'd do next year? I couldn't keep pretending to be part of the families of strangers forever. What kind of holiday tradition was that?

"Arnie's a Republican," Amy said, "and Melanie is a Democrat." I assumed these were their two children. "So there was way too much arguing. Melanie brought up the rape insurance that some Republican proposed."

I remembered the time one of Mom's boyfriends raped me.

"And Arnie brought up the disaster that the Obamacare website has been."

I thought about how the Affordable Care Act would have allowed me to stay on my parents' insurance while I was in school.

Of course, my mother had never had health insurance for me to be on.

She would probably have died of the cancer anyway, I told myself.

Weren't we as a country responsible for each other, I thought? Weren't we supposed to be each other's family? It not only took a village; it took a whole nation.

Maybe it even took the world.

"What party are you?" I asked, wondering if the question was a mistake.

Amy laughed. "We're Independents. Arnie can barely tolerate us. Even Melanie worries about us 'wasting' our votes. Someone's feelings always get hurt before the meal is over." She smiled wistfully. "Usually mine."

Were all families like this, I wondered? I sure wished some Mormons had responded to my ad. The Carters seemed nice enough, I supposed, but who wanted a family dinner with Rush Limbaugh and Al Sharpton in the room? Surely, every family everywhere wasn't a big mess, was it? This was now two out of three.

But perhaps they'd only had "nice" arguments.

I looked over toward the locked door.

"What do you do, Lucy?" asked Dexter.

"I'm working on a Psychology degree at UW."

"How lovely." We then spent the next forty-five minutes talking about me, my goals, my background, my worries, my hopes for the future. *That's* what I wanted out of parents. Maybe it was now two out of three *good* families.

I felt like Goldilocks. A story I'd read at school.

But the Carters were real people, too. What were *they* hoping to get out of me? A child who wouldn't berate them for their political views? A child who wouldn't attack their other children? A child who cared about *them*?

"I brought you some small gifts," I said. "It's nothing much."

"You shouldn't have."

Amy opened her Nutella, and Dexter opened his jar of okra right on the spot and ate one. "Never had that before. It's good."

I smiled.

"I'm afraid we didn't get you anything, dear," Amy said. "It being after Christmas and all."

"Oh, I'm fine. I'm just enjoying spending some time with you guys."

Sometimes, it was better not to receive a gift. My mom usually gave me a shirt she'd found at the thrift store, almost always some tarty style I'd have never chosen myself. I'd have to wear it and smile, pretending to like it. But I remembered one Christmas when my mother gave me a "special" gift. I was sixteen, and she'd just said something a couple of weeks before about hoping I'd become a teen mother, because teen mothers always needed their own mothers, and it would bring us closer together.

A few nights after that, I heard giggling and peeked through her bedroom door, which was slightly ajar, and saw her doing something odd with her boyfriend of the evening. She had a string of packaged condoms and was inserting a needle through each package just once. When I opened my Christmas present a week or so later, I understood. The condoms were for me.

So I was okay with Amy and Dexter not buying me anything. At one point during the conversation about the various careers I could pursue with a psychology degree, Dexter suggested I think about working for the police or FBI profiling criminals. That made me worry again about being drugged. What had I been thinking, going to a stranger's house like this? Dexter on TV fooled everybody. If my own mother was so untrustworthy, could I really trust someone I met through an ad? Hadn't someone been killed in Ohio when answering a Craigslist ad?

I wondered how non-Mormon single adults handled the world, going home with perfect strangers they met in bars, to an unknown house or apartment where anything could happen. Most of them led quite normal lives anyway, didn't they? Even got married and started families.

Perfectly normal families.

But what was normal? Happy families or unhappy ones?

You had to trust someone sometime. When Dexter handed me a glass of Coke, I thanked him and sipped it without hesitation.

Over dinner, I listened to Dexter tell me how he first met Amy at a Presbyterian church social and asked her out, and listened to Amy tell me how it took her several months to warm up to him. They told me how they lost their middle child at the age of three to pneumonia. Dexter was in a serious car accident once, and Amy had survived breast cancer. They'd separated for six months after Amy caught Dexter cheating, but after some counseling, they were happily back together again.

"Hey, maybe I do have something for you," said Amy, standing up, "if you don't mind recycled gifts."

"Oh, it's okay. Don't worry about it."

"No, I have it here somewhere." She left the kitchen and was gone a few minutes. I felt stupid. Dexter looked at his watch.

Amy came back a moment later with a folded piece of paper. She held it out for me. "It's origami. A dove." I must have looked puzzled because she went on. "I was shopping last week, and this woman was handing them out." She chuckled. "Most people wouldn't take them. Thought the woman was going to ask for money or something. But she just wanted to give everyone a little holiday gift."

She shrugged. "I took it because it made me remember that being kind to people you don't know is as important as being kind to people you do know. It's why I ended up responding to your ad."

"Now that you have the dove," Dexter said, "perhaps you can pass a little happiness on to someone else."

"I will," I said softly, looking over the carefully crafted paper. "I will."

We talked a bit more, and by 3:00, I decided it was time to head home. "You guys have been great. I can't thank you enough for taking me in, a total stranger. You're good people."

"Feel free to call us again any time you need to talk."

We hugged, and I headed for the bus stop. I sat in the shelter, pulling my jacket close around my face to ward off the cold, misty rain. All in all, I had to say I was happy with the way things had turned out. I was still alive, no small thing considering the chances I'd taken. But then perhaps there was no way to have what one wanted without taking a risk.

Maybe the best imperfect people could do was struggle together to find a little peace.

It wasn't very satisfying. The Church taught that it was supposed to be so much better. I wondered if even Mormon families had some of these problems and simply didn't talk about them. Maybe they *couldn't* let others see underneath the surface.

I wondered if a church that put so much emphasis on happy families was able to offer enough support to make those families a reality.

Of course, maybe Mormon families *were* great. Maybe it was all true.

I wanted a great family.

Perhaps I wouldn't have that until I died and met Heavenly Father.

When you followed a particular religion, weren't you accepting the Heavenly Parents it presented as your own? With a hundred different religions to choose from, you had to answer the spiritual ad that would bring you what you wanted. I had a Father and Mother in heaven, though the Mormon Heavenly Mother was a little distant. Still, the Church itself was my family now.

People who'd abandoned me at Christmas.

I'd have to speak with the bishop next Sunday and ask some questions. Maybe I could give a lesson to the others, a

Fireside or something, to teach parents what *not* to do, while I tried to figure out for myself what I *should* do.

There was a Single Adult dance this New Year's Eve. I should probably go to that.

My phone rang, and I answered. It was Phil from the restaurant. "Lucy?" he asked.

"Yes? Did someone call in sick? You need me to come in early?"

"I just wanted to let you know before you started spending any money. That tip was fake. Visa wouldn't cover it. Turns out the guy barely had enough to cover the meal."

I looked down at the wet cement, the lip of a beer bottle peeking out of a brown paper bag in the gutter.

"Thanks for letting me know," I said, hanging up. I stared at the wet paper bag for several minutes.

The bus pulled up, and I noticed an ad pasted on its side. Big Brothers Big Sisters of Puget Sound. There were photos of happy young faces staring out at me.

Standing up, I put my hand on my own face. It didn't feel particularly happy.

But maybe I could start taking in a stray or two myself. Catch girls early before they were as damaged as I was. That might be even better than missionary work. Assuming one damaged person could truly help another damaged person.

What other kind of person was there?

I climbed on the bus and looked around. There was an old white woman with a walker, with a slightly dazed expression. I sat next to her, looked her in the face, and smiled.

Making Hay

Joe Lee looked at the cow. She was still breathing hard, a little mucus dripping from her nose, but after the vet had given her an injection yesterday for the pneumonia, she was doing better. Joe Lee still had her separated from the other cows in a part of the covered pen he'd designed and built himself ten years ago, just before he retired and moved back to the country from New Orleans. He looked at the black cow one last time. It was late afternoon. He'd check on her again first thing in the morning.

Joe Lee started for the truck. His Angus were mostly here on his own land, but now it was time to go back to the house for supper. It was Myrtis's house really, but he'd moved in with her eight years ago when he turned sixty-two, the instant he retired and hurried back to Brookhaven as quickly as he could.

Climbing into the F150, he looked through the windshield at his tractor barn where his largest tractor and the covered wagon were stored. What was that over there, he wondered, frowning. It looked like smoke coming from behind the barn. He climbed out of the truck and casually walked behind the building.

He stopped and stared. Smoke was beginning to pour out of the hay barn behind the tractor barn.

Joe Lee ran immediately to grab the hose and pull it toward the barn, but it wouldn't reach.

Damn!

All his hay for the winter was stored in there. He'd just baled it a couple of days ago. It had still been too damp, though spread out on the ground for days. But since it had been about to storm, he'd baled it anyway, and now it had spontaneously combusted because he'd gathered it too soon.

He grabbed his cell phone and dialed.

"Hello?"

"Myrtis! Call 911! The hay barn's on fire!"

He hung up and ran into the barn. It wasn't officially the tractor barn, but he still had two small tractors in there, plus the Yukon. He didn't want to lose everything.

With the flames starting to build in the center of the barn, Joe Lee ran in again and again till all the vehicles were safely out.

It was all he could do, and he was relieved when the fire department showed up just a few moments later, even though he was several miles outside of town. They poured water on the hay, and soon it was just a smoldering black mess that they pulled out of the barn. The building itself was not damaged, thank goodness. Joe Lee knew instantly it was because he paid his tithing. He didn't go to church anymore, but he still did his duty, and God was watching out for him.

As the firefighters pulled off, Joe Lee called Myrtis again.

"Joe Lee! Are you all right? What happened?"

Joe Lee was breathing heavily. His chest hurt a little, and it took him a moment to speak. "Everything's fine. Just lost the hay. But it's early enough in the summer. I can still get some more hay before fall."

Joe Lee sat in the truck for a few minutes before making the drive a couple of miles to the house, resting for a moment first. Tithing, he thought. It really worked.

He remembered a time about twenty years ago, not long after he divorced Lisa, his second wife. That was back while he was still just a weekend farmer. One of his friends up here, Randy, had asked why his soybeans always did so well, even during a drought when everyone else's beans were suffering. "I pay my tithing," Joe Lee had said. Randy had laughed, but Joe Lee was serious.

But he'd really been burned on the Mormon Church after Lisa. She'd been Relief Society president in his Metairie ward, and he figured she'd be a good replacement for Ruth, who'd died of bone cancer a few years earlier. On her deathbed, Ruth had ordered Joe Lee to marry again, saying, "The only thing I ask is that she be a good housekeeper." Why that should matter to Ruth, who'd never been that good at housekeeping herself, puzzled Joe Lee, but he made sure to see that Lisa kept a clean house before he asked her out.

What a horror she'd turned out to be, though. She'd come home from meeting the other women in the congregation, telling all the secrets she'd learned as head of the women's program. It seemed inappropriate, but Joe Lee didn't say anything.

Then as their relationship quickly soured, Lisa, who worked for the Battered Women's shelter, used to push Joe Lee in the chest and say, "Hit me! Hit me!" when they argued. It wasn't long before they got a temple divorce, and not long after that before he decided to date a Catholic woman. No more Mormon women for him.

Mary had been nice enough, but their marriage started going downhill in just a few years, too, after her father died and Mary started putting up altars all over the house.

Joe Lee turned the motor over now so he could switch on the air conditioning in the truck. He pushed an old Faith Hill CD into the player and listened to her singing "Breathe" so sweetly and then "This Kiss" as he thought again of his two disastrous marriages.

Joe Lee realized he'd forgotten to feed the cat, so he stepped out of the truck and walked over to the tractor barn. He opened a plastic barrel and scooped out some food and put it in a dish. Then he emptied the water dish and refilled it with fresh water. It wasn't as if there was anything mice could get into here and ruin, but he liked having a cat around anyway. It made the place feel more alive. He wiped the sweat off his brow and rubbed his chest, slowly walking back to his truck.

Joe Lee wasn't sure he'd ever bother getting married again after that third try, but he started spending more and more time in the country, and one day he started chatting with a nice check-out woman at the country store not far from his land. He and Myrtis started dating while she was still putting herself through nursing school after her divorce, and then even more after she became a nurse.

Joe Lee knew he was sinning when they started having sex, but he didn't want to get married again. It was over two years after he moved in with Myrtis before they finally officially married. It was in the little Baptist church she attended. Myrtis's daughter Patsy came, and Joe Lee's daughter Karen and his son Larry came, too.

Joe Lee sat in the truck, his face enjoying the cool air from the vent. He was feeling better now. He could breathe again. He didn't want Myrtis to see him struggling. She'd make him go to the doctor, and he didn't want to go.

Joe Lee drove slowly back to the house, glad he'd been at the barn when the hay caught fire. It would have been awful if the hay had started burning while he was away. As soon as Joe Lee pulled into the driveway, Myrtis hurried out the kitchen door to meet him.

"You smell like smoke."

"I knew I was baling that hay too early. I won't do that again."

"You go take a bath and get out of those smoky clothes. Supper'll be ready in twenty minutes."

They talked more about the fire during supper, and about the cow with pneumonia, and a little about Myrtis's nursing. She took care of the babies at the hospital. Joe Lee liked hearing about her work, but sometimes there wasn't much to tell. Still, he liked to hear about the babies because even when they were sick, they almost always got well. It was comforting somehow to hear about new life.

"Adam's still practicing his roping every day," Myrtis said when the conversation dragged.

Adam was Myrtis's thirteen-year-old grandson. He lived half a mile away and came over a couple of times a week. He was a good boy, better than Joe Lee's own kids and granddaughter.

"When's his next competition?"

"Three weeks, in Dallas. He was so tickled to come in third place last month in Jackson that he's been practicing an extra hour every day."

Adam roped calves. He was training with a young man, Matt, who'd come in second at a national rodeo. Joe Lee was glad to see Adam involved in such a wholesome sport and doing so well at it. Matt seemed like a good role model, too, good-natured and healthy and strong.

Joe Lee's mind flashed briefly over his own son, Larry. Larry had been valedictorian of his high school and gone on to serve a mission to Mexico for the Church. While there he'd met a man named Rigoberto and brought him back to America. They became roommates, but it took a few years before Joe Lee realized they were also lovers.

Joe Lee had been shocked. Larry had always been so good, and now here he was excommunicated. His daughter Karen, on the other hand, had never been all that good, always in trouble at school, sassing teachers, cutting classes, pregnant at sixteen, with a shotgun wedding. Karen hadn't been to church in thirty years, and her daughter Jennifer was now living with a man she'd met in a bar.

They both smoked and drank and never came up to see him. Joe Lee had never treated them badly, not even when Jennifer had let slip once years ago she'd had an abortion.

Of course, having lived in sin himself for two years, Joe Lee knew he was hardly in a position to judge. And after having disapproved of Larry's relationship all these years, a couple of years ago when Larry and Rigoberto came up for Christmas, Joe Lee reflected on his two unhappy marriages and said, "If you can just find someone you like in this world, that's a good thing."

But it was still nice to see Adam so clean and masculine. Joe Lee thought of Adam as his own grandson, and it felt comforting to think of him as the legacy he'd leave behind after he was gone. He realized he hadn't spent enough time with Larry when he was a boy, and he wasn't going to make the same mistake with Adam.

"Adam also wants to learn the guitar," Myrtis said. "He says he can do both. And you know, I think he probably can."

"Well, if he wants a guitar, I guess we can afford it."

"I'd just hate to see him stop working on his roping when he's doing so well."

"He'll have to do what he wants. You can't decide things like that for other people."

"I know. It'd just be a shame is all."

"He'll keep roping. He's too good at it to quit."

Joe Lee and Myrtis watched a little TV and then the news. He looked up sometimes during the commercials at the hornet's nest he'd found a couple of years ago and hung from their ceiling, and at the wooden coat rack Myrtis had bought with the words, "I love my country home" carved in it, and at the circular saw blade Larry had given him one year with a cabin in the woods painted on it. Joe Lee loved being here in this wonderful place.

On Myrtis's piano was a photo of Patsy and her husband, and another of Adam, and one of Joe Lee with Adam hitching up the wagon. Larry had given him a photo of himself and Rigoberto together, but Joe Lee could never bear to put it out. Karen and Jennifer had never given him any photographs at all, so they weren't on display, either. But it gave Joe Lee hope to see Adam smiling out at him.

After the news was over, Joe Lee decided it was time to call his sister-in-law, Linda, down in Long Beach on the Gulf Coast. Linda and his brother, Aubrey, were eighty now and starting to go downhill, so he liked to keep in touch. He never knew when the last time he talked to them would really turn out to be the last time.

"Hey, Linda."

"How you doin', Joe Lee?"

"Oh, things here are fine. How about with you?"

"Well, Aubrey's getting worse every day. He's turning the stove on now and forgetting. And he wanders out of the house and forgets where he's going. I have to circle the block a couple of times a day to look for him. I try to check up on him every half hour or so, so he can't get too far away if he sneaks out."

"Do you need to come up and stay for a few days to get a break?"

"Oh, no. We're doing okay. I guess Aubrey hasn't got long, but he still knows who I am, so everything else is manageable."

They talked for several more minutes, and then Joe Lee joined Myrtis to watch a detective show he found to be a little too gritty. The world was sure a different place these days. There was even a gay character on this show. It always made Joe Lee feel uncomfortable to watch things like that. He often tried to study those people in shows to see if there was any of Larry in them, but tonight he started nodding off, and Myrtis had to wake him up finally and tell him to get to bed.

The next morning, Joe Lee went to check up on the cow with pneumonia. She was breathing a little better but still struggling. He dragged the burned hay out into the pasture and then drove out to another pasture a mile away where he kept more of his cows.

He could see from the truck that one of the cows had pink eye. Damn. And with all those flies lighting on them, it would spread to the other cows in just a couple of days if he didn't do something about it right away. He went immediately to buy some medicine and then had to go back and find the cow again. What a bother.

But he wasn't farming for profit. He was farming to stay busy, for fun, because it made him feel alive. So he treated the cow and then went to get his load of chicken litter from the chicken farm nearby. The waste made great fertilizer, and if he was going to grow a whole new crop of hay, he knew he'd better make the land stronger.

He was able to spread most of the chicken litter by 5:00, and even though he still had a couple of hours of light left, Joe Lee was feeling tired and breathing heavily again, and his chest hurt just a little. He waited till he was feeling better and then went back to the house and took a bath.

"Joe Lee," said Myrtis over supper. "You got a call from Randy and one from Bobby Lee. They both offered to give you some hay if you needed it."

"Well, I don't need it. But I'll take it. It'll make them feel good. And after I grow some more, I'll pay it back, and that'll make them feel good, too."

"And Shane called to see if you were coming to the tractor pull this Friday."

"Yeah, I told him I'd bring my sled over by 4:00 so he'd have plenty of time to get ready."

"You work yourself too hard, Joe Lee."

"It's better than having the tractor pulls myself like I used to." He'd hosted three each summer for four summers and was too exhausted to keep it up after that, so for last summer and this summer, he was only loaning his sled to others in the area who wanted to hold tractor pulls themselves.

In his younger days, Joe Lee had enjoyed competing. He'd even gone to Texas once for a major pull and become Texas state champion in his category. It had all been a lot of fun, a way to escape the tedious work of building houses in the suburbs of New Orleans.

He'd also been in charge of maintaining all the LDS churches in the New Orleans area for probably fifteen years. But when he moved in with Myrtis, he stopped going to church, and it was a relief to only worry about himself now.

But he did worry. Was he going to burn in hell for having sex before he got married? For not going to church anymore? For divorcing twice? For marrying a Baptist? For having a gay son? And a daughter and granddaughter who never went to church either?

If it had just been one problem, maybe God could have worked with him, but with so many failings, was there much hope? He thought he was a good man, but maybe he really wasn't. If he could help Adam grow up right, though, maybe that would count for something.

That night in bed, Joe Lee could tell Myrtis was in the mood, and he still enjoyed sex, so he quickly got in the mood, too. But every time he climbed on top of Myrtis, he couldn't help but think of his old friend, Lester. Lester and Myrtis had had an affair while they were both still married to other people.

Lester had been his friend for years, ever since Joe Lee began coming up to visit Ruth's family fifty years ago on holidays and occasional weekends. Lester lived on the next farm over from Ruth's parents, and he and Joe Lee had worked together a few hours here, a few hours there, for decades. After Ruth died, Joe Lee began spending more time in the country on weekends, and he found his friendship with Lester a real help during his next two tumultuous marriages.

Joe Lee hadn't said a thing when he learned about Lester's affair. It was none of his business. But Lester had eventually gotten cancer, and he was impressed that his wife let Myrtis move in and take care of him until the end. Somehow, knowing the woman he was having sex with now was the same one his best friend had had sex with in his last few years was comforting. It wasn't why he'd initially been attracted to Myrtis, of course, but it certainly helped that being with her was a connection to his old friend.

He never understood what Larry saw in other men. But he did like the intimacy he felt with Lester now as he pumped away at Myrtis. He could understand that part of homosexuality, anyway, the desire to feel permanently connected to a good friend. It was only after he moved in with Myrtis that Joe Lee finally began sending Rigoberto a Christmas gift along with Larry's each year.

Joe Lee felt that special tingling in his groin now and knew he was close. He put in a few final thrusts, breathing heavily by the time they finished.

"You okay, Joe Lee?"

"I'm fine."

He didn't like having Myrtis think of him as weak. It bothered him. He lay on his back and concentrated on his breathing. Myrtis had her head on his chest. He couldn't tell if she was just cuddling or trying to listen to his heart. But soon he was breathing normally, and before long he was asleep.

The next morning, Joe Lee finished spreading the rest of the chicken litter. He checked up on the cow with pneumonia and gave another treatment to the cow with pink eye.

Then he herded his pregnant cows into the opposite side of the pen from where the sick cow was. He had to keep her away from the others, but he also had to get them ready to take to the auction the next day.

Joe Lee decided to go on down the road to the barber. He got his hair cut about once a month. Myrtis had offered from the beginning to cut it for him, but Joe Lee liked going to see Luther.

The little shop was on the corner of two country roads just a couple of miles from the house. It used to be the only structure on the corner besides Luther's house, but now Luther's son Pete had opened a little country store with two gas pumps out front as well. The store was modestly stocked. There might be two quarts of oil, a single hammer, a single saw, one bag of feed, three loaves of bread, two boxes of matches, and so forth. But it was nice to have it so near.

Everything Joe Lee needed was out here in the country. He'd had no choice but to go to the city to make a living, but somehow, he wondered if he'd wasted his life doing things he didn't love.

"Hey, Joe Lee." Luther waved as Joe Lee walked in. He was cutting the hair of a man about fifty named Harlan. Luther was around sixty himself. His older sister had been just a few years behind Joe Lee in school. She'd died two months ago of a heart attack. Joe Lee rubbed his chest absentmindedly.

"Hey, Luther. Hey, Harlan."

"Hey, Joe Lee. I was just telling Luther here that the deer have been getting in my garden every night," Harlan complained from the elevated chair in the center of the room.

"I put up an electric fence around my garden," said Joe Lee.

"It's a shame you can't just shoot 'em off season." Luther clipped at some hair behind Harlan's ear.

"I know," said Joe Lee, "but society can't function without rules, can it?"

"I suppose." Harlan shrugged, almost causing Luther to nick him. "But I still think about poisoning those damn deer. Such pests."

"Well, I have something eating all my guinea, too," Joe Lee said. "I've only got one left, and she'll be gone before long."

"Life is short." Luther laughed.

Joe Lee smiled. Camaraderie was so much stronger among men out in the country than it had ever been in the city. It was nice to be back here where he belonged.

Joe Lee brought the weight sled to Shane's tractor pull that afternoon but didn't stay to watch the show. Those things could last for hours, and he needed to get up early Saturday.

At supper, Myrtis talked about a baby that came in with a broken arm. It looked suspicious, so she'd had to report it as possible abuse. "I hate seeing the ugly side of life," she said.

"Well, you're good, Myrtis," Joe Lee told her, putting his hand on hers. "All you can do is just be a good you."

She smiled but still looked troubled. Myrtis hated butting into other people's lives and had complained before about being forced into the position of tattletale. But she hated even more the thought of anyone harming an innocent young life.

Joe Lee decided to get out the DVD of *Stagecoach* Larry and Rigoberto had given him a while back. Myrtis liked movies, but Joe Lee hardly ever watched them, so maybe watching one with her now would put her in a better mood. Larry and Rigoberto had given him several John Wayne movies one Christmas, and he still hadn't watched them all.

Another year, they'd given him a photo album with pictures of all the houses he'd built over forty years. And then one Christmas, Larry had made a patchwork quilt with the design of a man plowing a field on a tractor. Joe Lee had been impressed, although quilting was something women were supposed to do. Rigoberto had given a quilt to Myrtis that year with a patchwork design of a rooster because he knew she liked roosters. Joe Lee smiled to think about the look on Myrtis's face that day.

But it was those movies that might come in handy tonight, so he pulled one out, and he was happy to see Myrtis's face light up again.

The next morning, Myrtis came over to the pen with Joe Lee, and his friend Randy came over as well. With the three of them working together, they soon had all ten of the pregnant Angus loaded onto the trailer.

"Joe Lee, you all right?"

"I'm fine, Myrtis."

"I think you'd better see the doctor Monday."

"I'm fine."

He was still annoyed by the time he and Randy pulled up to the auction barn a few towns over. But watching the unloading, then watching one of the auction workers put on a long plastic glove and slide his arm up to the elbow in each cow's butt to determine the progress of the pregnancies soon had him distracted.

Joe Lee sat on the third row in the auction hall, waiting patiently as the hogs and goats were sold first. Then came some horses, some calves, some bulls, and finally some cows. One poor woman in the first row got sprayed with feces when one of the cows had an explosive episode of diarrhea. She left to go wash up but was soon back. Then Joe Lee's pregnant cows were brought out. Every last one of them sold for at least a hundred dollars more than he'd been expecting, so it was an exciting morning. Livestock auctions were almost always fun.

When he got home, Joe Lee checked up on the cow with the pink eye, giving her another dose of medicine, and checked up on the cow with pneumonia, which was much better this afternoon, almost well. He breathed a sigh of relief. He picked up some hay from Bobby Lee and then went home for supper.

Afterward, Myrtis's daughter Patsy stopped by with Adam for a few minutes. Myrtis and Patsy stayed in the kitchen to chat, but Adam came out to the living room with Joe Lee. "How's the roping coming along?"

"Great," Adam said. "Matt's fun to work with. He's really helping me with my technique. And he's so friendly with everyone. He's a lot of fun to hang out with."

"He's not trying to get you to smoke, is he?"

"Oh, no, Paw Paw. He's a good man. He wouldn't do that."

"So you're still having a good time?"

"Oh, yes, sir." Patsy had trained him from early on to call people "sir" and "ma'am."

"Well, it's important to enjoy life."

The boy smiled up at him. "Hey, how was the auction today?" he said. "Did *you* have a good time?"

They talked about that for a few moments and then about some wooden duck calls Adam was learning to make. Adam shyly admitted he'd also started helping his mother in the kitchen and liked learning to cook. Joe Lee didn't know if he should be worried about that or not. His chest tightened a little, just thinking about it. But maybe it wasn't worth worrying about after all, he decided, sighing. Adam was a good kid regardless. And there was nothing you could do about these things anyway.

Joe Lee remembered now that with the first money Adam had ever won in a rodeo, he'd bought Joe Lee a beautifully colored, life-sized ceramic rooster. It was finely detailed and expensive looking. "I got it for you, Paw Paw, because I know you like roosters." It had struck Joe Lee even then as slightly odd for the boy to buy him a piece of art, but the boy was so masculine, he'd decided not to worry.

It wasn't that Larry *wasn't* masculine. He just seemed…sort of…refined somehow. He and Rigoberto got their hands dirty in their nursery, but it wasn't the same as getting your hands dirty plowing, or building fences, or hauling hay.

Patsy insisted that Adam not come over when Larry and Rigoberto were visiting. Joe Lee knew that made them feel bad, but what could he do? Patsy had to be able to make her own rules. She always made slightly insulting remarks about Larry, though, and Joe Lee never said anything.

Maybe he had to start making his own rules, too, that there not be any more remarks like that in his house. Joe Lee and Adam kept talking until Patsy was ready to leave. "See you at church in the morning, Mom," Patsy said, and then she and Adam left. Myrtis put on a CD of Brooks and Dunn. She and Joe Lee chatted for a while, until she had to wake him up to go to bed.

Myrtis was supposed to have this weekend off, but early the next morning, the hospital called and asked her to cover for someone out sick. Joe Lee thought of his daughter Karen, who was an LPN down in Metairie. When the hurricane had come a couple of years ago, she was scheduled to work that weekend at the nursing home but evacuated instead, leaving the nursing home understaffed. Two elderly residents had died over the next few days during all the chaos that followed the disaster. Joe Lee guessed you couldn't blame people for looking out for themselves, but he knew Myrtis would never have abandoned all those old people when they needed her.

Karen irritated him anyway. Joe Lee had probably given her at least $120,000 over the past twenty-five years, helping her make various payments. Karen would call, crying, saying the house was going into foreclosure if she didn't come up with some money, or her electricity was going to be cut off, or she couldn't buy groceries, or her car was going to be repossessed, or whatever.

She had divorced her second husband a few years ago, which was good. Neither husband had been very good to her, but she wasn't very responsible, either. Once, she'd bought an expensive exercise machine right after having begged for money to pay her water bill. Then she'd had the nerve to ask when she was going to get the $25,000 that was her inheritance from her mother's share of the house in Metairie. Joe Lee had come very near to cursing that day. His chest felt constricted just remembering the incident.

He wasn't entirely happy with Larry, either, but Larry had taken his $25,000 to put Rigoberto through school to study horticulture. They basically just ran a glorified flower shop, something too embarrassing for Joe Lee to tell his friends, but at least they didn't ask for money all the time.

Joe Lee remembered one weekend they'd come up to visit, and it coincided with the annual fundraiser at Myrtis's church. The pastor every year hosted a beauty pageant, with all the men in the congregation as contestants. It always drew a big crowd.

Joe Lee had been uncomfortable the first time he'd attended, but then he'd seen that everyone was just having fun. He remembered one of the contestants during the question-and-answer portion of the pageant. The heavy man had been asked, "What feature would you change about yourself?" The man had rubbed his stomach sadly and said, "My belly." He was wearing a maternity dress because it was all he could find that would fit. Everyone had howled.

Even the preacher wore a dress to host the show. Joe Lee could never bring himself to participate, but he'd thought it would be a good way to connect with Larry and Rigoberto during their visit, so he'd invited them along.

Larry had hesitated, saying, "We're not really into drag shows," but they'd gone, and they'd had a good time, with Rigoberto whistling at some of the contestants, and the two of them laughing continuously. Joe Lee had overheard Larry saying something about "country closet cases," but he didn't really know what that meant. Still, Larry and Rigoberto seemed more relaxed during the rest of that visit than they usually did, and that was good.

Joe Lee put on his John Deere cap now and went over to the farm. One of the horses he'd bought to pull his covered wagon looked like it was having trouble with its right front hoof. Joe Lee approached the horse, which was always gentle and easy to handle, so it didn't shy away when he reached down. He tried to get her to lift her hoof but had to keep pulling and pulling. Even when he could lift her leg briefly, she'd put her foot back down before Joe Lee had a real chance to look at it.

He kept pulling at her leg, and the horse kept resisting. Soon he was sweating in the 92-degree heat, and he was breathing heavily again.

The hoof could wait.

Joe Lee went back to the truck to sit down in the air conditioning. His chest felt a little tight, and he couldn't catch his breath.

He sat there sweating in the cool air, rubbing his chest. It usually got better after a few minutes, but today it wasn't getting better. After ten minutes, he started to get scared.

He tried to calm down, and his breathing got a little better, but his chest still hurt. He figured he'd better go to the emergency room. At least it would be his decision and not Myrtis's.

He drove slowly into town, not wanting to go too fast in case he had to pull over suddenly. But he arrived at the hospital safely and walked into the emergency room. As soon as he said his chest hurt, though, everyone began running around like he was dying. It was funny but a little irritating, too.

Well, maybe he *was* dying, he thought. He wondered if he'd done everything he should have. Somehow, even after seventy years, there still seemed to be so much more he wanted to do. He wondered if anyone besides Myrtis would even miss him. He'd left Myrtis most of his money, but he had also set aside some for Adam and Larry and even Karen.

He knew he was nothing more than a wallet to Karen, but she was still his daughter, and he couldn't cut her out. He knew there'd been many years when he hadn't been very good to Larry, though he'd tried to be better lately. He just hoped he'd done enough to make Adam feel loved.

He tried to relax and let whatever had to happen happen.

About two hours later, as he was lying on a bed waiting for the doctor to come back, Myrtis appeared by his bedside.

"Oh, hi, hon. What're you doing here?"

"Joe Lee, you're going to be fine, but you have a 75% blockage in one of the arteries in your heart. They're going to put in a stent."

"Okay."

"You'll have to take Plavix from now on to keep the blood from clotting around the stent, but you'll be perfectly fine. You'll be able to keep doing everything you've been doing."

"Okay."

She gave his hand a squeeze and leaned over to kiss him. "I've got to get back to work, but I'll stop by again in a little while."

Joe Lee watched her go. Myrtis was a good woman. People in general were so undependable and disappointing. He was lucky to have her. He still wondered if he was going to heaven or not, but it seemed that if he had someone like Myrtis to vouch for him, he might just have a chance.

He thought about his heart, and wondered if he'd be seeing Ruth again, and what she'd say to him. In some ways, he got along better with Myrtis than he ever had in his twenty-five years with Ruth. Would that upset her? Or would she simply be mad he hadn't also married Myrtis in the temple so they could all three be together in the afterlife? Myrtis was a good housekeeper, after all, so Ruth would probably approve. Not that there would be any housekeeping to do in heaven. But still.

Joe Lee was awake as the doctor inserted the stent. He could hear people talking about which size to use, but he didn't pay much attention to the procedure. None of it hurt much, though something a nurse injected burned a good bit. Before long they wheeled him into a room where he'd have to spend the night.

"I'll make sure the sick cow has water and feed," Myrtis told him when she stopped by before going home for the evening. "And Adam will help Randy unload some of his hay in your barn tomorrow."

"We still going to the Smoky Mountains next month?"

"Of course."

"And on the wagon train ride after that?"

"We can still do everything we want to do. This isn't going to change your life in any way."

Joe Lee nodded. It simply *felt* like his life should change in some meaningful way after all this.

"Myrtis, I just want to tell you that you make me very happy. I wanted you to know that."

"Don't talk like you need to have closure. You're not going anywhere."

"I know. But I still wanted you to know."

"Well, I want to get home before it gets dark. Anything else you need me to do tonight?"

"Call Adam and tell him I'll be counting on him."

"All right."

"And call Larry and tell him what happened."

"Karen, too?"

Joe Lee didn't answer right away. "No," he finally said. "Just Larry."

Myrtis hesitated a moment before answering. "All right," she said. Then she sighed and grabbed his hand again. "I'll have a good supper for you tomorrow night," she said brightly, "but I'm afraid I'm going to have to cut down on the fried foods."

Joe Lee smiled. "Okay."

He watched her leave and thought about turning on the TV but decided against it. It was still early, but he was tired. He might just try to get some sleep instead.

A young, pretty nurse came in to check his vitals, and he smiled at her, wondering if he'd ever been that young. Or if she'd ever be as old as he was now.

He'd have to make more of an effort to watch movies with Myrtis. And he'd get Adam a nice guitar next week.

Perhaps he'd even ask Adam to cook a special meal for them one Sunday. Life was too short not to be doing what you wanted as often as life would let you.

Maybe he'd look at TV a little tonight, after all, he decided, maybe that sitcom with all those zany characters out in West Hollywood or wherever it was. The show Larry always tried to get him to watch. Joe Lee waited just a moment before reaching for the remote control, to rest a bit. And before he could concentrate long enough to push the on button, his head settled deeply into the soft hospital pillow, and he was snoring gently and peacefully for the first time in a long while, a slight smile clearly visible on his sleeping face.

The Homeless Bishop

The idea was born during services the Sunday before Thanksgiving, when I listened to my congregants talking about the things they were thankful for. "I'm so grateful Heavenly Father has allowed us to buy a second home down in Palm Springs," said Brother Knightly, our High Priest group leader. "Now we can get away during some of these dreary Salt Lake winters. It's such a blessing."

"I'm truly grateful Heavenly Father has blessed us that we can now afford to go First Class when we fly," said a young man, Brother Erickson, with his smiling young wife by his side. "It makes learning about this great world so much easier. And you know the saying, 'The World is Our Campus.'"

The following young man to speak was that elder's best friend, Aaron Smith. "I'm so blessed I can now afford to fly on private jets and no longer have to bother with commercial airlines." Aaron winked at Brother Erickson, who didn't wink back.

"I'm thankful for Heavenly Father helping me realize how important it is to save our planet," said Brother Randolph, another High Priest. "Our family used to have six cars. But then we realized we had too big a footprint on the planet, so we downsized to five. I'm grateful Heavenly

Father has kept us humble despite our wonderful business successes."

By "family," I suppose I should mention he was referring to himself, his wife, and his ten-year-old son. It wasn't as if he had three teenage children, or four wives.

The entire service progressed in much the same manner, every speaker trying to one-up the previous speaker in demonstrating how blessed they were. Somehow, though, the voices didn't sound overly thankful. They sounded like they felt they deserved more.

It struck me that my congregants could have been performing a parody skit, but they were quite serious. And *that* was the problem.

Not a single person mentioned anything truly spiritual. If people would only stop concentrating so much on their financial prosperity, I thought.

But if I went through with my idea…

When I arrived home after meeting with my first and second counselors, I proposed the idea to Jacqueline, my wife. She wasn't impressed. "You're just doing this to show up everyone, Daniel. You want to embarrass them and prove they're not as righteous as they think they are."

"I simply want to see how they'll react. I think it will be a learning experience for everyone."

"*You* don't want to learn anything. You want *them* to learn."

"What's so bad about that?"

"It comes across as condescending. You're the great, wise bishop who knows everything and *you* must teach the little children."

"Actually, I'm particularly interested in seeing how the children in the ward will react."

"You only want to prove to everyone how superior you are."

"Do you realize that the richest eighty-five people in the world have the same amount of wealth as the poorest three and a half billion?"

Jacqueline didn't even look at me as she spoke. "The poor will always be with us," she replied.

I was miffed. I thought my idea to show up to church in a couple of weeks dressed as a homeless man was pure genius. I'd already told my counselors today I had to go out of town and they'd have to conduct services themselves. No one would be expecting to see me. And apparently, Jacqueline wasn't going to be giving me away with any loving glances, so maybe her disapproval would come in handy.

Veronica would have understood.

I sighed and wished I hadn't agreed with Jacqueline's demand I destroy every remaining photograph of Veronica. Veronica had been my college sweetheart, a couple of years older than I was and already working as a co-pilot while I was still just a senior. Then there'd been that terrible day when I turned on the news and learned her flight had gone down after a fire broke out onboard. The plane had dived almost vertically into the ground at the end.

One of the officials from the regional airline she worked for advised me not to listen to the cockpit voice recorder. "There's a horrible scream at the end. You don't want to hear it."

"But I do want to hear it," I protested. "I *want* to be haunted by her scream. Someone who loved her should feel at least some of the terror she felt at the end. I *want* to lie awake at night and remember what I hear."

Against his better judgment, the official let me listen to the recording.

I heard that heartrending scream every night in my mind for the next several months. When I broke the commandments and rented the R-rated movie *Blow Out*, I was deeply moved by the concluding scene, when the John Travolta character listens to the sound of his girlfriend's dying scream as he uses it to dub an inadequate actress in a film he's working on.

He did the right thing, I thought. No one should forget such a scream.

After I met Jacqueline and tried to move on with my life, I acquiesced to her prerequisite I get rid of every photo of every girlfriend I'd ever had. Letters, cards, emails, gifts, anything that had come from another woman had to go. I felt I was losing the possessions that made my life rich and full. But I told myself possessions didn't matter. What mattered was that I'd found love again. I was going to make an eternal family. And our eternal family would always have a home, at church and, most importantly, in the Celestial Kingdom in our Heavenly Father's house.

The day after I told Jacqueline of my plan to appear as a homeless man, I contacted a make-up artist, Kelly, and we arranged to meet early in two weeks on Sunday morning. Fortunately, our block wouldn't begin until 10:00, so at least we wouldn't have to get up at the crack of dawn to do the make-up.

The following evening after I contacted the make-up person, I stopped at Deseret Industries on my way home from work to buy an ugly, ill-fitting outfit and the most unattractive jacket I could find. Then that Saturday, even though it was freezing cold outside, I jogged and did work on the house without wearing any deodorant. It took a while in that weather to work up a sweat, but I continued to wear the clothes the rest of the day, to let the sweat ferment a little. I knew I'd succeeded when even little Florence, our two-year-old, finally turned up her nose when I came near.

"Don't think you're getting close to me tonight," Jacqueline said as we sat down to dinner. I'd already changed clothes at this point, of course.

"I took a shower," I pointed out.

"What you're doing still smells, Daniel. No nookie tonight."

"No nookie!" Florence shouted gleefully, unaware of what she was saying. I looked at Jacqueline disapprovingly.

On Wednesday during my lunch break at work, I decided to take a walk. There were always several homeless people in the area, even in weather like this, with a few inches of snow on the ground. One man was huddled in an alleyway between two buildings, his coat looking quite insufficient. A woman held out a cardboard sign, "Veteran. Please help."

I gave her a dollar, but the look of misery on her face didn't change. Finally, I came to a bus stop, where the half-partition gave a little relief from the slight wind blowing today. A man about sixty was hunched over, mumbling angrily to himself.

Must be schizophrenic, I thought. Who could even fathom what he was angry at? I'd seen people like this shouting at every passerby, upset at the whole world.

But this man was saying things in disgust as well as anger, judging from his expression, and now he was hitting himself in the head as he mumbled. Oh, my, I thought. He hates *himself*.

It just seemed too awful, so I sat down beside him and offered my hand. "How are you doing today?" I asked. "Pretty cold, isn't it?"

Without even looking at me, the man stood up and walked away. I'd driven him from the bus shelter. Good job, Daniel.

After lunch, when I went back to the office, one of my coworkers stopped by my desk. "I saw you during your break," Brad said. "It's nice you're making some new friends." He smirked but didn't walk away.

What was it to him? It wasn't as if I was going around chastising my coworkers for being moral bums.

"Everyone can use a kind word," I returned, hoping he'd catch the sarcasm. I was only human, after all.

He didn't catch it. "Gonna baptize anyone?" he asked.

"Not everyone has an ulterior motive for everything they do."

"Of course we do." Brad laughed.

That night at dinner, I tried again to get Jacqueline on my side. After she served the scalloped potatoes and green beans, I took a sip of my milk. "I talked to a homeless man today."

She didn't even look at me as she responded. "I don't want to hear it." She scooped a spoonful of cauliflower with cheese onto her plate and took a bite. Then she helped Florence eat a green bean.

"Do you know how many children are homeless in Salt Lake?" I persisted.

"I said I don't want to talk about it."

There was no nookie that night, either.

Lying in bed next to Jacqueline, I thought about Veronica. I remembered one day when we'd gone to the park, about a month before I proposed. It was springtime, and birds were singing, and there was a light, fragrant breeze. I noticed some children nearby playing on the swings, but my attention was directed primarily toward Veronica.

After several moments, she stood up and walked over to the swings. There was a boy about eight on the one swing that was functional. A six-year-old girl waited patiently for her turn, but the boy, I now realized, was laughing at the girl, saying things like, "*I've* got the swing. It's *my* swing. You can wait all day, but *I'm* the one having fun."

Veronica stood next to the girl and looked at the boy flying back and forth through the air. She didn't reprimand him. She smiled and said sweetly, "Wouldn't it be better to let her take her turn? And then you can take another turn. And then she can take her turn again. Don't you really think that would be better?"

The boy didn't say anything at first, but after a moment, he stopped swinging and let the girl on, waiting now for his next turn.

The last year of our relationship, Veronica was stationed in Cincinnati, so we didn't get to spend much time together, Skyping when we were able so we could at least see each other's face. It would only be another year before I graduated and we could marry. I planned to look for a job in Cincinnati. Six weeks after she'd set up her apartment, she called me on a Sunday afternoon. "There's an old woman in the ward," she said. "She sits in the back row in Sacrament meeting. No one sits near her or talks to her."

"That's a shame," I said.

"So the last couple of weeks, I've been making a point of speaking with her." Veronica laughed. "I understand now why people avoid her."

"Why's that?"

"She's one of those people who doesn't stop talking once she starts. And it's always some boring, pointless story with far too many details."

"What are you going to do?"

"I'm going to keep talking to her, of course. The woman needs human contact even if she isn't perfect. Goodness knows I'm not perfect, either."

I lay in bed and pinched my arm till it bruised. Was I sinning by thinking about Veronica while married to Jacqueline? Normally, Jacqueline was a perfectly fine woman. We watched *Person of Interest* together and *Sleepy Hollow*, and we played with Florence together every evening for at least half an hour. We didn't take turns bathing Florence but did it together as a couple. We read at least four pages of the scriptures together every evening before bed.

We even had fun sexually sometimes, those days when Jacqueline was willing to participate, me pretending to be a missionary and she pretending to be an investigator. We did lots of role-playing and kept things interesting. She was mad about the homeless "stunt" I was about to pull, but every married couple had disagreements. That didn't mean we weren't right for each other.

I turned onto my side and looked at Jacqueline in the dim light as I drifted off to sleep. I could hear Veronica screaming distantly in the night.

The rest of the week went well, and on Saturday morning, with two new inches of snow on the ground, I dressed in my "costume" and caught the bus downtown, getting off near Pioneer Park on the southwest end of downtown. The bus driver gave me a suspicious look, and no one sat near me on the bus. The homeless were spread out in the city, but there was one area where I'd seen several, so I headed there. Once I arrived, though, I didn't know what to do. A couple of men were hanging out together, but most of the people I saw were alone. Where were all those families I'd read about?

It wouldn't have hurt for me to go to a shelter and talk to some professionals. Why was I doing this "research" without taking advantage of people with experience?

One man looked at me as he passed. He was missing several teeth and had a five-day growth of beard. Another man walked by as well. His skin was covered with lesions, the kind I'd seen on meth addicts in a TV commercial once. A black man gave me a piercing stare, and another white man looked at me and licked his lips. Was he hungry? Or was he plotting something? I hadn't brought much money, but I might still get mugged, I realized. What if someone hit me with a rock? These were crazy people and alcoholics and people with nothing to lose. Anything could happen.

I already knew how my congregation would react when I showed up. They'd react like I was, full of fear and suspicion. What was the point of "testing" them?

I walked up to a man who appeared to be in his fifties. "Hey," I said.

He nodded.

"So what's your story?" I asked.

He looked at me for a long moment. "You must be new," he said softly.

"What do you mean?"

"No one else asks questions like that."

"Yes, I'm new," I admitted. But I still wanted to know. "So what happened?"

The man was leaning against a brick wall and looked about for someplace dry to sit, but there was nothing. He turned back to me. "I worked as a real estate agent until the crash. Then I got divorced. My wife took most of the friends. My family is all Baptist and disowned me after I was baptized a Mormon."

He was Mormon? I guess I knew that must happen, but I couldn't help but wonder where his bishop had been. Why wasn't this man on Church welfare?

"I stayed with one friend for three weeks on his sofa, and with another friend for a month, but no one wants people like us around for long."

"You couldn't find another job?" I asked.

"Couldn't you?" he returned.

"Well…"

He shrugged. "Actually, I did find another job, just at minimum wage, and only part-time. I couldn't afford rent on that. I have a bank account and have enough money to eat, but I have to live on the street. I wash my clothes at the Laundromat once a week. It's not the worst life in the world."

How could he say that?

"But…but what can people do?"

"What people?"

"People who can help."

"There's no one who can help. Everyone's just trying to take care of their own life." He looked at me. "Did *you* ever think of helping before it happened to you?"

Yes, I thought. That's why I was there. But I couldn't say that. And really, I wasn't sure it was even true. What good did "thinking" about it do? What good did "feeling sorry" do? "Understanding"?

The Church offered Church welfare, which was great, but why didn't individual wards volunteer at soup kitchens? Or have a ward fundraiser to support homeless shelters? Why did we only care about "our own" and forget that there was a whole wide world out there which needed help? Maybe I could do something with my congregation, after all.

I slipped back into the house and changed clothes without letting Jacqueline see me. I let her take a nap while I watched Florence, and then I chopped up some vegetables and started a stew in the early afternoon. Jacqueline put on a Taylor Swift CD, and we danced for half an hour, Florence joining in most of the time.

Then late in the afternoon, about an hour before dinnertime, Jacqueline and I went in the bedroom. I thought about role-playing and wanted to ask if we could pretend to be homeless people trying to find some privacy for sex, but I knew that would turn Jacqueline off, so instead I didn't suggest anything, and we made love just as Daniel and Jacqueline.

I'd never had sex with Veronica and wondered what that might have been like.

I wondered if she could be my second wife in the Celestial Kingdom.

Would she even want to be? And would Jacqueline allow it?

Why did I feel homeless, even at home?

That evening, we watched Amy Adams in *Enchanted* while I rubbed Jacqueline's feet. She went to bed around 9:30, and I stayed up, reading articles about the homeless on the Internet. One appalling story explained how the Japanese government was developing a plan to help get their homeless back to work—by offering them jobs cleaning up the radiation contamination at the Fukushima power plant.

Another story was about how some teenagers had beaten a homeless man to death in Denver. Finally, a third story described how the city of Phoenix had found housing for every one of its homeless military veterans. Non-veterans were still homeless all over the city, but at least one small segment of the dispossessed had been helped. At least for now.

In the morning, I was off early to meet Kelly, the make-up artist, at her apartment. I brought my outfit and changed into it after she'd finished, so as not to offend her with the smell any more than necessary. I did still ask her to drive me to church. She went in first, already a member and knowing how to navigate, even if it wasn't her home ward. I walked back and forth outside, afraid to go in, unnerved even by the worried and suspicious glances I received from families walking past on their way to the foyer.

Finally, I headed inside and watched as the sea of people parted in front of me, just like a miracle from Exodus. I didn't panhandle for money, thinking that would be in poor taste even for a real homeless person who'd come to church. I simply sat on the back row in the chapel, about six feet from the doors, and watched as my congregants walked by.

Some of the women pulled their children away from me as they passed. The men narrowed their eyes. An older woman literally walked by with her nose in the air. Another older woman looked at me with sad, sympathetic eyes, but she didn't approach, either. Jacqueline strolled by, holding Florence, ignoring me completely.

To my surprise, not a single person came over to shake my hand. I'd expected the number to be small, but I didn't expect it to be zero.

Also to my surprise, I found that my feelings were hurt.

I sat throughout the meeting, struggling to sing along with the hymns, pretending to be a person who couldn't cope. I partook of the sacrament when it was passed, getting several stern glances for my audacity, and listened to the talks. I had planned near the end of the meeting to stand up and walk straight to the podium, taking off the matted wig and revealing my identity. A kind of poor, wayfaring man of grief moment.

But I found I no longer wanted to do that. It felt as obnoxious as Jacqueline said it would be. But more than that, I simply no longer had the energy.

I wanted to curl up in a corner. I sat through the closing prayer and then walked back out into the parking lot. The other congregants would be going on to their next meetings, but soon Kelly came out and walked up to her car.

"Was it everything you'd hoped for?" she asked with a smile.

"I want to clean up and go home," I replied.

We drove back to her apartment, where she removed the make-up. I put on my regular clothes and drove off.

Only I didn't feel like going directly home, even knowing that Jacqueline wouldn't be there to poke fun. I went to Liberty Park and started slowly walking along the roughly cleared sidewalk. I came upon an iron bench and sat down, staring at the desolate trees in front of me. The wind blew snow gently across the snow-covered grass.

I could give a talk next week, saying I'd "heard" that a homeless man had come the previous Sunday, and see if we couldn't organize some kind of useful response to the problem. I could take what little I might have learned personally and use it for good, without upsetting anyone else in the process. If nothing else, I could join a program that was already set up and donate a couple of hours a week.

As if bishops ever had a couple of free hours a week.

I looked at the leafless trees in front of me, their branches covered in snow that was being softly blown away.

Then I looked at my hands, pink in the cold air. Weren't our bodies our temples? If Veronica was bodiless, was that like being spiritually homeless?

If no one remembered you anymore, were you like a tree that had fallen in a forest with no one to hear?

I watched as an older man trudged by. He wasn't homeless, just lonely.

What was that old woman in Veronica's ward doing now without her?

I saw a plane flying by slowly in the west and felt a tear on my cheek. I stood up, shaking my head. I couldn't do it. I just wasn't the man Veronica wanted me to be. I couldn't help all those helpless people. I wasn't strong enough.

I would tell no one what I'd done, and this entire episode would soon fade away into the past. My real job, my only job, was to make my family a Celestial family. Everything else was secondary, even serving as bishop. I would go home and prepare Jacqueline's favorite meal.

I started walking back toward the car. The wind picked up a little, creating a low howl through the barren trees.

It sounded like a scream.

Mis ing Parts

Miranda sat brooding at her window, looking out toward the dimly lit parking lot. She was sure Rita was behind it all. Why else would Lizelle have gotten a note under her door which said, "Tell your friend we hope she gets the hint!" It had to be Rita who was hiring someone to steal the parts off her car.

It had started three weeks ago when her battery was stolen as her car was parked under the overpass on Claiborne near Charity Hospital. Then the new battery had been stolen just over a week ago, and then over the past few days three tires and the new disc brakes had been taken as well. Miranda had reported all of it to the police in addition to the security guard, who said she didn't see anything.

Miranda knew she had, of course. She was probably in on it, too. The nuns in the elevator certainly were. She could tell by the way they looked at her, with their frowns and superior gazes. They thought she was trash because of all the things Rita and her friends had been telling them.

After two semesters at nursing school, Miranda wasn't sure she could live with these people the rest of the time it would take to graduate. The dorm was cheaper than an apartment, and she'd spent the last of her mother's inheritance years ago on clothes to impress Keith.

She'd moved out of her father's house after he threw a chair at her one time too many. Besides, the house had too many bad memories, with her father kicking out the missionaries who'd come to visit, when Miranda was sure one of them liked her, and her foster siblings all being taken away one by one over the years.

But living with Susan, her one friend from church, was no good either, because she was the one who'd introduced Miranda to Eric, whom she'd dated before meeting Keith. Every time Susan called now to invite her back to church, all Miranda could think of was her miscarriage, and how Eric had used that as an excuse to dump her, telling everyone he couldn't marry someone who'd had an abortion.

So now she didn't know where she could live. Hopefully, Keith would ask her to move in, but even if he didn't, she'd have to do something. These other students were just too horrible.

First of all, they barged into her room at all hours without more than a quick knock. Of course, she always said, "Come in," but they should know better than to interrupt her studies all the time. They borrowed her clothes, and she always offered part of her dinner if they came while she was eating, which they often did. Which brought up the fact that they always knew when she cooked, even if she cooked at different times. It must be them who reported her dirty pans in the kitchen to the floor supervisor.

Which of course brought up the fact that Miranda was the only one the supervisor ever bitched at for leaving dirty dishes in the kitchen, when everyone else did it, too. How could the floor supervisor notice *her* pan and not the others? Someone had it in for her, and who else could it be but Rita?

Rita had befriended her when Miranda first moved in, a semester after Rita did. Rita had shown her the ropes, which proved she knew them well enough to manipulate now, and Miranda had trusted her sufficiently to confide her affair with Keith.

And *that* was the whole reason for all the trouble since. Once Rita learned that Keith was a nurse in the emergency room, and once Miranda had pointed him out at lunch in the cafeteria, that was the beginning of the end.

Miranda had seen Rita with Keith since then, talking and laughing, and Keith had been colder to Miranda since. Of course, he'd said for years now he didn't love her, that he only called her up for sex when he was horny and it was late, but Miranda knew he really cared, or why would they still be seeing each other after almost seven years?

It *couldn't* be for the sex because Miranda always complained about the things Keith wanted to do to her. But she was thirty-one now and didn't have much time to invest in another relationship. She knew Keith would eventually marry her, and yet now Rita was trying to ruin everything. Rita took her clothes, her food, was trying to take her man, and now she was taking her car, too, bit by bit.

She looked down into the parking lot again. It was almost midnight, but a couple of black men were passing one way, and a white woman was walking the other way. No one was looking at her car, not that there was much to look at anymore.

But Miranda was going to stay up until she saw someone going after that last tire. She had the phone ready and would have the police down before they could finish getting the tire off. Then she could prove the connection to Rita. *Then* Keith and all the other nursing students on the floor and all the nuns in the elevators would know Rita had been lying about her. She smiled grimly and kept staring.

She hoped staying up late wouldn't hurt her chances on the final pharmacology exam the next morning, but with all this crap going on, it wasn't as if she could study or sleep anyway. That was probably Rita's strategy in the first place. If Miranda failed even one exam, she'd be out of school, and Keith wouldn't want her for sure.

With the phone at her fingertips, Miranda debated over whether to call Keith. He'd probably ask her over if she did, and she'd fail her exam for certain after he tied her up for two hours. More importantly, she'd miss catching Rita. Keith would have to wait.

She heard footsteps going past her door and was tempted to cross the room to peek down the hallway. She resisted, but a few minutes later, some other footsteps approached, stopping right in front of her door. They were obviously plotting something, but Miranda wouldn't make a sound.

Then came a knock. Miranda jumped, glanced again at her car, and reluctantly crossed over to the door, opening it. "Lizelle!"

"Were you sleeping?" the young woman asked apologetically. "Oh, I know you were, but I've got that final tomorrow, and I just need some help. It's the Basics course you took last semester."

This was Lizelle's first semester in the dorms, and she was one of only a few students who were still nice to her. Miranda had already told her yesterday what the exam had been like the semester before, but she quizzed her one more time anyway. She needed to keep *some* friends with so many enemies about.

Lizelle left after about half an hour, and Miranda decided she'd better get to sleep after all. She'd catch Rita tomorrow night. She stretched and went down the hall to the bathroom and then drank a glass of water.

Back in her room, she kicked off her shoes and debated again whether to call Keith. She glanced briefly at some pharmacology notes, turned off her lights, and then went to the window for one last look down. She squinted at first, but then her eyes grew large.

Her tire was gone!

She gasped and stared in horror. Then she swirled toward her closed door. So Lizelle was in on it, too! *Everyone* was. Lizelle had been sent by Rita to divert her.

She sat down and hugged herself, whispering softly. "Oh my God. Oh my God." She sat there for several minutes, staring in the darkness at her door, feeling small and alone. Then a siren screamed outside, and she looked absently out the window. Then she looked down at her car. The poor thing. At least the engine was left. Maybe she should sell it while she still could. Or maybe that could yet be bait.

She raised an eyebrow and thought, and then she decided on a plan. First, she'd *pass* that test in the morning and show everyone. She nodded. Then she'd find a way to prove what Rita and Lizelle were up to. Yes, she'd prove it. Then those nuns would know the truth. And Keith would know. Those girls thought they were so clever, but Miranda would show them. She'd show them all.

She sat in the darkness, holding herself and smiling softly.

Becoming an Ammonite

I became a serial killer innocently enough.

Tony and I were sitting on our front porch in the New Orleans suburb of Harvey when a carload of teenage boys drove by.

"Faggots!" one of the boys shouted out the window.

I leaned over and kissed Tony. I wanted to show those cretins we weren't intimidated. The boys continued cursing but drove off. I smiled at Tony.

"You think that was wise, Ernest?"

"We can't pretend we don't exist. Unless you want to live in a gay ghetto somewhere, we have to be able to be ourselves in our own home."

"But they might come back and egg the house. Being right isn't the same as being wise."

"We have a security camera. We'll give the video to the police."

"Like they'd care."

"I came out to my entire congregation during Fast and Testimony meeting. I'm not going to hide under a rock again."

"Okay. Okay. Let's just not flaunt it."

It was what my bishop had said when he excommunicated me from the Mormon Church. "Only someone with internalized homophobia would say that."

"Can we please change the subject?"

"Any time you want."

It was 3:00 on Sunday, so after soaking up some of the late afternoon sun, we went inside, cooked some chicken stroganoff, and put in a DVD of *The Brave One*. We were both Jodie Foster fans, though *The Accused* was our favorite of her films. Then Tony and I had some good sex and fell asleep cuddled in each other's arms around 10:00. I'd be waking up at 7:00 to get to my job as a court reporter while Tony would be getting up at 7:30 to head over to his job at the cable company.

Tony sometimes shouted in his sleep, so we liked to go to bed early to make up for having to wake up two or three times during the night. Tony could never remember what dream had sparked the cries, so we just took it all in stride. I would simply pull him close afterward and hug him tightly until he fell asleep again.

Around 2:00, a fairly routine time for Tony, he shouted, and we both woke up.

"There, there, it's okay," I whispered.

"Sorry, Ernest, I—"

He stopped when we both heard a sound out in the hall. That wasn't the normal creaking and settling noises our house made. Tony grabbed my hand.

I wriggled loose and sat up, reaching over to the bedside table where I kept my gun. I had just retrieved it and still hadn't had time to check the safety when our bedroom door flew open and two figures came through the doorway.

"Fucking faggots!" someone yelled. There was a shot, and then another, and then several more. Tony screamed.

Then there was silence. I reached over and turned on the lamp. Tony was sitting up in bed with the sheet pulled to his chin, shaking uncontrollably. There was a bullet hole in the sheet, and another in the wall above the bed.

"You okay?"

"I think so."

I looked to see where the intruders had gone. My mouth fell open when I saw two bodies crumpled in the doorway. "Oh my god."

"Call 911, Tony."

"Shit, shit, shit."

The police were there within five minutes, and an ambulance arrived a few minutes after that. It turned out we didn't really need the ambulance, however. Both intruders were dead.

It seemed clear enough this was a home invasion. The two teens were among those I'd seen in the passing car earlier. I didn't mention the car or the epithet the young men had shouted, though I don't really know why. It wasn't as if that would have tipped off the officers the two men obviously sharing a bed were gay. For some reason, I felt the need to keep something back.

You could never be sure even when things seemed clear cut, so I was relieved when the police didn't arrest me and the bodies were carted off. Now it would just be a matter of replacing the carpet and sheets and repairing the wall.

And getting over the fact that someone had tried to kill us for being gay.

Tony and I both called in sick to work in the morning and went to a carpet store, where we paid extra to have the new carpet put in that day. Before the installers arrived, I spackled the wall and let it dry, and after the installers left, I used some of our leftover paint for the bedroom to touch up the spot.

We had other sheets already in the linen closet, but after dinner, we still went out to buy a new set.

"Won't we always associate these new sheets with what happened?" Tony asked uncertainly.

"It'll remind us it's okay to stand up for ourselves, that it's okay to be gay. I know as a Baptist, you keep doubting that."

"I wish I could go back to being ten, before I ever thought about sex."

"Sex is a good thing. It's not a sin."

"What about all those rapists and serial killers who get their jollies through sex? It's got to be a *little* wrong in the first place for so many people to be corrupted by it."

"Is religion bad? Look at all the people who kill others in the name of God. Is believing in God a bad thing, at least just a *little*?"

Tony let the subject drop, but while I'd simply been arguing for argument's sake, I began to wonder. Maybe there *was* something wrong with religion if it caused so much suffering in the world. There were hateful televangelists and popular preachers who loudly proclaimed gays were bringing about the end of civilization and needed to be stopped at any cost. It clearly led to the kind of thing that had happened here.

When people could slap bumper stickers on their cars that read, "Kill a queer for Christ," it was only a small step further to actual murder.

Maybe there weren't hundreds of Matthew Shepards out there, but there were some. Ten years ago, I'd had a friend, a fuck buddy really, who'd been stabbed to death by a gay basher. He'd lived just long enough to identify his killer. The killer was caught and confessed, saying he'd stabbed my friend because my friend was gay, and if he was put in prison, he'd kill anyone there he thought was gay, too. He got fifteen years. That story never made the news at all.

Suddenly, the oppression no longer seemed acceptable. I'd long thought it wrong, of course, but now it simply became intolerable. If vigilante straight people could attack gays to "protect" society, then I could attack those straight people, in order to protect the gay community, to protect the healthy and progressive part of American society.

While Tony was watching TV that evening, I went to my computer and googled New Orleans TV preachers. There were a couple with cable shows, one local and one syndicated. I researched their attitudes toward gays and found both to be horrific. "Gays will bring about the extinction of America," said Bob Butchart, the local show preacher, typical hate speech.

But the other creep, Andrew Killeen, went further. "If we allow the rest of society to say gays are okay, that they should be treated as if they were decent human beings, then God will smite *all* of us with a plague far worse than the one He's already inflicted on gays. He will allow terrorists to release biological warfare. He'll have no reason to protect us. We *must* insist our political leaders deny 'rights' to these people who are so, so wrong."

I'd thought for years of these people as intellectual soda straws, conduits for sugary drinks full of empty calories. But now I saw them for what they were—enemies.

"What was the name of your preacher who told you he'd pray every day for you to get leprosy so you'd suffer more than you would if you just got AIDS?" I asked Tony in bed.

"Oh, God, did you have to bring that up?"

"What was his name?"

"Teddy Kyzar. Why do you care? He's a nobody, off in Wesson, Mississippi, where no one pays any attention to what he says."

"You do. Every time you get a flake of dandruff or a patch of dry skin, you worry about developing leprosy."

"That's just because I have a weak personality. Anyone with a spine would just have told him to go fuck himself."

"There are a lot of spineless people out there. And some of them have very big mouths."

"Whatever. Can we talk about something else?"

"I'm going to make Teddy Kyzar pay for what he did to you."

"I said let's talk about something else."

"See? You *do* have a spine, and he still broke your back."

"I'm going to hit you."

"How about spanking instead? You haven't spanked me in a long while." I got up on my hands and knees and wiggled my butt in the air.

Tony laughed then and slapped me playfully, and we had some healthy sex. I loved seeing his beautiful brown skin against my pale white body. While Tony spanked me as I was fucking him, suddenly another thought came to my mind. What if spanking wasn't innocent? What if it really was a sign we'd had the idea we needed to be punished ingrained too deeply in us?

What if this insidious religious hatred still infected us years after we'd gotten over the initial acute case of internalized homophobia? What if the disease lurked just barely detectable in our systems for life, doing its secret damage unnoticed till it was too late?

"Ow. Go easy there, Ernest."

"Sorry."

After I came inside Tony, I sucked him off, letting the cum linger on my tongue for a moment. Tony was positive, but I didn't feel there was much risk with oral sex, so I brought him to climax as often as I could in my mouth. As I knelt there with HIV rolling around on my tongue, I instantly knew what I had to do.

The next day after work, I stopped by a pawn shop and bought a new handgun. I couldn't use the same one I'd used on the two intruders. There would be a ballistics record on those bullets, even if I hadn't been prosecuted.

I did more googling and whitepaging.com and found Bob Butchart's address. I drove to his home a couple of times to familiarize myself with the area, and on Saturday, I was lucky enough to catch the man leaving church in the afternoon. I followed him to a house that wasn't his.

It was probably that of a congregant. I'd rather have confronted him at his own home, but I might not get another chance. I quickly parked behind him, and before he could get to the door to knock, I walked up to him and shot him twice.

I ran to my car and sped off, my heart beating rapidly.

What if I got caught? It would be a big blow to Tony. And I wasn't thrilled with the idea of going to jail, even if I could do the opposite of my friend's killer and attack anyone in prison I thought was a homophobe. Besides, I was too weak to do anything without a weapon. Jail would be a disaster.

But I'd killed one homophobe now. That was something. Wait, I thought with a start, it was three, wasn't it? It meant I'd accomplished a tangible good already. My life had meaning finally beyond my own existence.

Murder was a sin, of course, but this wasn't really murder. It was self-defense. Would it have been a sin for a Jew in World War II to kill a Nazi guard, even if the guard hadn't personally killed any Jews? He was part of a system that murdered others, part of a system that caused others to be murdered, however you wanted to look at it.

People were responsible for their affiliations, for their passive contribution to evil. And Bob Butchart had contributed directly to hatred. If you lived by the sword, you died by the sword.

"Are you having an affair?" Tony asked when I got home.

"What?"

"You've been gone a lot this week. Are you trying to feel more alive after nearly dying? Or are you just tired of me? Are you disgusted with me for being a wimp?"

I walked over and hugged Tony. "I love you. I've just been driving around thinking about life. I haven't been seeing anyone. Really."

"You swear?"

"I swear. I made a commitment to you, and I'm keeping it."

"I don't want you to 'keep your commitment.' I want you to love me."

"I do love you."

"Promise?"

"I promise."

As it turned out, the news eventually announced that a preacher had been killed outside the home of a woman he was reported to be having an affair with. I laughed when I heard, though I felt guilty for it.

I put off doing anything else for the next couple of weeks. But I knew from the start that eliminating just one or two jerks wasn't enough to change the world. So before long I was following Andrew Killeen as well. There was no way to do this without arousing Tony's suspicions, but I was determined and eventually caught Andrew alone one morning walking to his car. I shot him and then headed to the courtroom for work.

I'd seen the preacher drop his satchel when he fell, but it wasn't till I watched the news later that I heard pornography had spilled out onto the driveway next to him. I laughed again.

I knew enough from John Kennedy's assassination, and Robert Kennedy's, and Martin Luther King's, and Gandhi's, that it really did make a difference who was leading. Maybe others would try to fill the void, but it took *that* person to promote a specific agenda in a specific way successfully.

I wasn't sure the two preachers who would replace the ones I'd killed would be any less awful. Chances were, they wouldn't be. But eventually, someone with some humane opinions would be in a leadership position. I could only do so much, yet I had to do what I could.

Still, just like I occasionally felt a residual stab of guilt over being gay, I also wondered now if killing could ever really be justified. There were dozens of wars in the Bible and Book of Mormon where the righteous killed the wicked. It was the religious right in this instance who insisted they were in a war against gays. If they were the ones who declared the war, if they were leading state legislatures across the country to pass anti-gay laws, didn't we have a duty to fight back?

The U.S. sometimes went to war for financial reasons, to protect business interests, not for any high moral purposes. When my last partner had died six years ago, he hadn't left a will, and his sister had inherited the house, the car, the life insurance, the pension settlement. All told, I'd lost over $250,000. I knew that story was repeated hundreds if not thousands of times in the gay community because self-righteous preachers condemned gay marriage and blocked it every chance they got.

If soldiers were guiltless for fighting financial wars, why couldn't that alone justify what I was doing, regardless of my other reasons? And if people were going to use the Bible as a weapon because they were too weak to fight on their own, they had to expect others to make moral judgments about them, too.

"You've been very distant lately," Tony said.

"Have I?"

"You know you have. Talk to me. Tell me what's going on."

"Nothing. I'm fine."

"Ernest, I know you. Something's up. If it isn't an affair, what is it? You didn't finally test positive, did you?"

"No, no, I'm okay."

"So what is it?"

"I just—I just—"

"What?"

I shrugged. "I started praying for God to smite those wicked preachers, and—"

"You think God has been answering your prayers by killing people?" Tony shook his head. "If you have that power, why don't you pray for gay marriage bills to pass instead? Or for there to be some really good gay movie that will influence people to like us? Or anything else that's positive?"

"It seems easier to create change by doing something negative."

"Well, if God is all-powerful, isn't he strong enough to do the harder thing and make a positive change? Shouldn't we at least be praying for that?"

"Can we change the subject?"

Tony laughed. "Isn't that my line?"

I made more of an effort to act normally around Tony, but soon I was waking him up during the night with my own shouting as often as he was waking me.

During the evening, we played cards or watched *Lost* or listened to Melissa Etheridge. On weekends, we hung out with friends or had sex. One Saturday, we walked for the March of Dimes. Another weekend, I read a book by Jodi Picoult. Tony and I went one day to a mineral shop and picked out a new fossil for our collection, an ammonite shell this time, to add to our fern and fish impressions, our megalodon tooth and saber-toothed tiger tooth.

It was fascinating to look at the remains of extinct life, to know that this life was no longer here but that we were, to know that God had allowed this life to cease existing for some reason. What had this poor ammonite done to deserve such a fate?

Still, all the while we were going about life normally, I was planning my next move. Representative Darren Khouros of Metairie had recently announced his opposition to gay marriage, wailing about how it would destroy the family. This just weeks after he was caught with a prostitute. He didn't spend a lot of time here locally, but I did manage to catch him coming out of his house one morning.

His wife didn't look particularly broken up when interviewed on the news later.

But there was the first bit of speculation that the recent killings I'd done were related. It was announced that the bullets in all three killings matched. I kicked myself. I probably should have bought two or three different guns.

A couple of days later, there was conservative talk about the wicked, secular left now out to murder the good, holy people of the right. It was ever so subtly hinted that perhaps the right would have to start their own military campaign against liberal leaders.

This was already a serious cultural war. Could I be provoking a literal civil war as well?

Soon, calmer voices were talking about the "lone kook" out there who had to be stopped but insisting there was no evidence of a larger conspiracy. Still, the lack of these three leaders didn't seem to be swaying the right-wing public to feel any kindlier toward the left. I knew it would take time, but what if it simply had no positive effect at all?

Executing Ted Bundy may not have had the result of changing society for the better, yet it still got rid of Ted Bundy. I wasn't sure he was all that different from Mormon leaders, just killing in different ways. So I was seeing that justice was done to these other hatemongers in my city, regardless of the overall effect on the rest of the inhabitants. I was getting rid of ministerial Ted Bundys.

I was worried about only having an influence in New Orleans, though, so when Tony and I took a week's vacation in San Francisco, I snuck off to buy a gun there, and I followed in our rental car a Catholic priest who'd made several comments about AIDS being divine retribution and how it was immoral to use taxpayer dollars to fund either treatment or research. I picked him off in his confessional.

When parishioners were interviewed to discuss how saintly the man had been, two young men claimed the priest had molested them regularly when they were boys.

I was afraid of the conspiracy accusation being made again now that the killings had spread, yet I was still excited when the following day there appeared to be a copycat assassination in Los Angeles of a televangelist who claimed the city would be destroyed by a massive earthquake within five years unless all gay characters were removed from television. A couple of days later, his autopsy revealed he had a latent syphilis infection. I giggled.

"Why are we watching the news so much?" Tony asked wearily. "It's our vacation."

"I just like to keep up with what's going on in the world."

"Did you enjoy your hustler the other day?"

"What hustler?"

"What other reason could you possibly have for going off without me in San Francisco?"

"Okay, you're right. I'm sorry. But he wore leather and you refuse to."

"Bitch."

"I still love you. Let's go hire someone for you, too."

"I don't wanna."

"You keep saying you want to piss in someone's mouth, and I won't let you."

"Well..."

I wondered for a second if maybe we were in fact degenerate, but this was all between consenting adults, so who cared?

The right wing cared, that's who.

The Mormons had taught me there were two plans presented in the Pre-existence. Satan had offered to come to earth and force everyone to be good. Jesus had offered instead to come down and atone for everyone's sins when they made inevitable bad choices. God had selected Jesus's plan.

But religious leaders of all types ever since seemed to have retroactively chosen to follow Satan's plan. They wanted to coerce gay people to be straight, force all people to live the way *they* thought we should.

I hired a hustler for Tony, and he was smiling when he came back to the hotel room later.

"I believe in monogamy," he said, "but maybe once a year we can hire someone."

"Okay," I said. I still hadn't had sex outside the relationship and didn't want to, but I could make this accommodation for Tony. Without realizing it, he was certainly making a much larger concession for me.

Back in New Orleans, I made a list of other possible targets. I realized I couldn't possibly get to them all without being caught, so I tried to figure out a way to at least have some impact in their lives. I decided to mail get well cards, each filled with a spoonful of flour, hoping that the threat of anthrax would make the preachers and politicians think twice.

I typed on the computer little notes to include with the cards. One read, "Equality for all." Another said, "Fetus rights, but no rights for gay adults?" Still another read, "Oppression for the oppressors." I mentioned the necessity of saving the environment, the importance of national health care, and the need to intervene in the Sudan. I tried to advance as many humanitarian claims as I could.

And I killed one more preacher, in Baton Rouge.

Somehow, though, none of this seemed to make the right back down. Everyone was up in arms. There were more calls to arrest anyone suggesting the U.S. needed to change. Protestors were treasonous for not believing the country was great the way it already was.

"The Founding Fathers didn't say gays deserved rights. Anyone who wants to change that correct principle is going against the fundamentals of our nation and is a dangerous socialist who needs to be put away."

Several church leaders made pronouncements, but it was the one from the First Presidency of the LDS Church that hit home. "We thoroughly condemn the grievous assassinations which have occurred recently. It seems clear that encouraging tolerance of fringe elements serves no useful purpose. It simply instills in the wicked a desire to take even more from those trying to live a God-centered life. We encourage lawmakers to redirect their efforts at stopping these horrendous crimes. Rather than vote for hate crimes legislation which punishes those who target people who commit abominable sins, such as homosexuals, it might be wiser to implement legislation which imparts harsher punishments on those who kill others merely for upholding high moral principles."

My mouth fell open. The Mormon leadership was singling out gays even though there was no evidence all this was gay-related, only that it was anti-religion. I'd left no notes to police regarding any of the people I'd killed, stating my reasons. For the Church to assume gays were the culprits infuriated me. They were right, of course, but still.

Three senators and two representatives also spoke out against gays, making claims that "the future of Christianity is at stake. There are those who would put us back in the Coliseum with lions. Our very lives are at risk. We must stand strong against evil."

"I wish all these killings would stop," Tony said. "I'm tired of the constant violence. Can't we all just get along?"

"Rodney King's famous words."

"And did all those riots in Los Angeles solve anything?"

"I suppose not."

"Gandhi and Martin Luther King had it right. The only way to create successful positive change is through non-violence. A Jew kills an Arab, and the Arabs feel the need to kill a Jew, and then Jews get angry at Arabs and attack them. Everyone feels wronged, and the fighting goes on for centuries."

"But sometimes, if it's a specific enemy, fighting does solve things. America freed itself from England, didn't it?

Now we have liberty *and* a good relationship with England. Win-win. We fought the Japanese and lots of people died, but we have freedom and peace and good relations there, too."

"What about the Civil War? There's still bad blood 150 years after that ended. Blacks couldn't march peacefully even a full hundred years after the war."

"But you can now, can't you? And is marching peacefully the answer anyway? Gays marched peacefully after Harvey Milk was assassinated, but Dan White still only got eight years for murder. If you don't stand up for yourself, no one else will, either."

"And after the verdict, gays did riot, and did that help any? Dan White ended up only serving five years."

"He turned up dead, didn't he?"

"Ernest, killing people is wrong. This won't end well for anybody."

"We'll see. I don't think this guy is ready to quit."

I wasn't. I went to my local Mormon congregation to find out who the bishop was, and then the following Sunday morning, I shot him as he headed to church hours ahead of the rest of his family. The news that evening reported how he'd left behind three young children, one of whom was suffering from leukemia.

"We forgive the person who did this," the bishop's wife said to the news camera. "We know for someone to commit this kind of act, he must have been pushed by pain as great as what we're feeling now."

The comment irritated me. I didn't need her forgiveness. I'd done nothing wrong. I remembered Hitler's secretary saying she thought he was a nice man. The bishop and all these other preachers could seem nice to a lot of people, but if they were creating a culture of hatred, they were far from innocent. I was *glad* I'd killed those people.

Then suddenly, the memory of Yigal Amir laughing as he talked of killing Yitzhak Rabin came to mind. I'd been appalled at the time, thinking, "Even if you thought you were justified, your response should be, 'Killing is a terrible thing. It was necessary, but it's an awful, awful thing to have had to do.'" Timothy McVeigh in Oklahoma City had laughed, too.

And I had laughed as well, I remembered now.

I went to the bedroom and knelt beside the bed to pray. "Heavenly Father, when I was in Chile on my mission, I was stoned with rocks as big as my fist. I didn't dust my shoes or take any kind of revenge. When I came out at my first job after college and got fired, I didn't seek vengeance. Turning the other cheek is one thing, but when does an attack become a Pearl Harbor that warrants an atomic bomb?

"The religious right allowed AIDS to go untreated and unresearched until millions were infected. Now millions are dead. Isn't that a bigger crime than the thousands killed in the World Trade Center? *Am* I doing the right thing by fighting back?"

I strained with all my spirit, but I didn't feel a clear answer, only confusion. The Mormons taught that confusion was a negative answer. Yet to accept that was to assume

Mormon teachings on answers to prayer were correct in the first place.

I knew the Mormon Church couldn't be true if it said being gay was wrong. Still, after so many years of indoctrination, it was impossible not to keep believing just a little. I picked up my Book of Mormon and opened it at random and started reading. I had kind of been hoping to open to the part where God kills all the wicked people in America with terrible disasters during Christ's crucifixion.

Instead, I turned to a section talking about the Anti-Nephi-Lehies, the small group of Lamanites who had been converted to the truth by Ammon and seceded from the larger, evil contingent of Lamanites by becoming Ammonites. They had committed so many murders as Lamanites they were afraid God would never forgive them, so they committed to lives of non-violence, refusing even to defend themselves when the other Lamanites attacked them.

Then, as the Lamanites watched them humbly allow themselves to be slaughtered, many thousands of them converted to the truth as well.

I slammed the book shut in disgust and pulled Tony over and fucked him. Then I sucked him off and let him piss in my mouth.

"I love you," Tony breathed as he let the stream flow through my lips. I swallowed and tickled his balls in response.

The next day at work, I made several mistakes in my court reporting. It was the trial of a battered woman who'd chosen to kill her husband rather than simply divorce him.

"He'd have followed me anywhere and never left me in peace," she claimed. I accidentally wrote, "He followed me everywhere and never let me pee." I was letting my personal life affect me too much.

Tony and I watched the news during dinner, and there was another preacher being quoted. I sighed deeply. "Gays cannot procreate. They can only prolong their kind by recruiting. But they are naturally bringing themselves to extinction with AIDS, and we must do whatever we can to ensure they do become extinct. It's either them or us. If we are sinful enough to allow their kind to flourish, God will exterminate us all."

"Turn that shit off," said Tony. "I'm so sick of it."

"I saw on the internet there's going to be a gay peace rally this weekend. Gays are getting together to ask for peace on both sides."

"Yeah?"

"You want to go?"

"Do *you*?"

I nodded. "I think so."

"What if some right-wingers attack us? Are you going to bring a gun to the rally?"

"No." I paused. "Do you suppose sometimes even the innocent can become religiously contaminated, like the preachers are, and do terrible things in the name of righteousness?"

"It happens all the time."

"I'm not sure living is worth the trouble if you have to become a murderer to do it."

"Those two boys deserved what happened to them."

"Yes, they did. But it was just as much a sin for them to force me to shoot as it was for them to try to kill us in the first place."

"You'd rather we let them murder us?"

"If we die for proclaiming that love is more important than hate, doesn't that make us martyrs?"

"Who wants to be a martyr?"

I wondered. Was allowing the wicked to trample on us unchecked the same as condoning their actions? Would I be responsible for promoting hatred if I didn't oppose it as strongly as possible?

All I knew was that I was making an oath now to never shed blood again, even in my own self-defense. Or in the defense of the man I loved.

I doubted that would count in my favor on Judgment Day. I'd be responsible for my own partner's death as well. That couldn't be good, either.

I thought again of the Ammonites. While they never broke their oath, their children weren't under the same obligation. When they were old enough, they fought to defend themselves against the Lamanites. They shed blood righteously.

I frowned. Was such a thing even possible? Perhaps that story alone proved the Book of Mormon wasn't true.

After dinner, Tony and I listened to Toni Braxton and Brandi Carlyle and R.E.M. as we played Hangman and then gin rummy. We drank a cup of coffee, and I wondered for the thousandth time if I was sinning for taking a sip. God, why was religion so ridiculous in its oppression?

When Tony went to take a shower, I took a brief drive to throw my pawn shop gun into a canal. We went to bed at 10:00 and slept fitfully for a few hours, kicking each other several times. I finally relaxed and began dreaming, of Paradise, something I rarely dreamed of. There were flowering trees, and tulips, and daffodils, and a kitten playing with a puppy. Tony and I were standing under an arbor covered with jasmine. We were getting married. I knew I loved him, and I could feel his love for me.

I smiled in anticipation as Tony leaned over to kiss me.

Then I felt a sharp pain in my leg and jerked awake when Tony screamed. For some reason, I screamed, too.

"There, there," I whispered into Tony's ear, my arm across his chest, pulling him close.

"Sorry about that."

"It'll be okay."

He sighed. "Will it?"

"Yes, everything's going to be fine."

Just then, the light above us flashed on, and in the glare, I could see someone in our bedroom doorway. It was the third teen from the passing car all those weeks ago. He was pointing a gun at us. My registered one was in the bedside table.

At least the police wouldn't find the other one here.

Tony clutched my hand.

I watched as the boy's finger moved slowly on the trigger. Then he smiled and squeezed.

Tony didn't shout, and neither did I.

Mormon Movie Marathon

"You got the popcorn?" I asked.

"Sure do, Steffan," Audrey replied. "You got the beer?"

"Two six-packs."

"That'll get us through the first movie, anyway." She laughed.

We put our goodies in the car and took off for Sheri's house on the far side of Denver. It was the first weekend in April, time for General Conference, but the Ex-Mormon Club didn't have the patience to listen to ten hours of staid conference talks over a two-day period. Still, our inner culture called for us to gather like monarch butterflies, so we instead sat down to a weekend movie marathon. The only catch was that we had to watch Mormon movies.

Hence the beer.

Irene often sprung for the pot, now that it was legal. Most of us still didn't like smoking, so Irene usually gave the marijuana to Sheri to put in her brownies. Cal usually brought cookies, chips and dip, David brought pizza, and Viridiana brought soda. Audrey and I were the only couple attending these meetings. Cal and David both had wives who were still active in the Church. Sheri and Audrey had left before marrying in the temple and married non-members who weren't interested in anything Mormon. Viridiana was still single.

The Ex-Mormon Club met once a month, usually on the first Saturday. We sometimes sang Primary songs or belted out our favorite hymns in the language of the countries where we'd served missions. I sang in Spanish, Audrey in Italian, Cal in Dutch, David in Japanese, and Viridiana in French.

But over the last couple of years, our meetings had turned more and more to simply watching a Mormon movie and discussing it. Sometimes, we watched "good" films, like *The Best Two Years* or *The Other Side of Heaven*, but to be honest, there weren't many in this category.

So we more often watched films we could laugh at, such as *God's Army*, *The Home Teachers*, or *Mobsters and Mormons*. Some films were intentionally funny, but there were far more that were humorous for their naïve intensity. Some just made us shake our heads, like *Day of Defense*, an imaginary tale of two missionaries put on trial in the U.S. for preaching. Mormons were nothing if not paranoid.

Then again, there was *The Saratov Approach*, the true story of two elders kidnapped, beaten, and held for ransom in Russia.

I thought about the time a group of teenagers had stoned my companion and me back in Ecuador.

"What's on the playlist today?" I asked as Sheri let us into her house.

"*Beauty and the Beast: A Latter-Day Tale, Baptists at our Barbecue,* and *American Mormon in Europe,*" she replied. "You know, it's the sequel to the film we saw last month, *American Mormon.*"

"A classic." Audrey rolled her eyes.

That film had been a documentary about the ridiculous things non-Mormons believed about Latter-day Saints. Ignorance was never all that funny to me. There were plenty of legitimate things not to like about Mormons, plenty of truly outrageous things they did or believed. There was no need to invent fantasies about them.

Though I did miss the Celestial Room, I had to admit. And I'd always found the one-piece garments rather comfortable.

"Hi, Cal," Audrey said, giving the man a hug. "Hey, David." Another hug.

David irritated me a little. He was still hung up on polygamy, only now in his "enlightened" state of mind, he was also into polyandry, and had on more than one occasion mentioned wife-swapping. "Not today, buddy," I would say each time he made the suggestion.

"Maybe I'm asking the wrong person, Steffan," he told me last time. "Next time, I'll just ask Audrey."

The comment made me grumpy for weeks. Of course Audrey had the right to make these kinds of decisions on her own.

But she was *my* wife.

"It's almost 10:00," said Viridiana. "Anyone want to watch the opening prayer and opening hymn before we get started?" General Conference in Salt Lake was always televised.

"Not particularly." Irene waved. "You need any help with those brownies, Sheri?"

"Under control."

Soon we were settled around the living room, and Sheri put the DVD of *Beauty and the Beast* into the player. It was the story of a sweet woman, Belle, who goes to work for a crotchety man because her father had accidentally broken an expensive vase the man owned. During the course of her stay at his house, she learns he really isn't such a bad guy after all. Life is great, and everyone lives happily ever after.

"She's almost as pretty as you, Audrey," David said at one point.

"Can it," I told him.

"Mormons certainly believe in true love," Viridiana said after the film was over. "Did you guys ever see that many perfect marriages in the Church?"

David and Cal looked at each other. "My marriage wasn't perfect even before I left and Sandy stayed," said Cal. "We argue now over how to raise the children, how to spend the weekend, what movies we or the kids can see, what organizations we can donate to. The Church is right about one thing—mixed marriages are a problem."

"My husband goes to church almost every week," Sheri countered, "but he doesn't much care that I don't go. He does his thing, and I do mine."

That hardly counted, I thought. Her husband wasn't even a member.

"You sound close." Viridiana smirked.

"We read books together and take walks and have wild, passionate sex. What else do we need?"

"You doing anything next Friday night, Sheri?" David asked.

She ignored him.

During the last several months, this kind of banter had begun to get on my nerves. They were just trying to have fun, but their fun had begun to feel decadent. "Can't we talk about something more pleasant?" I asked.

"Sure," said Irene. "Like what?"

I grabbed a handful of chips and put a couple in my mouth. I didn't want to talk about work, which was driving me bonkers. The kids were giving me nightmares, and politics was an even worse topic than religion. "Anyone seen any good movies lately?" I managed.

Everyone laughed, thinking I was making a joke, and I felt my cheeks burning. Last month, we'd watched *Passage to Zarahemla*, the story of two wayward teenagers who leave Los Angeles to stay with relatives in Utah, but on the way, there is a big earthquake, and a time portal whisks them back in time to a battle between the Nephites and Lamanites, where they learn the true importance of being good.

I actually considered renting it for my own young teens, but I knew Audrey wouldn't approve.

It was almost noon. General Conference had a two-hour session beginning at 10:00, another starting at 2:00, and an evening Priesthood session for the men beginning at 6:00. I remembered the days when that had felt fulfilling. But our little group didn't have the patience to spend an entire day together to mimic that schedule. David put two pizzas in the oven, and the first beers were passed around.

I still didn't approve of drinking, so I continued to pour Viridiana's 7-Up for myself. I was always the designated driver when we went anyplace Audrey might have alcohol. I'd deliberately brought only enough to provide two beers per person, not wanting any of the group to drive home intoxicated. Plus, I thought it might help Audrey feel guilty if she had a third or fourth, knowing there wouldn't be enough for the others.

"Time for *Baptists at our Barbecue*," Sheri announced, slipping the new disk into the DVD player.

We sat back to watch again. I put my hand on Audrey's shoulder and stole a glance at David, who was looking at Irene. The pizza seemed appropriate for a movie about a barbecue, certainly less messy than wings. I tried to relax and enjoy myself. The movie was a comedy, after all, the story of a small town with 262 Mormons and 262 Baptists, who keep feuding until everyone learns their place and a fledgling romance can bloom.

The others laughed at the appropriate places, but the only thing I could think of again was mixed marriages. What would Audrey do if I started going back to church?

I had a couple of brownies. For some reason, eating them didn't seem as offensive as smoking or drinking. I was quite sure the Nephites had done something similar, that the reason it wasn't mentioned in the Book of Mormon was because it wasn't sinful.

Not that there was any truth to the Book of Mormon in the first place.

For that matter, there was no condemnation of tobacco or alcohol in the Book of Mormon either. So why those vices bothered me in any event, I didn't know.

And who cared what the Book of Mormon said anyway?

Audrey was on her third beer by the time the film ended, laughing at every joke in the screenplay.

I missed structure.

I remembered other movies we'd seen, stupid films we were supposed to scorn, like *The RM*, about a returned missionary who doesn't receive the blessings he thinks he deserves for his service, considers leaving the Church, but who in the end does the right thing for the sake of doing the right thing, regardless of his earthly blessings. And *The Singles Ward*, where a newly divorced man basically experiences the same dilemma but miraculously ends up with a new love interest anyway.

It was odd to see gospel principles in action, fleshed out in the lives of others, even if those others were caricatures. It was a bit…haunting.

"This is fun," said David, motioning for Audrey to give him a sip of her beer, which she did grudgingly. "We ought to do it more often than just General Conference."

"You want to have another movie marathon for the Days of '47?" Irene asked.

"Sure!"

I could feel my lip curling.

David winked at Audrey. She seemed oblivious, eyeing the kitchen as if contemplating a fourth beer.

"Would you like some 7-Up, dear?" I asked.

Now it was time for her lip to curl.

"I'd like another brownie," Viridiana announced. "And a cookie."

"I'm not in the mood for *American Mormon in Europe* anymore," said Sheri. "I brought an alternative just in case. How do you guys feel about *Pride and Prejudice: A Latter-Day Comedy?*"

There were some groans, since it sounded so similar to the first film we'd seen today, but I wasn't particularly in the mood for a documentary, either, so I agreed along with everyone else, and Sheri put the film in the machine. It was almost funny watching a Jane Austen tale adapted for LDS standards, since really Jane Austen even by Jane Austen standards fit quite well within the Church's moral universe. The biggest difference in this version was that the characters were all attending Brigham Young University in Provo, but otherwise, the story was familiar.

And a bit lackluster.

And yet…there was something appealing about watching a classic story with Mormon characters. It was validating somehow.

I wanted to see *The Hunchback of Notre Dame* retold as a Mormon story. And *Angels and Demons*. And *A Tale of Two Cities*. And *Hamlet*.

Or even versions of other movies. *Foul Play, Finding Nemo, Romancing the Stone, Sister Act*.

But I wasn't sure any of those could truly be told from an LDS point of view. Thinking about it as I watched the closing credits, I felt a longing I wished I didn't feel.

It was so hard to escape Mormonism. Sometimes, I wondered if celebrating "the culture" was doing us more harm than good. Mormons always criticized those who left, asking pointedly, "Why can't you ever really leave?" I wondered if maybe Audrey and I should stop coming to these meetings altogether.

I missed the sons of Mosiah.

Audrey stumbled on a cast off shoe on her way to the kitchen, and David rushed to support her. I could hear them giggling in the kitchen. "We need more beer," I heard Audrey shout.

"It's time to go home anyway," I returned.

"Aw nuts," was her reply. Then more giggling.

Both Audrey and David were wiping their lips when they came back from the kitchen, David with a leering grin on his face, like the guys on the Cialis commercials.

I thought of the movie we watched in December, *Christmas for a Dollar*, about a poor family who make each other's dreams come true with love, not money.

"Good to see everyone," I said, taking Audrey's arm. "It's always fun to be with you guys."

"I need to get going, too," Cal said, putting his shoes back on.

"Me as well," said Irene.

"Need some help cleaning up, Sheri?" David asked.

"I'm good, thanks."

Soon Audrey and I were in the car, heading back for the other side of Denver. Audrey was resting her head against the back of the seat, her eyes closed. I looked up at the bright blue sky above us, with just a couple of tiny white clouds drifting by.

I missed the gilded Moroni on top of the temple, holding his horn aloft for everyone to see.

I wasn't all that sure I wanted to attend any more of the club's activities. But I wasn't sure I wanted to let Audrey attend by herself, either.

Mixed marriages.

We'd stay up late this evening watching our regular Saturday night suspense movie. And come morning, I'd let

Audrey sleep in, while I put on my suit and tie and went back to the ward meetinghouse for the first time in almost five years.

I wondered what stories I'd hear from my old friends.

I wondered if any of them would be as good as *Charly*.

Circumcising the Hivites

"Thankful! Oh, Thankful!"

"Coming, Mother." The eleven-year-old finished tying the blue bow onto her blond hair and smoothed out the lace on her collar. Just three more hours until her cousins came. Three more hours before the fun began, before she could get back at her parents.

"Thankful! Thankful Root! You get down here this minute, young lady! We'll be late for church."

Thankful swooshed down the stairs in her knee-length blue dress, waiting on the bottom step for her mother's approval. Whenever she'd try to simply head from her room straight for the car, her mother would grab her by the shoulder and turn her around to inspect her. Now, Thankful posed on the bottom step to get it over with.

"Aren't you just lovely!" her mother cooed. "Andy, isn't she lovely?"

"Yeah," said her father. "Come on. Let's get on the road."

Thankful sat carefully in the back seat so as not to wrinkle her dress, and her father started the car. Soon they were on their way through the rolling hills to the little LDS church in the southern Mississippi countryside. It was one of the few Mormon congregations in the south that had been around for over a hundred years. Thankful had been told many times she should appreciate that she came from good Mormon stock. Fourth-generation Mormons weren't common outside of Utah. She had responsibilities because of her great blessings.

Thankful peered out the window, counting the bulls in the pastures they passed. Cows didn't interest her much. Only the bulls seemed worth noting, perhaps because there were fewer of them. Especially Brahmas. She liked the way they reminded her of that hunchback movie from the 1930's she'd sneaked up late one night to see.

"Oh, look at the bunny rabbit, dear," said her mother, pointing. "Isn't that adorable?"

"It's beautiful," breathed Thankful, but she was looking at a rusty tractor half hidden by weeds. That was the best part of living in the country, she thought. Her cousins had to live in the suburbs up in Jackson where everything was always so clean, where her uncle mowed the lawn each week and her aunt shopped in the closed-in malls. Her two cousins, Terry and Leslie, had such boring, city names. You couldn't even tell which one was the boy and which was the girl. They weren't really bad sorts as far as cousins went. A little dull, but so were the kids at school.

Thankful might even like her cousins if only her mother would stop saying, "Oh, Thankful, couldn't you be more like Leslie? She's always so clean." Every time Thankful heard it, she wanted to push Leslie into the pond. On their last visit, Leslie had made a casual comment at the dinner table that she really liked Thankful's 1909 edition of *A Girl of the Limberlost*. Thankful had found it in near perfect condition at a rummage sale her mother had dragged her along to, and she loved that old, beautiful book.

But once Leslie had complimented Thankful's mother on the book, her mother insisted that Leslie take the book with her. "Thankful's read that book three times already. It would make us both happy if you could enjoy the book, too."

What was Leslie going to walk away with today, Thankful wondered. She didn't believe Leslie was deliberately calculating, but even her innocent praise could bring grief to Thankful, so she had hidden a few of her more precious things.

But what if Leslie simply ended up taking some of Thankful's dignity? If Thankful's mother said anything today about how pretty Leslie looked, or about how nice her manners were, or about how well she spoke, Thankful just wasn't sure she could take it. She might have to spill some gravy on her at dinner.

And if Leslie talked about her china doll collection for half an hour again, maybe Thankful would simply have to throw up on her. She'd never vomited on cue before, but she could try. Perhaps it was a bit extreme, she thought, but at some point, innocence wasn't an excuse. Leslie had to pay for the trouble she was causing.

Thankful's father pulled into the gravel parking lot of the church and stopped the car. Thankful climbed out but then stood in front of her mother's door, waiting for the last inspection before she could run off to join her classmates. Her mother brushed a strand of hair behind Thankful's ear and then kissed her lightly on the nose.

"Now, you have a nice time in Sunday School, dear. I want to hear all about it on the way home. Listen for something nice to share with Leslie." They'd come an hour late today, missing the first meeting, coming only for Sunday School and Sacrament, having stayed late at the house getting it ready for the visit. Thankful didn't mind, though. Sometimes, church seemed too much like living in the suburbs.

Thankful kissed her mother and then skipped off into the building ahead of her parents. Once inside, she sighed and walked the rest of the way to her classroom. She could see the other students covering their mouths as they whispered to each other, and it was plain that Sally Kyzar was plotting something with Nelda Lee Smith. And all because of what had happened the other day at the creek.

Well, it wasn't her fault. If Thankful's mother hadn't made her invite all the girls from her class on a picnic, she'd never have had Sally pull up the string on the bridge. But the back pasture was her territory. No one else was going to invade it. Even Terry and Leslie she only took to the big pasture or along the road. The back pasture was for her, the cows, and for the bull.

Thankful sat down in a metal folding chair by the window and looked outside. A lizard crawled along the outer sill and then across a lower pane. Thankful stared at its underside, trying to memorize it so she could draw it later.

"You like lizards?" someone asked.

Thankful turned. It was Jerry Lyn White, who'd never once talked to her before. In fact, he hardly ever talked to anyone, probably because the others laughed about how ugly his hair looked, poorly cut by either his mother or his father, or maybe by himself. Once, Nelda Lee had told him, "Why don't you just shave your head? It'd be easier on all of us." Even now, Nelda Lee was whispering to her friends and pointing at him.

"Yes, I like them," Thankful said bluntly. "Lizards don't hurt anyone." She wondered if she should have answered, though. It felt strange talking normally to someone else.

"Ooh, sick!" said Nelda Lee, holding her stomach. "It figures. She probably likes snakes, too!" Then she stomped off to the other side of the room.

Thankful was glad Nelda Lee had gone because she didn't want the other girls to know about the snakes, not so much because she worried they'd like her even less, but because she didn't think them worthy of hearing about even her minor likes and dislikes.

She probably shouldn't even have mentioned the lizards, but she'd been surprised to hear someone who seemed interested in her. Sure, Jerry Lyn was a nobody, but it was clear if anyone else was going to be interested in her, it would be another nobody. That was certainly a lot better than being liked by the popular kids.

"*Do* you like snakes?" Jerry Lyn asked, dropping his eyes shyly, glancing nervously across the room at the others, as if afraid they'd hear or see him talking to her. He probably realized he was going to be teased later for this. It touched her that he was willing to make the sacrifice. She hadn't expected this.

"Just the harmless ones," she said. "You know, the black snakes, the garter snakes, the king snakes. You have to be careful with the king snakes, though, because some of them look a lot like coral snakes."

"Can you tell the difference?" asked Jerry Lyn.

"Of course."

He smiled, and Thankful smiled back. She hadn't realized there could be someone else out there who was interested in the same things she was. She wondered if he liked to climb up silage pits and look for honey trees, too. The chair next to Thankful was empty because no one else ever wanted to sit next to her, so Thankful motioned to it and Jerry Lyn sat down.

The lesson today was about selling Joseph into Egypt, and Thankful wondered what kind of animals the brothers meant when they told their father about the beasts that were supposed to have eaten Joseph. She wondered if there were still a few dinosaurs around back then, or at least a saber-toothed tiger.

When the class was letting out, Thankful wanted to say something to Jerry Lyn, maybe invite him over one day to go on a walk or something, but he headed off as soon as the door opened. Thankful shrugged, pushed past Sally and Nelda Lee, who were blocking the aisle, and joined her parents for Sacrament meeting in the chapel.

Thankful liked the worship service because she didn't have to make a report of the talks and therefore didn't have to pay attention. Instead, she opened her Bible and read. She had a couple of stories she liked to read over and over. From the Book of Mormon, she liked the story of Coriantumr cutting off Shiz's head, and Shiz still trying to get up and fight.

But there were even better stories from the Bible. One was about the time Jacob's family made all the Hivites get circumcised and then killed every one of them while they were still sore. Another was about the horses trampling Jezebel and the dogs eating her. And she especially liked the one about Elisha cursing the little children who were mocking him about his bald head, and how two she-bears came out of the woods and killed forty-two of the horrid brats.

Thankful's mother never asked which stories she was reading but instead just smiled down at her for a second and then looked back toward the pulpit.

As she was going out the front door of the building after the meeting, Thankful saw Sally and Nelda Lee laughing and talking to Jerry Lyn. She'd never seen them talk to him like that before. What could he have to say to popular kids like them? Before Thankful could turn away, Sally glanced over and pointed. Then all three of them moved their arms in a wavy fashion and laughed again.

He did it, she thought, a chill running down her spine. He told them. Thankful felt her face harden and hoped she wasn't turning red. She glanced quickly down at the gravel in the parking lot.

"Oh, your friends are waving goodbye, Thankful. Why don't you wave back?"

Thankful thought about refusing or about saying she already had, but instead she smiled sweetly and waved enthusiastically back at the others.

Soon she was home, and while she was able to get out of her good dress, Sunday was the one day each week Thankful still had to wear a dress around the house. That usually meant she had to read instead of play outside, but she liked to read and didn't really mind staying inside one day a week. It was nicer to read about people than to be with them, so she sometimes liked reading on other days, too. She had an old copy of *The Witches* that she liked a lot, but she was certainly going to keep that hidden today.

Reading was better than having to practice the piano, anyway, because playing always led to a recital in front of people who hoped she'd make a mistake, letting their own child look better. Thankful remembered the time her mother had insisted she practice her music, right while she was in the middle of a good book.

Thankful had gone to the piano, sat down at the bench, and run one hand absentmindedly up and down the keyboard while she held her book in the other hand. She'd managed to get away with it for almost fifteen minutes.

Today, though, rather than read, Thankful had to help cook dinner because her aunt, uncle, and cousins were coming down for a visit. Thankful cut the tomatoes, set the table, and put a rubber spider on the chair where she knew Leslie always sat. Her father, sitting in the rocking chair near the kitchen door and reading the paper, saw her put the spider down and slowly shook his head. Thankful sighed and put the spider away.

She wanted to do something to get back at these people, but she didn't like the idea that she was stooping to their level. It was too difficult deciding what to do, as she almost always did something worse than she should have. One time, a couple of years ago, Leslie said her mother told her not to pet Thankful's cat because it probably had ticks. She wasn't supposed to get too close to Thankful either since Thankful touched the cat.

Thankful had waited a little while and then showed Leslie her walk-in closet. She'd closed the door behind them, saying she had something special to show Leslie, and had then given her a long hug and a kiss, telling her how much she loved her as a cousin. Leslie had looked uncomfortable enough just for that, but then Thankful had shrieked that something was crawling on Leslie's neck, and the girl had run screaming out of the house.

Thankful wondered if Leslie remembered that day. Thankful did, and smiled, but though it was fun getting people, it made her feel cold inside, too, and she wished she didn't have to feel that way. But it was always their fault. They forced her to do these things. She was sometimes amazed she didn't do anything worse than she did.

She wondered if she'd have to do anything today. If her mother said just one thing about Leslie's hair, Thankful wasn't sure she'd be able to resist. The pond had some algae on it right now. That might improve Leslie's complexion.

By 1:00, the relatives had arrived, and everyone sat down to dinner. Leslie was Thankful's age and sat next to her, but Terry was two years younger and sat next to his sister rather than on the other side of Thankful. It had been six months since they'd last been together, up in Jackson, but Terry must have remembered the day when they'd come upon a dead dog that had been badly mangled, lying in the road, and Thankful had said, "Looks like my mother's homemade jam."

Terry had run off toward the house, and he'd refused to eat any of the strawberry jam or chicken salad or anything else Thankful's mother had brought. He seemed willing enough to eat now, Thankful noticed, as long as he wasn't close enough to hear her say anything about the food. The funny thing was that Thankful hadn't even been trying to gross him out. She wondered if she really were just a little sick. But as soon as that thought entered her head, she felt stifled. She wanted to get up from the table and run outside.

"Have some of the fruit salad," Thankful's mother said, gesturing toward Terry and Leslie. "Thankful made it herself. She's getting to be quite a help in the kitchen these days."

"Oh, no, Mother," said Thankful. "I could never have made it without your recipe. You make it so easy to do well in the kitchen."

Thankful's mother beamed and handed the large bowl of fruit salad to Terry, who took it halfheartedly and peered into it for several seconds before picking up the spoon. Thankful smiled and passed the rolls to her aunt.

After dinner was over, the two women stayed in the kitchen to talk, and the two men drifted out to the living room. Divisions bored Thankful, so she ran outside, and Leslie and Terry followed after her.

"What would you like to do?" Leslie asked.

"Shoot baskets?" suggested Thankful. She had talked her father into nailing a basketball hoop up on the tree in the front yard a few months earlier. Her mother had protested at first, but when Thankful had promised to embroider a cloth for her dresser if she'd relent, her mother finally gave in.

"No, I don't feel like it," said Leslie.

"What do you want to do?" Thankful asked.

"Let's go swimming in the creek," said Terry.

"We just ate," Leslie argued. "We can't go swimming. We'll get a cramp and drown."

"Want to climb a tree?" asked Thankful. She was still in a dress, but her mother would just have to make some allowances if she got dirty today, since she was obligated to entertain her cousins.

"Nah."

Well, what *did* they want to do, Thankful grumbled to herself. She wasn't about to show them any of her special places. City kids ought to be satisfied with simple country things. They didn't need her special ones.

"How about walking in the garden?" suggested Thankful.

"Boring," said Leslie.

If Leslie didn't watch it, Thankful thought, she was going to have her pull up that string on the bridge like she had Sally do.

"Want to look at the pond?" asked Thankful. Or the algae, she thought.

"No."

"I want to look at the creek," Terry insisted.

"Let's cross the creek and go look at your cows," said Leslie.

"Yeah," agreed Terry. "Let's. Let's."

"Let's do," said Leslie.

Thankful turned away from them and glared at their car for a moment. She tried desperately to think of some other activity she could suggest, but she was too angry to think clearly. Why did everyone want to invade her? Why couldn't they just leave her alone? She was not going to give up without a fight. They'd be sorry they'd been so hard to please. They'd see what they'd get when they tried to take away her private alone space.

Thankful's eyes set again on the car. Then she turned back with a little smile. "Okay, let's go," she said, scattering two of the chickens pecking nearby as she started off toward the fence. She'd take her cousins as far as the creek, anyway. But they weren't about to get any further. She walked past the feed room, Leslie and Terry following.

"Where's your cat?" asked Leslie. "Didn't you used to have a cat?"

"Died two weeks ago," Thankful said. "Someone poisoned him." She held the top barbed wire of the fence up and motioned for the others to crawl through.

"Poor thing."

Thankful led the way around the barn and past the pond. Then they walked through the little gullies and down across the bottoms, the level pasture that led to the creek and which sometimes flooded during heavy rains. Thankful paused at the maple gum tree, one of the few trees left to dot the pasture to provide shade on really hot days. It was the same tree she'd climbed and stayed in overnight the day her parents butchered her pet pig.

Thankful remembered the day they'd bought the pig years ago, how her parents had said Thankful could help raise it, that she could give it a name, that it would be her pig. Thankful had loved feeding Fat Pat table scraps, and she'd loved scratching behind his ears.

Thankful's mother tried to stop her from playing with him so much, but Fat Pat always rushed to the fence to greet her and loved to have her come in and play for a bit, always in a clean part of the pen, of course.

But one day a couple of years later, Thankful's mother told her not to go out to the pen, that Fat Pat was old enough and big enough now to help with the food bill. Thankful had run out of the house toward the pen, but before she could get there, she'd heard a shot, then a high-pitched squealing noise, and another shot.

Thankful had sat by the pond the rest of that day while her parents strung up the pig in the back yard, cut him up, and prepared all the meat. The next day, when Thankful opened the refrigerator door and saw Fat Pat's face and heard her mother say, "Would you like some hogshead cheese, dear?" Thankful had run screaming out of the house and down to the bottoms, where she'd climbed the tree and stayed all night.

Two weeks ago, that hadn't been far enough. When a spiteful neighbor, tired of having his cats get pregnant, poisoned her cat, John-boy, her mother had merely said, "Well, we must be forgiving. We must be thankful we had him as long as we did."

The pond wasn't far enough to go then, and neither was the bottoms. Thankful had crossed the creek and gone on to the back pasture, where she liked to play more and more because her mother never went out that far. But when Thankful went back to the house and her mother suggested she invite the girls from her Sunday School class on a picnic down by the creek, to show God how she could be loving and think of others even when she was sad, it just seemed too much.

Without protesting, Thankful agreed, but then she calmly walked back outside and picked up the sack her mother had put the cat in until Thankful's father could come back to bury it. Thankful got a long piece of twine from the barn and carried the sack down to the creek.

After tying one end of the twine to the middle plank on the wooden bridge, she tied the other end to the cat's neck and lowered him into the muddy water. When the Sunday School girls came along a few days later, Thankful had asked one of them, that nasty Sally Kyzar, to pull up the string, saying there was a picnic surprise at the end of it.

"There's the creek," Terry said. He picked up a twig and tossed it into the water, watching it slowly float off. "Gee, it must be nice to live out here. All we've got is a row of bushes with wasp nests in the front yard, and one pecan tree in the back."

"Yeah," said Leslie. "We never have as much fun at home as we do here. There's too many kids around for us to take walks at home. You always run into a bully. Or a dog."

"Don't you think we're all a bunch of hicks out here in the country?" Thankful asked, walking out onto the bridge and then stopping. She glanced down briefly to make sure the string was still tied to the plank.

"They have just as many hicks in the city," Leslie replied. "They're just a different kind of hick." Thankful smiled in spite of herself but forced the smile away.

"Ooh, honeysuckle!" said Terry, trotting across the bridge to smell the sweet white flowers.

Leslie broke off a few blades of grass and then stepped out onto the bridge. Sitting down, she tossed the first blade into the water and watched it drift off. "I'll bet you come here a lot, don't you?" Leslie asked Thankful, who stood watching the blade of grass as it bumped along one side of the bank and finally snagged in some briars.

"What do you mean?" Thankful was afraid of giving away her secrets and didn't want to admit to anything just yet. She looked down at the string which disappeared into the water.

"When I want to get away from my folks, the only place I can go is my room, and my mom still walks in on me. It must be nice to come out here. I know I'd like it if I could get away."

"Yeah," shouted Terry from the bank. He leaned over to watch a beetle crawl over the dirt path and into the grass, and then he came back out on the bridge.

Thankful looked at them and wondered for the first time if maybe they weren't trying to escape into rather than invade her territory. Or were they fake refugees like Jerry Lyn? Or was she the one who was like Jerry Lyn, pretending to take an interest while all along plotting a way to hurt them?

Was she like those guys who'd made the Hivites vulnerable and then went in for the kill? Thankful tried to shake the idea from her head. It would be too dreadful to learn a lesson from the scriptures. She couldn't have that.

But there was Leslie, sitting on the bridge, watching the minnows dart about in the muddy water, and she was smiling. How could she know Thankful needed a private place, or even if she did, that this was it, and that no one else could be allowed to enter?

And when Leslie had suggested this might actually be that private place, hadn't she said it in a reverent way, in a grateful way for the chance to be there for even a few minutes? Hadn't Leslie been admitting she needed Thankful's help?

Thankful stared at Leslie's back, thinking. It might still be a trick, of course. She tried to remember any clues her cousin might have dropped that could help her decide. Why did people have to be so hard to figure out? It wasn't fair. Maybe—

"Hey, what's this?" asked Terry, pointing to the twine and kneeling to look over the side of the bridge. "It goes down into the water." He started to tug at the string.

Thankful looked at Terry, whose face glowed with the anticipation of finding Indian treasure at the base of a fifteen-year-old bridge, and she saw Leslie looking over with mild interest, still holding a blade of grass in her hand.

"Let's go," Thankful said suddenly, pulling Terry to his feet.

"Huh? Why?" asked Terry.

"I want to show you the cows," said Thankful. "And our bull. Y'all are only staying for the afternoon. And we still haven't climbed up the banks along the road yet. Or played in the silage pit. We've got a lot to do."

She grabbed Leslie by the hand and began running with both cousins into the back pasture, heading toward the cows chewing contentedly, and the lone bull staring dully out toward them.

Books by Johnny Townsend

Thanks for reading! If you enjoyed this book, could you please take a few minutes to write a review online? Reviews are helpful both to me as an author and to other readers, so we'd all sincerely appreciate your writing one! And if you did enjoy the book, here are some others I've written you might want to look up:

Mormon Underwear

Zombies for Jesus

A Gay Mormon Missionary in Pompeii

The Golem of Rabbi Loew

Marginal Mormons

Mormon Bullies

The Mormon Victorian Society

Going-Out-Of-Religion Sale

Gayrabian Nights

Missionaries Make the Best Companions

Invasion of the Spirit Snatchers

The Washing of Brains

Interview with a Mission President

Weeping, Wailing, and Gnashing of Teeth

Behind the Bishop's Door

The Moat around Zion

The Last Days Linger

Mormon Madness

Human Compassion for Beginners

Dead Mankind Walking

Breaking the Promise of the Promised Land

I Will, Through the Veil

Am I My Planet's Keeper?

Have Your Cum and Eat It, Too

Strangers with Benefits

Constructing Equity

Wake Up and Smell the Missionaries

Racism by Proxy

Orgy at the STD Clinic

Life Is Better with Love

Please Evacuate

Recommended Daily Humanity

The Camper Killings

Kinky Quilts: Patchwork Designs for Gay Men

Inferno in the French Quarter: The UpStairs Lounge Fire

Latter-Gay Saints: An Anthology of Gay Mormon Fiction (co-editor)

Available from your favorite online or neighborhood bookstore.

Wondering what some of those other books are about? Read on!

Invasion of the Spirit Snatchers

During the Apocalypse, a group of Mormon survivors in Hurricane, Utah gather in the home of the

Relief Society president, telling stories to pass the time as they ration their food storage and await the Second Coming. But this is no ordinary group of Mormons— or perhaps it is. They are the faithful, feminist, gay, apostate, and repentant, all working together to help each other through the darkest days any of them have yet seen.

Gayrabian Nights

Gayrabian Nights is a twist on the well-known classic, *1001 Arabian Nights*, in which Scheherazade, under the threat of death if she ceases to captivate King Shahryar's attention, enchants him through a series of mysterious, adventurous, and romantic tales.

In this variation, a male escort, invited to the hotel room of a closeted, homophobic Mormon senator, learns that the man is poised to vote on a piece of anti-gay legislation the following morning. To prevent him from sleeping, so that the exhausted senator will miss casting his vote on the Senate floor, the escort entertains him with stories of homophobia, celibacy, mixed orientation marriages, reparative therapy, coming out, first love, gay marriage, and long-term successful gay relationships. The escort crafts the stories to give the senator a crash course in gay culture and sensibilities, hoping to bring the man closer to accepting his own sexual orientation.

Inferno in the French Quarter: The UpStairs Lounge Fire

On Gay Pride Day in 1973, someone set the entrance to a French Quarter gay bar on fire. In the terrible inferno that followed, thirty-two people lost their lives, including a third of the local congregation of the Metropolitan Community Church, their pastor burning to death halfway out a second-story window as he tried to claw his way to freedom. A mother who'd gone to the bar with her two gay sons died alongside them. A man who'd helped his friend escape first was found dead near the fire escape. Two children waited outside a movie theater across town for a father and "uncle" who would never pick them up. During this era of rampant homophobia, several families refused to claim the bodies, and many churches refused to bury the dead. Author Johnny Townsend pored through old records and tracked down survivors of the fire as well as relatives and friends of those killed to compile this fascinating account of a forgotten moment in gay history.

A Gay Mormon Missionary in Pompeii

What is a gay Mormon missionary doing in Italy? He is trying to save his own soul as well as the souls of others. In these tales chronicling the two-year mission of Robert Anderson, we see a young man tormented by his inability to be the man the Church says he should be. In addition to his personal hell, Anderson faces a major earthquake, organized crime, a serious bus accident, and much more. He copes with horrendous mission leaders and his own suicidal tendencies. But one day, he meets another missionary who loves him, and his world changes forever.

Missionaries Make the Best Companions

What lies behind the freshly scrubbed façades of the Mormon missionaries we see about town? In these stories, an ex-Mormon tries to seduce a faithful elder by showing him increasingly suggestive movies. A sister missionary fulfills her community service requirement by babysitting for a prostitute. Two elders break their mission rules by venturing into the forbidden French Quarter. A senior missionary couple try to reactivate lapsed members while their own family falls apart back home. A young man hopes that serving a second full-time mission will lead him up the Church hierarchy. Two bored missionaries decide to make a little extra money moonlighting in a male stripper club. Two frustrated elders find an acceptable way to masturbate—by donating to a Fertility Clinic. A lonely man searches for the favorite companion he hasn't seen in thirty years.

The Golem of Rabbi Loew

Jacob and Esau Cohen are the closest of brothers. In fact, they're lovers. A doctor tries to combine canine genes with those of Jews, to improve their chances of surviving a hostile world. A Talmudic scholar dates an escort. A scientist tries to develop the "God spot" in the brains of his patients in order to create a messiah. The Golem of Prague is really Rabbi Loew's secret lover. While some of the Jews in Townsend's book are Orthodox, this collection of Jewish stories most certainly is not.

The Last Days Linger

The scriptures tell us that in the Last Days, wickedness will increase upon the Earth. When leaders of the Mormon Church see a rise in the number of gay members, they believe the end is upon them. But while "wickedness never was happiness," it begins to appear that wickedness can sometimes be divine. At least, the stories here suggest that religious proscriptions condemning homosexuality have it all wrong. While gay Mormons may be no closer to perfection than anyone else, they're no further from it, either. And sometimes, being gay provides just the right ingredient to create saints—as flawed as God himself.

Mormon Madness

Mental illness can strike the faithful as easily as anyone else. But often religious doctrine and practice exacerbate rather than alleviate these problems. From schizophrenia to obsessive-compulsive disorder, from persecution complex to sexual dysfunction, autism to dissociative identity disorder, Mormons must cope with their mental as well as their spiritual health on a daily basis.

Am I My Planet's Keeper?

Global Warming. Climate Change. Climate Crisis. Climate Emergency. Whatever label we use, we are facing one of the greatest challenges to the survival of life as we know it.

But while addressing greenhouse gases is perhaps our most urgent need, it's not our only task. We must also address toxic waste, pollution, habitat destruction, and our other contributions to the world's sixth mass extinction event.

In order to do that, we must simultaneously address the unmet human needs that keep us distracted from deeper engagement in stabilizing our climate: moderating economic inequality, guaranteeing healthcare to all, and ensuring education for everyone.

And to accomplish *that*, we must unite to combat the monied forces that use fear, prejudice, and misinformation to manipulate us.

It's a daunting task. But success is our only option.

Wake Up and Smell the Missionaries

Two Mormon missionaries in Italy discover they share the same rare ability—both can emit pheromones on demand. At first, they playfully compete in the hills of Frascati to see who can tempt "investigators" most. But soon they're targeting each other non-stop.

Can two immature young men learn to control their "superpower" to live a normal life…and develop genuine love? Even as their relationship is threatened by the attentions of another man?

They seem just on the verge of success when a massive earthquake leaves them trapped under the rubble of their apartment in Castellammare.

With night falling and temperatures dropping, can they dig themselves out in time to save themselves? And will their injuries destroy the ability that brought them together in the first place?

Orgy at the STD Clinic

Todd Tillotson is struggling to move on after his husband is killed in a hit and run attack a year earlier during a Black Lives Matter protest in Seattle.

In this novel set entirely on public transportation, we watch as Todd, isolated throughout the pandemic, battles desperation in his attempt to safely reconnect with the world.

Will he find love again, even casual friendship, or will he simply end up another crazy old man on the bus?

Things don't look good until a man whose face he can't even see sits down beside him despite the raging variants.

And asks him a question that will change his life.

Please Evacuate

A gay, partygoing New Yorker unconcerned about the future or the unsustainability of capitalism is hit by a truck and thrust into a straight man's body half a continent away. As Hunter tries to figure out what's happening, he's caught up in another disaster, a wildfire sweeping through a Colorado community, the flames overtaking him and several schoolchildren as they flee.

When he awakens, Hunter finds himself in the body of yet another man, this time in northern Italy, a former missionary about to marry a young Mormon woman. Still piecing together this new reality, and beginning to embrace his latest identity, Hunter fights for his life in a devastating flash flood along with his wife *and* his new husband.

He's an aging worker in drought-stricken Texas, a nurse at an assisted living facility in the direct path of a hurricane, an advocate for the unhoused during a freak Seattle blizzard.

We watch as Hunter is plunged into life after life, finally recognizing the futility of only looking out for #1 and understanding the part he must play in addressing the global climate crisis…if he ever gets another chance.

Recommended Daily Humanity

A checklist of human rights must include basic housing, universal healthcare, equitable funding for public schools, and tuition-free college and vocational training.

In addition to the basics, though, we need much more to fully thrive. Subsidized childcare, universal pre-K, a universal basic income, subsidized high-speed internet, net neutrality, fare-free public transit (plus *more* public transit), and medically assisted death for the terminally ill who want it.

None of this will matter, though, if we neglect to address the rapidly worsening climate crisis.

Sound expensive? It is.

But not as expensive as refusing to implement these changes. The cost of climate disasters each year has grown to staggering figures. And the cost of social and political upheaval from not meeting the needs of suffering workers, families, and individuals may surpass even that.

It's best we understand that the vast sums required to enact meaningful change are an investment which will pay off not only in some indeterminate future but in fact almost immediately. And without these adjustments to our lifestyles and values, there may very well not be a future capable of sustaining freedom and democracy…or even civilization itself.

The Camper Killings

When a homeless man is found murdered a few blocks from Morgan Beylerian's house in south Seattle, everyone seems to consider the body just so much additional trash to be cleared from the neighborhood. But Morgan liked the guy. They used to chat when Morgan brought Nick groceries once a week.

And the brutal way the man was killed reminds Morgan of their shared Mormon heritage, back when the faithful agreed to have their throats slit if they ever revealed temple secrets.

Did Nick's former wife take action when her ex-husband refused to grant a temple divorce? Did his murder have something to do with the public accusations that brought an end to his promising career?

Morgan does his best to investigate when no one else seems to care, but it isn't easy as a man living paycheck to paycheck himself, only able to pursue his investigation via public transit.

As he continues his search for the killer, Morgan's friends withdraw and his husband threatens to leave. When another homeless man is killed and Morgan is accused of the crime, things look even bleaker.

But his troubles aren't over yet.

Will Morgan find the killer before the killer finds him?

What Readers Have Said

Townsend's stories are "a gay *Portnoy's Complaint* of Mormonism. Salacious, sweet, sad, insightful, insulting, religiously ethnic, quirky-faithful, and funny."

D. Michael Quinn, author of *The Mormon Hierarchy: Origins of Power*

"Told from a believably conversational first-person perspective, [*A Gay Mormon Missionary in Pompeii*'s] novelistic focus on Anderson's journey to thoughtful self-acceptance allows for greater character development than often seen in short stories, which makes this well-paced work rich and satisfying, and one of Townsend's strongest. An extremely important contribution to the field of Mormon fiction." Named to Kirkus Reviews' Best of 2011.

Kirkus Reviews

"The thirteen stories in *Mormon Underwear* capture this struggle [between Mormonism and homosexuality] with humor, sadness, insight, and sometimes shocking details....*Mormon Underwear* provides compelling stories, literally from the inside-out."

Niki D'Andrea, *Phoenix New Times*

"Townsend's lively writing style and engaging characters [in *Zombies for Jesus*] make for stories which force us to wake up, smell the (prohibited) coffee, and review our attitudes with regard to reading dogma so doggedly. These are tales which revel in the individual tics and quirks which make us human, Mormon or not, gay or not..."

A.J. Kirby, *The Short Review*

"The Rift," from *A Gay Mormon Missionary in Pompeii*, is a "fascinating tale of an untenable situation...a *tour de force*."

David Lenson, editor, *The Massachusetts Review*

"Pronouncing the Apostrophe," from *The Golem of Rabbi Loew*, is "quiet and revealing, an intriguing tale..."

Sima Rabinowitz, Literary Magazine Review, *NewPages.com*

The Circumcision of God is "a collection of short stories that consider the imperfect, silenced majority of Mormons, who may in fact be [the Church's] best hope....[The book leaves] readers regretting the church's willingness to marginalize those who best exemplify its ideals: those who love fiercely despite all obstacles, who brave challenges at great personal risk and who always choose the hard, higher road."

Kirkus Reviews

In *Mormon Fairy Tales*, Johnny Townsend displays "both a wicked sense of irony and a deep well of compassion."

Kel Munger, *Sacramento News and Review*

Zombies for Jesus is "eerie, erotic, and magical."

Publishers Weekly

"While [Townsend's] many touching vignettes draw deeply from Mormon mythology, history, spirituality and culture, [*Mormon Fairy Tales*] is neither a gaudy act of proselytism nor angry protest literature from an ex-believer. Like all good fiction, his stories are simply about the joys, the hopes and the sorrows of people."

Kirkus Reviews

"In *Inferno in the French Quarter* author Johnny Townsend restores this tragic event [the UpStairs Lounge fire] to its proper place in LGBT history and reminds us that the victims of the blaze were not just 'statistics,' but real people with real lives, families, and friends."

Jesse Monteagudo, *The Bilerico Project*

In *Inferno in the French Quarter*, "Townsend's heart-rending descriptions of the victims…seem to [make them] come alive once more."

Kit Van Cleave, OutSmart Magazine

Marginal Mormons is "an irreverent, honest look at life outside the mainstream Mormon Church….Throughout his musings on sin and forgiveness, Townsend beautifully demonstrates his characters' internal, perhaps irreconcilable struggles….Rather than anger and disdain, he offers an honest portrayal of people searching for meaning and community in their lives, regardless of their life choices or secrets." Named to Kirkus Reviews' Best of 2012.

Kirkus Reviews

The stories in *The Mormon Victorian Society* "register the new openness and confidence of gay life in the age of same-sex marriage….What hasn't changed is Townsend's wry, conversational prose, his subtle evocations of character and social dynamics, and his deadpan humor. His warm empathy still glows in this intimate yet clear-eyed engagement with Mormon theology and folkways. Funny, shrewd and finely wrought dissections of the awkward contradictions—and surprising harmonies—between conscience and desire." Named to Kirkus Reviews' Best of 2013.

Kirkus Reviews

"This collection of short stories [*The Mormon Victorian Society*] featuring gay Mormon characters slammed [me] in the face from the first page, wrestled my heart and mind to the floor, and left me panting and wanting more by the end. Johnny Townsend has created so many memorable characters in such few pages. I went weeks thinking about this book. It truly touched me."

Tom Webb, *A Bear on Books*

Dragons of the Book of Mormon is an "entertaining collection….Townsend's prose is sharp, clear, and easy to read, and his characters are well rendered…"

Publishers Weekly

"The pre-eminent documenter of alternative Mormon lifestyles…Townsend has a deep understanding of his characters, and his limpid prose, dry humor and well-grounded (occasionally magical) realism make their spiritual conundrums both compelling and entertaining. [*Dragons of the Book of Mormon* is] [a]nother of Townsend's critical but affectionate and absorbing tours of Mormon discontent." Named to Kirkus Reviews' Best of 2014.

Kirkus Reviews

In *Gayrabian Nights*, "Townsend's prose is always limpid and evocative, and…he finds real drama and emotional depth in the most ordinary of lives."

Kirkus Reviews

Gayrabian Nights "was easily the most original book I've read all year. Funny, touching, topical, and thoroughly enjoyable."

Rainbow Awards

In *Lying for the Lord*, Townsend "gets under the skin of his characters to reveal their complexity and conflicts….shrewd, evocative [and] wryly humorous."

Kirkus Reviews

Lying for the Lord is "one of the most gripping books that I've picked up for quite a while. I love the author's writing style, alternately cynical, humorous, biting, scathing, poignant, and touching…. This is the third book of his that I've read, and all are equally engaging. These are stories that need to be told, and the author does it in just the right way."

Heidi Alsop, *Ex-Mormon Foundation Board Member*

In *Missionaries Make the Best Companions*, "the author treats the clash between religious dogma and liberal humanism with vivid realism, sly humor, and subtle feeling as his characters try to figure out their true missions in life. Another of Townsend's rich dissections of Mormon failures and uncertainties…" Named to Kirkus Reviews' Best of 2015.

Kirkus Reviews

In *Invasion of the Spirit Snatchers*, "Townsend, a confident and practiced storyteller, skewers the hypocrisies and eccentricities of his characters with precision and affection. The outlandish framing narrative is the most consistent source of shock and humor, but the stories do much to ground the reader in the world—or former world—of the characters….A funny, charming tale about a group of Mormons facing the end of the world."

Kirkus Reviews

"Townsend's collection [*The Washing of Brains*] once again displays his limpid, naturalistic prose, skillful narrative chops, and his subtle insights into psychology…Well-crafted dispatches on the clash between religion and self-fulfillment…"

Kirkus Reviews

"While the author is generally at his best when working as a satirist, there are some fine, understated touches in these tales [*The Last Days Linger*] that will likely affect readers in subtle ways....readers should come away impressed by the deep empathy he shows for all his characters—even the homophobic ones."

Kirkus Reviews

"Written in a conversational style that often uses stories and personal anecdotes to reveal larger truths, this immensely approachable book [*Racism by Proxy*] skillfully serves its intended audience of White readers grappling with complex questions regarding race, history, and identity. The author's frequent references to the Church of Jesus Christ of Latter-day Saints may be too niche for readers unfamiliar with its idiosyncrasies, but Townsend generally strikes a perfect balance of humor, introspection, and reasoned arguments that will engage even skeptical readers."

Kirkus Reviews

Orgy at the STD Clinic portrays "an all-too real scenario that Townsend skewers to wincingly accurate proportions...[with] instant classic moments courtesy of his punchy, sassy, sexy lead character..."

Jim Piechota, *Bay Area Reporter*

Orgy at the STD Clinic is "...a triumph of humane sensibility. A richly textured saga that brilliantly captures the fraying social fabric of contemporary life." Named to Kirkus Reviews' Best Indie Books of 2022.

Kirkus Reviews

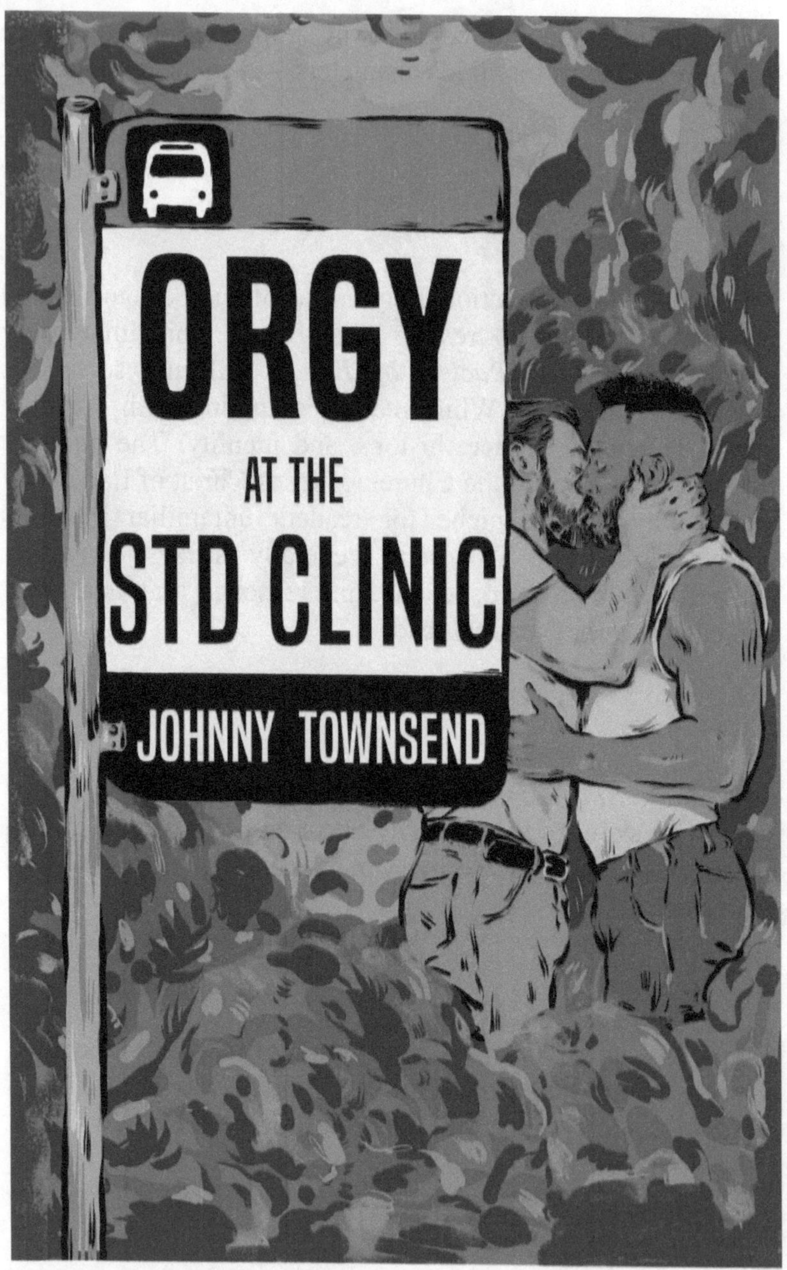

ORGY
AT THE
STD CLINIC
JOHNNY TOWNSEND

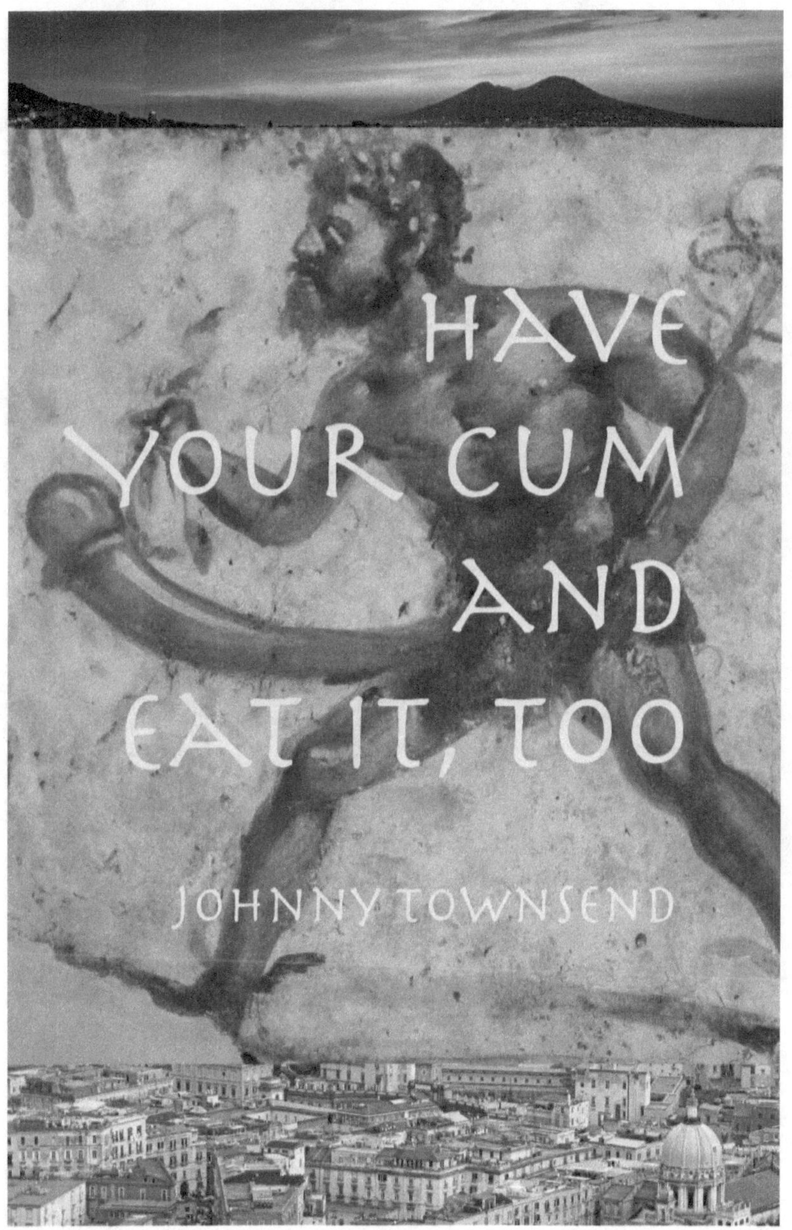

HAVE YOUR CUM AND EAT IT, TOO
JOHNNY TOWNSEND

Going-Out-Of-
Religion Sale
JOHNNY TOWNSEND